BENEATH

Brazen Skies

OREGON PROMISE SERIES
by Lynnette Bonner

Through Dust and Ashes – BOOK ONE
Beneath Brazen Skies – BOOK TWO
Across Barren Plains – BOOK THREE (Coming soon.)

OTHER HISTORICAL BOOKS
by Lynnette Bonner

THE SHEPHERD'S HEART SERIES

Rocky Mountain Oasis – BOOK ONE
High Desert Haven – BOOK TWO
Fair Valley Refuge – BOOK THREE
Spring Meadow Sanctuary – BOOK FOUR

SONNETS OF THE SPICE ISLE SERIES

On the Wings of a Whisper – BOOK ONE

THE WYLDHAVEN SERIES

Not a Sparrow Falls – BOOK ONE
On Eagles' Wings – BOOK TWO
Beauty from Ashes – BOOK THREE
Consider the Lilies – BOOK FOUR
A Wyldhaven Christmas – BOOK FIVE
Songs in the Night – BOOK SIX
Honey from the Rock – BOOK SEVEN
Beside Still Waters – BOOK EIGHT

Find all other books by Lynnette Bonner at:
www.lynnettebonner.com

BENEATH
Brazen Skies

OREGON PROMISE – BOOK 2

Lynnette BONNER
USA Today Bestselling Author

Pacific Lights

Beneath Barren Skies
Oregon Promise, Book 2

Published by Pacific Lights Publishing
Copyright © 2024 by Lynnette Bonner. All rights reserved.

Editing by Lesley Ann McDaniel Editing – https://www.lesleyannmcdanielediting.com
Proofreading by Sheri Mast – https://faithfulediting.com
Book interior design by Jon Stewart – http://stewartdesign.studio

Cover design by Lynnette Bonner of Indie Cover Design, images ©
Depositphotos:149855280 – Tall Grass
Depositphotos: 657661110 – Man's Face
Depositphotos: 64546223 – Leather Rein
AdobeStock: 482613519 – Horses and Wagon
MidJourney: Woman's Face, and Man and Horse

Paperback ISBN: 978-1-942982-34-0

Philippians 4:13

I can do all things through Christ who strengthens me.

Prologue

Lexington, Missouri

For at least thirty minutes, Hoyt Harrington, the drunk at the bar, had been loudly proclaiming his good fortune to have secured the purchase of an Independence mercantile. He was a young man, doughy of build and arrogant in manner, interacting with those around him in a way that screamed of a wealthy upbringing. He'd obviously been raised with plenty of servants to boss around.

Corbin Donahue, sitting at a table in a dim back corner, twisted the whiskey he'd not yet touched. He hadn't realized this job would be so easy. His mark wouldn't know what hit him.

Good. Smoother that way.

"Build me an empire, I will!" The drunk yelled, his jowls jiggling with each effort at speech. "Just see if they don't regret telling me I'd never amount to anything!" He slumped over his drink then and stared into it morosely.

Corbin stood and dropped a few coins onto his table. He tugged his hat low, nudged his coat collar high, and strode over to slide onto the bar stool next to the man. "Hey there, friend." He kept his tone casual and friendly.

The drunk muttered darkly—something about his father.

"Going to Independence, are you?"

The drunk jerked up straight and blinked slowly, as though just then realizing someone sat so near. But when his bleary search finally focused on Corbin's face, he apparently found no danger, just as hoped. "Bought me a mark . . . merk . . . mercan . . ." He gave up with a sloppy wave. "A shtore," he slurred with a sullen nod.

Corbin dropped his hands onto the counter and motioned to the barkeep. "His next round is on me. Make it two."

The barman eyed him with speculation and curiosity, but Corbin was long used to such perusal, so he just turned his focus back to the young man beside him. "Heading that way myself." He stretched a palm out to shake the man's hand. "Name's Bill Stone."

Even the man's handshake felt fleshy. "Hoyt Harrington. I'm gon' start som'thin' big."

"So you've said. Say . . ." Corbin leaned back and waited to ask his question until the barman set the two shots in front of them and stepped away. He used the lip of the bar to cover his twisting of the compartmentalized ring to the inside of his hand, then reached to swap the drunk's nearly empty glass for the new full one. That was all it took to flick open the ring's top and transfer the arsenic into the cup. He slid it toward the man, but then drew it back sharply, knowing the sloshing of the rye would help the powder slip below the surface of the dark liquid. "When do you take possession of this new store?" It was a moot question. Corbin already knew all the details he needed to know to pull off this job. All that would be left to do would be to slip into Hoyt's hotel room this evening to procure the necessary paperwork.

The drunk leaned close as though to offer a tightly guarded secret. "Takin' over tomorrow. Two 'clock."

"You don't say!" He clapped young Mr. Harrington on one shoulder. "I'm heading on to Oregon, myself. I have a job I'm about to get paid for, and then I plan to travel west and make my fortune in cattle. I wish you the very best." Careful to use his left hand and keep his ring far from his own glass, he lifted his whiskey. "To the future."

Hoyt smiled sleepily, lifted the glass, and downed the drink in one gulp. "Thankee ver' mussshh." He smeared one hand over his face and then passed out on the bar. Perfect.

Corbin met his own gaze in the mirror above the back counter. One more job in the books. Once he reached Oregon, he would have all the money he needed to live the high life. He would be an upstanding citizen there—at least perceived as one.

As he stood, he patted the drunk on his back as though they were old friends. He leaned close and whispered into the man's unhearing ears, "Hope you have a better afterlife, my friend." The man would be dead inside a week. Certainly too sick to travel by tomorrow. By that time, no one would remember a passing conversation he had with a stranger in a bar.

Chapter 1

Willow Chancellor stood at the mercantile register, trying to ignore Gideon Riley, who worked to grease one of the hinges for the portion of the counter that could be raised. If only she could get the numbers in her ledger to come into focus, she could maybe forget about how she had made such a fool of herself last year when he'd first come to town—okay, and for a few months after.

But once the man had made it clear he had no interest in her other than as a friend, she'd determined to set him from her mind. She'd put her head down and concentrated on her work—or, at least, she tried to.

For months, she'd hardly spoken to him other than a polite greeting when necessary, and he'd seemed just fine with that, treating her in kind.

She pinched her lips into a tight line and returned her gaze to the top of the column. Some of her addition must be off.

In his defense, much of today's anxiety had nothing to do with Gideon Riley—none whatsoever. For just this morning, Papa had informed her that he was selling the store, and they would be traveling west with the first of the spring wagon trains to leave Independence! He'd known for months, he'd said, but he hadn't wanted to burden her with the knowledge until he felt absolutely certain of the undertaking.

She lifted her head and tapped her pencil against her lips. Tears blurred her vision as she swept a look across the store. The corner window provided her earliest memory—Mama and her arranging a new selection of china all the way from England. The basket of eggs nearer to the counter reminded her of the time she had rushed in all aflutter over some accomplishment at school and knocked them to the floor in her twirl of excitement. She'd received a hug from Papa instead of the expected punishment. Here behind the counter she could still envision Mama bending to give her a hug as she'd dashed off to school on the day they'd unexpectedly lost her.

She sighed and rubbed one palm over the smooth boards of the counter. This was the only home she'd ever known!

And now Papa was using words like "certain of the undertaking." So certain, in fact, that the buyer was due to arrive today.

Hadn't Papa realized that it would be better for her to have time to reconcile with their departure rather than finding out only hours before the sale of the store? Had he even paused to consider her opinion on the matter? She pressed her fingers into the hollow at the base of her throat, swallowing down pain. And this shredding of her heart was taking place only a couple of weeks before they were to have a wagon packed with all the essentials they might need for the next six months!

On top of all that, the books needed to be properly reconciled for today's buyer, which she'd been putting off for two months without knowing she would regret that particular bit of procrastination to the utmost. Now, she had an hour or less to reconcile the books before she needed to present the store to one Hoyt Harrington.

"Your problem is here." Gideon made her jolt as he reached past her on the opposite side from where she'd last seen him to stab a broad, blunt finger at a set of numbers. "Seven and nine is sixteen, not fifteen."

Of course. Defensiveness rose inside her. She'd been so concentrated on her feelings of loss that she hadn't heard him approach. Nor felt him reading over her shoulder. "You're right, of course. I do know that." Allowing her pique to reflect in her features, she tossed him a glance.

He was wiping grease from his fingers onto a rag, which would explain why he stood on the wrong side of her—the rag bin sat under the counter on the far end.

Gideon lifted his blue eyes to hers. "I know you do for all the arithmetic help you've given the boys."

His reference to his nephew and the son of Mercy Adler, who now courted his former brother-in-law, eased some of her irritation. A reminder of some of the good that would come about because she wouldn't need to say farewell to those who had become friends over the past few months, for they would travel to Oregon together now. And, well, if she were more glad about not having to say farewell to one man in particular, he would never know about it. Even now, the way he watched her made her heart patter as though she'd just finished a romp with the boys he'd spoken of.

She slid her books farther down the counter and moved to join them, creating more room between herself and Gideon without comment. Putting her eraser to good use, she bent over the book and, once the column was tabulated correctly, stood to arch out the ache in her back.

Gideon remained where she had left him—still watching her. When the silence between them stretched to near its limits, he said, "Your father informs me that he plans to start another store once we reach Oregon. In a few years, you'll have another place that's just as near and dear to your heart as this one."

Not "just as," but perhaps he was right that a new place would also become dear.

Realization dawning, she narrowed her eyes, plunked her fists to her hips, and pivoted to face him. "And just when did he have time to share this information with you?" After Papa had told her the news, he'd promptly left to meet their buyer as soon as he arrived in town.

A furrow ticked Gideon's brow.

She stabbed a finger in his direction. "Caught out! How long have you known?"

He seemed solely concentrated on cleaning his fingers again. His teeth worried one side of his lower lip.

Willow sniffed, unexpectedly hurt by the sudden realization that she might just be the hindmost to know of her father's plans. "Am I the last he told?"

He shook his head. "If it's any consolation, neither Micah nor Mercy were aware of your father's plans until I told them this morning—as Wayne asked me to do. Further . . ." His lips pressed into a tight line for a moment before he continued. "I felt he should have told you sooner. You are strong, Willow. Could have handled the knowing. But just as you could have handled it then, that strength will see you through now. And . . ." his gaze seemed to turn even more serious. "If your strength seems uncertain, remember the Lord's is not."

Her chin shot higher, more as a precaution against allowing her tears to fall than from any of the other plentiful emotions surging through her. She could not acknowledge his encouragement of her strength, or she would prove him very wrong by collapsing into a puddle to bawl out her lament. Instead, she clarified, "Father asked you to tell them—Micah and Mercy?"

A single nod. "He did."

She gave a sharp sniff and resumed her focus on the accounting book. "I have to finish this. I don't have more time to talk now. If you'll excuse me."

Despite her words and her vision blurring against numbers that refused to make themselves clear, all her attention lay attuned on the man who didn't move for the longest of moments.

Finally, from the corner of her eye, she saw him lower his hands and stride toward her, which he would need to do to get out from behind the counter, provided he'd even finished his work on the hinge.

He paused behind her. "Wayne knew that you'd be some upset and didn't want Mercy and Micah worrying over what troubled you. That was all."

Despite herself, she spun toward him. "And yet, you've known for months!"

She blinked as she realized just how close her spin had brought her to the man. From here, she could see the light glinting in the stubble he hadn't shaved for the past few days. See that today, the blue of his eyes had drifted nearer to the color of a storm-tormented lake than the vibrant blue of placid waters under cerulean skies.

He didn't seem perturbed. He only inclined his head. "Yes, I've known for months. Because last fall, your father extracted a promise from me that I'd keep you safe if ever anything happened to him."

"If ever—" A frown tightened her brow. "Why would something happen to him?"

A look of consternation touched Gideon's face. He raised one hand to scrub his jaw with the back of one thumbnail. "Didn't he tell you why he's selling in the first place?"

Willow's heart began to hammer, and she felt a bit of dampness touch her palms. "Not a word. Only that we are selling and leaving for Oregon."

Gideon lowered his gaze. "I think it's best you ask him his reasoning then." He started past her.

Her hand shot out and clamped on his forearm before she thought better of it. "Gideon Riley, if you know of some danger my father is in, you better tell me this instant."

Gideon looked to where she held his arm firmly and then inspected her face. Sincerity shone in his eyes when he said, "Willow, this really isn't my story to tell. But you can rest easy in knowing that neither your father nor I believe him to be in any immediate danger." He eased his arm from beneath her hand. "I need to go help Micah finish the transfer of his crates from his old wagon to the new. Try to ease your mind so you can finish the books."

He took a step, hesitated, turned back to her, and raised one hand to skim the point of her chin with the knuckle of his first finger. As though the gesture surprised him, he snatched his hand to his side and left her.

It was such a light graze that if it wasn't for his reaction, she might have thought she'd imagined it. She remained still and watched him walk to the hinged portion of the counter, step out, and then lower it into place.

He raised and lowered it a couple of times, smiling slightly in satisfaction at the lack of a squeak. Then, with one more flick of a glance in her direction, he took Papa's wooden toolbox and disappeared out the back door of the mercantile, which would take him across to the barn.

With a sigh of resignation and more questions than she'd started the conversation with, Willow returned to her calculations. But not before she rubbed her palm several times on her skirt in hopes of removing the feel of Gideon's strong forearm from her memory.

"Is it done?" Grant Moore wished that the sound of trepidation hadn't vibrated so strongly in his voice.

The meeting of two was taking place in the dim interior of a small brick room at the back of Moore Brewing's Independence offices. A room with access from a back alley that would prevent most from seeing who came and who went.

Grant didn't know what he'd expected his hired assassin to look like. Certainly not like this short man with handsome features and a charming smile.

Corbin Donahue looked at him placidly. "I am hired by men such as yourself on the basis of my reputation, Mr. Moore. If I don't complete a job, word begins to travel, and then I have trouble securing the next." There was a moment of pause where his smile fell away, leaving only a cold stare in its place. "I always get the job done."

Grant Moore hated that the lifeless eyes suddenly had him adjusting his necktie. "And he won't be found?" He cleared his throat and forced his fidgeting hands to his knees beneath the desk.

The man sighed as though Grant's questions taxed his patience. "He will be found. But it will be assumed that he died of his own excesses."

Grant nodded, opened a drawer, and slid a stack of bills across the table. A very thick stack. "Payment for the first part of the job being done. And, of course, as agreed, you will receive the remainder once you complete the next. You are supposed to arrive in less than an hour. Don't be late."

Donahue snatched the money and fanned one end as he leveled all the animosity of his icy stare at Grant. "I won't be late. You just be sure that my payment is ready in full."

Grant narrowed his eyes and met the man look for look. In a game of machismo there was one hard-and-fast rule. Never let them see your fear. He didn't bother forming a response. They both knew he would have the man's money when the time came. Not to have it would mean certain death.

Finally, with a nod, Donahue sauntered through the outer door into the alley. In one last act of defiance, he left the door swinging open.

Grant waited until he felt certain the man could not hear him before releasing a sigh of relief and rising to shut the door. After closing it tight, he slid the bolt lock into place and turned the deadbolt, too.

A shiver worked down his spine.

His eyes fell closed in a fleeting regret for what he'd set in motion but then with a deep breath, he silenced his conscience. Business was cutthroat, especially here on the edge of the untamed west. It was good that he had the courage to be the kind of businessman who could make it in this new era. Too bad his brother-in-law had gone behind his back and tried to sell the store out from under him. But no matter. All would soon be his despite Wayne Chancellor's best efforts.

His brother-in-law may be barely making a living off the store. But Grant had better plans. This was the last stop before immigrants headed across the barren midlands. Once he put Independence's other mercantile out of business, he would own the only store the wagoneers could access near the pushing-off point. He would be able to ask any price he wanted.

A thin smile touched his lips.

Soon. Very soon.

Chapter 2

Gideon arrived at the Chancellors' barn with a heavy heart. He tucked Wayne's toolbox into its rightful place on the shelf in the tack room and then headed for Micah's wagon, which stood at the far end of the barn. They had finished transferring his own supplies to his new wagon the day before. Thankfully, Wayne's calculations had been correct and there would be room for him to sleep on a tick at the front of the wagon because on the way here from Virginia last year, he hadn't planned too well, and he'd grown mighty tired of sleeping on the cold ground beneath his wagon.

Mattox, Micah's big black dog, rose from beneath the wagon and wagged his tail in greeting.

"Hey, boy." Gideon bent to ruffle his ears. Micah wasn't in sight. He wouldn't be too far, however, for the dog never roamed far from his master. "Where's Micah, huh?" He stooped further to roughhouse with the dog's big paws. "Where'd he go boy?"

Mattox sank his front end low while his back end remained in the air, tail furiously wagging. He barked, spun in a circle, and then crouched playfully again.

Gideon played with the dog for a few minutes longer, but finally, he pointed back beneath the wagon. "All right, enough. I've got work to do. Lay down."

Mattox grumbled a protest but obeyed and had already closed his golden eyes by the time Gideon rounded the end of the wagon to see how much of Micah's task still needed to be done. To his surprise, more than half of Micah's wagon was loaded. Maybe he'd needed a break for water.

Just then, young Declan Boyle came into the barn with a load of horse blankets in his arms. He gave Gideon a nod. "Afternoon, Mr. Gideon. Right glad ta see ye could pull yourself away from Miss Willow 'n' join us men in the work o' loadin' this wagon."

He offered the joke with such dry wit that Gideon did a double take before taking note of the twinkle in the boy's green eyes.

He surged toward the lad, who was almost more man than boy, and served him with several pulled punches. "I'll have you know that the hinges Mr. Chancellor asked me to oil are moving as smooth as a ship through open seas now. And that took some doing, rusty as they were."

The boy pinched his lips to one side. "Truly? For when I popped in there a bit ago to fetch Mr. Micah's canned goods from the larder, it looked like ye were leanin' o'er Miss Willow's shoulder, all cozy-like."

Gideon felt a coil of unease tighten his stomach at the boy's teasing. He wouldn't deny that her beauty and upbeat personality were attractive to him. When he'd first met her, he'd thought her much younger than she actually was. However, despite her being older than he'd thought, he was still her senior by a good seven years, and best he remember it. Besides, even though she'd made her feelings for him plain when he'd first arrived in Independence, she'd cooled to him measurably months ago. And that was a good thing!

Probably. Yes, probably a good thing.

He willed away the memory of the strand of red hair that had rested against Willow's neck and tempted his fingers to brush it into the plait of her braid. Refused the memory of the way his fingers had longed to linger against the warmth of her skin when he'd unexpectedly turned and brushed her chin there at the last moment. He couldn't—shouldn't—be doing things like that. The girl obviously wanted something better than a world-weary widower who wouldn't have anything to offer her when they reached the Oregon Territory.

He swallowed and blinked. He pegged Declan with a look instead. "Miss Willow and I are friends and nothing more. What you saw was me helping her with a column of sums that she had mistallied. And what do you know of getting cozy with a lass, anyhow? Anything I should be mentioning to Mr. Chancellor?"

Declan ducked his head, a distinct swath of red sweeping both his ears. "Nae a thing, Mr. Riley. Just got eyes, is all."

Gideon pointed to the horse blankets. "Best you put those eyes to use, stashing those where Micah asked you to store them, don't you think?"

Declan nodded. "Aye, sir."

The lad moved to settle the blankets into a small compartment Micah had built into the bottom of his wagon. It was only about six inches high, but Gideon hadn't added a similar space to his. He hadn't wanted to risk losing the clearance between the ground and the bed of his wagon in case it became important to have it while crossing a river or some other unknown terrain on the way west. Despite not having them on his own, he couldn't help but admire Micah's ingenuity. Micah had separated the compartment into smaller sections and had fixed each with small cupboard-like doors in several places around the perimeter. In the first compartment, he stored his shovel, adze, hatchet, saw, drill, and ax. In the second, he'd added double the length of rope required, along with a completely new oilcloth tarp for replacement, should the first one become damaged.

Gideon had to admit that as he'd watched Micah pack, he'd been half sorry that he hadn't followed suit. He had all the same supplies, but he would need to navigate them in the back of his wagon instead of having them conveniently tucked into out-of-the-way compartments beneath.

At least it was only him who would need to navigate the cramped compartment and not a wife also!

Gideon shook away the thoughts and glanced at his pocket watch. They were to meet their wagon master in less than thirty minutes. Packing the rest of Micah's wagon would have to wait. "You seen Micah?" he asked.

Declan grinned. "Speakin' o' cozy-like…" He gestured toward the back of the barn, where the double sliding doors were propped open to allow in light. "He seen Ms. Mercy traivelin' by the creek 'n' lit oot like his tail was afire."

"He saw Ms. Mercy walking." Gideon automatically corrected before waving his comment away. "Never mind. I'll fetch Micah, and you remember to meet us at the central green at the end of town to chat with our wagon master and meet the other members of our wagon train."

Declan nodded. "Aye, sir." A bit of sadness flitted through the boy's eyes, but he blinked it away, and if Gideon hadn't known him so well, he might not have noticed it at all.

He reached to squeeze the kid's shoulder. It couldn't be easy not knowing what might have happened to his father, who had gone west with the promise that he'd return—a promise that, at least so far, he hadn't kept. It must weigh on the kid not knowing whether he was an orphan or had simply been abandoned by his father. Yet, with his father gone for several years now, Gideon was glad the boy had chosen to travel with him—them—to the West. Really, it was Willow who had talked the lad into joining them.

He headed out the back doors of the barn and started toward the creek.

Mercy Adler tucked her hands behind herself and leaned against the bark of the willow tree. The drooping branches, flush with the tender green leaves of spring, hung in a curtain of privacy around her and Micah. A conflagration of emotions flamed through her at the question he'd just asked her—happiness, terror, joy, concern, and a whole host of other emotions she couldn't quite put her finger on.

Micah stepped closer and propped his forearm on the trunk above her head. The intensity of his blue eyes softened when they swept over her features.

Mercy's heart raced, though she did her best to appear calm. She looked toward the burbling water. She'd yet to allow Micah to kiss her, though they'd shared plenty of intimate conversations over the past few months. He'd filled her in on the abuse he'd suffered as a boy at the hands of an uncaring father. She'd haltingly filled in the details he hadn't known of all she'd suffered at Herst's hands.

They'd talked of Micah's hopes for the future. How he hoped to buy land in Oregon and start a small ranch. His plans for cattle drives with good sturdy cows from Texas, where they could be purchased for less than five dollars per head. And how he hoped to cross them with the Hereford bull he'd purchased from a Virginian that had arrived in Independence just as the snows were melting. Micah and Gideon had each purchased twelve pairs of oxen in addition to the bull, which Micah had hired Declan to ride herd on all the way to Oregon, much to the young man's delight. Six oxen at a time would rotate in pulling their wagons.

They'd shared time over Bible readings with their boys, his son Joel from his first marriage and her son Avram from hers. They'd talked of their awe over how the Lord had revealed the depth of His love to them.

Just the other day, as she'd watched Micah carefully instruct the boys how they should act around the steers on the way to Oregon, it had hit her fresh how much she loved him. And yet, she'd not spoken of it with him yet. To be honest, she felt terrified at the depth of her feelings. The terror started a tremor in her chest that threatened to vibrate right to the very tips of each finger and toe. And yet . . . Micah was not Herst.

And . . .

He'd just asked her to marry him.

Before the wagon train left in two weeks!

"Determined to keep me in suspense, I see." Micah's deep voice rumbled in her ear. The warmth of his breath tickled the escaped curl by her temple.

His skin had bronzed as the days grew sunny, only heightening the contrast of his light eyes against his dark coloring. She remembered how stern she'd thought him when they'd first met. How grieved he'd been after the loss of his wife—a loss that could be laid squarely at Mercy's feet. And yet, what a wonderful God they served who could weave so much joy and happiness from so much tragedy.

She knew hope hung there. All she needed to do was reach out to pluck the fruit of friendship, love, and family that Micah had offered to her time and again.

Micah's finger traced her brow and tucked the curl behind her ear. "What are you thinking behind that frown?" He tapped the puckered skin between her brows.

"I'm thinking that you're not Herst."

He seemed to still, even though he hadn't been moving much anyway. His scrutiny grew intense. One brow arched slightly upward. "This is something I know." The corner of his mouth quirked up.

She smiled at his teasing tone. Looked away. Looked back. Her tongue darted out to moisten her lips, and she swallowed to wet her suddenly parched throat. "You say you love me, Micah, but we haven't even . . ." Flames licked her cheeks, and she plucked at a bit of fluff on the sleeve of her sweater. She clamped her teeth in frustration with herself, then lifted her chin, determined to get the words out. "We haven't even kissed. What if you . . . don't like it?"

His second brow joined the first in his hairline. He eased back from the tree, arm lowering.

She had shocked him! And he was pulling back.

Heat crashed through her face, and she prodded at a bit of moss with the toe of her boot. "That is, maybe I won't—What I mean to say is—" *Oh, Lord of Heaven, what do I mean to say?* "I know I've been . . . slow, and I don't want to disappoint—"

Micah's palm settled against her cheek. His thumb pressed gently to her lips, while his first knuckle caressed the underside of her chin. "Have you ever been kissed by a man who loves you?"

She must be as red as the apple that Avram had insisted on taking to his teacher this morning. She rolled her lips inward and pressed them together. Shook her head. Noted that he hadn't assured her she wouldn't disappoint him, and poked at the moss again.

But Micah's hand remained to nudge her chin up. His eyes were soft as they searched her own. "When two people love each other, a kiss is not something to be measured. It's . . . well, it's as though two hearts are clambering for unity. When you love someone, there can be nothing disappointing about a kiss."

"I know that here." She touched her temple. "But here . . ." She touched her heart. "Even just standing here with my back to this tree and you blocking my escape makes my palms feel clammy and—"

Before she could even blink, his hands were around her waist and he spun them so that his back pressed to the tree. "Forgive me. I didn't think how that might make you feel."

Mercy settled one hand on his chest and dropped her forehead beside it, closing her eyes. This was such a good man, and she didn't want to hurt him. "It's not logical, Micah—this panic that swells inside of me. I know you would never . . . That is, like I said, I know you aren't Herst . . . But then the flashes of . . ." She drew a sustaining inhale. Flapped one hand. "Memories . . . My back to a wall with his hand crushing my throat so tightly that I couldn't breathe as he held his pistol pointed at Avram in my belly." She felt a ripple work through Micah's body. She should stop talking but wanted Micah to understand her hesitations. "His mouth crushing mine until my lips were bruised and bleeding as he took his pleasure without concern for my . . . cries of pain."

Micah's arms slid slowly around her. One of his big hands gently cupped the back of her head. She heard him swallow. "Lord forgive me, but I'm glad that man is dead."

She lifted her head then, and Micah's hands fell away. He tucked them behind himself as though he wanted her to know she was completely free to retreat whenever she liked.

But she didn't want to retreat. She wanted this. This intimacy with a man who truly cared for her.

The muscles of his chest were firm beneath her palms, and his lips were so close—firm and masculine in the thick black stubble that surrounded them. A unity of two hearts. She wanted that. Oh, how she wanted that.

"I love you, Mercy." The words seeped into her and watered dry places. He dipped his head to catch her attention as though he wanted to make sure she'd heard him.

"I know you do. And . . . I love you, too, Micah." There. She'd gone and done it now. Did ever any other words render a person so vulnerable?

With her focus fastened to his lips, she leaned closer, But Micah shifted. She froze and raised her gaze to his.

"Don't feel you have to kiss me, Merce." Sincerity shone in his eyes. "I'm content to wait until you are certain of my love for you. And I'm praying that God will release you from these bonds that Herst still has around you."

She blinked, leaned more firmly against him, and turned to study the creek. "You're right. He does still have me bound. But I'm determined to do as Parson Houston said in his final sermon on Sunday—'forget what is behind, and strain toward what is ahead.'" She searched the face that had become so dear to her over the last few months.

She had said enough. It was time to put her determination into action. "I think I'm going to kiss you now."

"Then I will be the happiest of men." His lips tilted up softly at the corners. His hands remained tucked against the willow's trunk. He tilted his head in anticipation but didn't move toward her.

Mercy rose on her tiptoes, wishing her pounding heart wasn't making it so hard to breathe. She leaned—

"Micah?"

Mercy froze at the sound of Gideon's voice. She met Micah's gaze for one flash of a moment before Micah's eyes fell closed, and his nostrils flared.

"Mercy? You out here?" Gideon's call, accompanied by the crunching of his boots in the sand, came from just outside the perimeter of their tree.

When Micah opened his eyes again, they were narrowed with ironic humor. "Hang on while I toss him in the creek," he whispered.

Mercy giggled quietly. She tucked her lower lip between her teeth, hoping she looked normal despite the quavering that tripped through her. She eased away from him and brushed at her skirts.

"We're here, Gid," Micah called, pushing himself off the tree.

Gid cleared his throat, remaining outside the drape of concealing branches. "Sorry to interrupt. Just a reminder that our meeting is at the other end of town in a few minutes."

"Right. We'll be right there." To Mercy, he offered softly, "We will resume this conversation. I'm still waiting for an answer to my question. And . . ." He gave her a pointed look. "I've still got a debt of fifty cents waiting for collection." He winked.

She blushed at the reminder of the first time he'd teased her about awaiting repayment in the form of a kiss. He'd purchased some mittens for Avram and her, and she'd repaid him the fifty cents, which he'd quite promptly returned to her with the teasing comment that if she wanted to repay him, he could think of better ways. Since then, he'd not missed an opportunity to mention how he continued to wait for repayment of the debt she owed him.

"Micah?" She snatched his hand before he could stride from their shelter.

He stilled.

"The answer is yes. I will marry you."

He turned to face her more fully, a smile slowly spreading across his lips. But then it faded. "You understand that I have nothing to offer you but a passel of hard work? We don't even have land because we missed the deadline."

"You understand that I come weighed down with plenty of baggage?" she rejoined.

He worked to slip his fingers between hers and gave her a nod. "I used to scoff at those who claimed God would help them through, but I'm happy to say that I honestly believe God will help us, Mercy— likely not give us a life without any problems, but help us find the strength to make it through the valleys."

She nodded and curled her opposite hand around his forearm as she leaned into his side and looked up at him. "I think so too."

His gaze lowered to her mouth. "We could skip the meeting," he offered teasingly.

Mercy chuckled. If he could tease her, then she could tease him back. "Maybe we'll find time for a kiss once we are settled in the Oregon Territory."

His brows shot up, and then he laughed. "I had no idea I was courting a woman who would enjoy torturing me."

She only grinned.

With a wry shake of his head, he reached to part the fronds and led her out.

And as she followed him to the meeting, she pressed one hand over her stomach. Had she done the right thing, agreeing to marry the man? He undid her, that was what. In his presence, she couldn't seem to think straight.

She drew in a long sustaining breath, trying not to focus on the tumultuous roil of knots forming in her stomach.

Chapter 3

Willow was still working at tallying the books when Gideon poked his head back into the store half an hour later. "You and Wayne coming to the wagon train meeting?"

Willow sighed and pressed her fingers to her temples to massage away the surging despair. She would not ponder on all the precious places she'd be leaving behind. She shook her head. "Father hasn't returned yet from his meeting with the buyer. He was to meet the man and return with him here. I expected him a while ago. And I'm still working on these books, and besides, I can't leave the store unattended."

Gideon frowned. "I hate to leave you here all alone when the rest of us will be at the other end of town. Will you please lock up and come with me to the meeting? If the buyer was running late, he and your father are likely already there."

"Hoyt Harrington."

His brow furrowed. "The buyer?"

"Yes."

"Right." He nudged the door a little wider as though to encourage her to join him. "Will you come with me? Please?"

Willow couldn't deny that a great deal of curiosity burned through her at the thought of the meeting. And if Father was still waiting for

Mr. Harrington, at least one of them should attend the meeting so that they knew what to expect.

She tossed down her quill, capped the ink, and raised her skirts just enough to ease from behind the counter. "Just let me lock the back door."

He nodded. "I'll wait."

True to his promise, he was pacing the store's porch when she returned to the front. After locking that door, she accepted his offered arm and strode beside him down the boardwalk. She tried not to notice the work-hardened muscles beneath her hand or the way her heart kicked into a gallop from standing this close to him.

Calm decorum. Poised serenity. These were the emotions she endeavored to exude. Then she wouldn't have to endure any more rounds of rejection.

She swallowed the dryness from her throat. "Did you and Micah finish loading his wagon?" There. A perfectly poised and serene question!

He shook his head. "He and Declan got more done than I expected, but we'll have to finish this evening or tomorrow."

"There's still time."

"Yes. But your father will be wanting help with his wagon now, too, though he's loaded a good portion of it already, I dare say."

Despite her determination to be unflappable, she found her jaw hanging open.

With a grin, Gideon chucked her chin. "I've been surprised that you didn't ask anything about the third wagon in the barn."

She ground her teeth, refusing to acknowledge that comment. There had been a third wagon for months now. What had she thought would happen with that one? She figured Papa would sell it, she supposed.

They walked on in silence to the meeting in the green at the end of town. Several families had already gathered, and she thanked the Almighty for a reason to withdraw her hand from Gideon's arm and step farther from his side when they stopped by the group. Being so near the man positively discombobulated her. Everything inside churned with distinct cognizance of his every move when he was near. And yet, she refused to throw herself at a man who'd made his feelings so patently clear. She'd learned that lesson the day she'd found out Gid had proposed to Mercy and been rejected. Willow had no desire to be any man's second choice.

Speaking of Mercy . . . She stepped up beside them with her hand tucked into the crook of Micah's arm, and Willow couldn't help but feel a little pang of jealousy over how happy they looked as Micah settled one of his large hands over Mercy's small one and smiled down at her softly. Not that she wanted Micah, just the promise of one day having a family of her own—other than Papa and Declan.

Thoughts of her father and the lad they'd taken in last winter had her searching them out. There. They were across the circle of gathered people, standing by a handsome dark-haired man with a broad forehead and a blunt chin. The man said something quietly, and Papa laughed.

Then the man's eyes landed on Willow.

His brows peaked when he found her watching him so intently, and he swept her with a leisurely gaze that lingered in ungentlemanly places and filled her with unease. However, the smile he offered her seemed innocent enough. Maybe she'd misjudged his scrutiny?

She squirmed and studied the yellow petals of a dandelion. Was he Hoyt Harrington? At least that meant he'd be staying behind when the wagon train left.

She felt Gid's gaze on her and saw him flick a disapproving glance from her to the man beside Papa and back. Had he thought she'd given the man an inviting look of some sort?

Anger, hot and sure, swept through her. If he thought that, he didn't know her at all. Except . . . What was he to think when she'd done that very thing to him when he first arrived in town? Well, she was done making a fool of herself! The whole male species could fall off the face of the earth, as far as she was concerned! She was an independent woman who could maneuver through life on her own!

Where was a fan when she needed one? Too bad she'd left hers back in the mercantile. The sun suddenly felt brutal.

The man by Papa gave a sketch of a bow in their direction.

Gideon's feet shuffled, but he did return the man's greeting with a short, sharp nod.

Willow only swallowed, and moved her attention to Parson Houston, who stood next to another dark-haired man who obviously spent most of his time outdoors. His deep brown skin had that leathery look, but she'd guess him to be Gid's age. No matter his age, he didn't look like a man to be trifled with. Beside him stood a man of color, but of mixed blood because his skin was almost lighter than the suntanned man beside him, and he had light colored eyes—blue she would guess, though she couldn't exactly tell from this distance. He met her gaze too, but instead of raking her with a look like the man by Papa, he offered an easy smile and a quick, polite tug on the brim of his hat.

Willow liked him instantly. She gave him a nod and a smile.

Beside her, Gid shifted again, but when she looked at him to see why, it wasn't the friendly man he glowered at but instead the other man by Papa's side. When she glanced that way, it was to find that man still scrutinizing her.

Again, she wished for a fan, if only to give her hands something to do. Whoever he was, she supposed Papa would introduce him in good time. And then she hoped never to see him again.

She shivered despite the heat and focused on the others in the circle, many of whom she recognized as having been around town for at least a few days, and others that she didn't recognize at all.

From their left, an older man stepped forward. Maybe in his fifties with long gray hair, a good number of crow's feet etched the corners of his eyes. "If I could have everyone's attention, please!"

Willow worked the inside of her lip and forced herself to ignore the dark look Gideon continued to level on the man by Papa and focus on the speaker at the front of the group. "My name is Caesar Cranston, and I'm going to be your wagon master, as you all know."

The wagon master's gaze met hers briefly before continuing a sweep over the tops of the heads in the crowd, and she suppressed a wave of despair. This man would lead her and Papa into the unknown, leaving all they knew and held dear behind.

Lord, I don't know if I'm strong enough. She'd never planned to leave Independence.

Mr. Cranston held a folded newspaper above his head. "I have grand news for most of you!"

A ripple of curious murmurs swept the crowd.

"Congress has decided to extend the Donation Land Act in the Oregon Territory!"

"What?" Gideon exchanged a huge smile with Micah and then the men clapped each other's shoulders and practically shook the life out of each other.

Many around the circle whooped and one man tossed his hat clean into the air.

Caesar Cranston whistled sharply for everyone's attention. "Before you get too excited, please know that the tracts of land have been divided—half of what they were previously."

Murmurs of disappointment replaced the whoops of excitement.

Caesar placated them by patting his hands against the air. "I know it's mixed news, but I wanted you to hear it from me first. Now, there are a few other people I'd like to introduce before we hit the trail." He gestured to his right. "This is Cody Hawkeye. He is my second in command."

Willow studied the man he'd indicated. Though he stood a few inches shorter than the wagon master, he had long black flowing hair that somehow emphasized the sternness of a wide brow and serious brown eyes. At his belt, a tomahawk hung within inches of strong brown hands. His broad, ready stance and the long rifle protruding above one shoulder proclaimed him a man who'd been down the trail a time or two.

"If ever there is a time on the trail when you can't find me for some reason, Cody is the man to talk to." Caesar held up his hands to silence a rising wave of alarm. "I promise folks I'm going to be there for you every minute of every day. But with sixty-two of us—twenty-five wagons—there might come a time when Cody is closer to you than I am. I just want to assure you he's a safe man to confide in if you need one."

Willow felt her stomach churn. All these strangers. And the leaders could spout their trustworthiness until they were blue in the face, but that assurance meant nothing until they proved themselves.

Caesar continued, "And scouting for us this trip, we have Striker Moss and Jeremiah Jackson." He swept a gesture to the two men beside Parson Houston. "They'll be hunting and keeping an eye on the trail around us. Letting us know of any dangers we should be aware of."

Striker stepped up next to Cranston with the handsome, black man trailing. She tucked their names away. Jeremiah, at least, was a man she wouldn't mind having a conversation with. Had he been a slave? Was he a runaway? If so, she hoped he made a clean getaway.

Cranston continued. "We'll take off half an hour after dawn on the twenty-second. Please bring your wagons to the field on the western end of Main Street the night before. We'll make camp that first day only about seven miles west of here. A nice short day to get us started. Any questions?"

Several hands went up.

Willow felt someone's perusal then and turned her head to meet Striker's dark eyes. Like Jeremiah beside him, he only seemed to be assessing those who would be in the wagon train. He gave her a nod and moved his assessment on to Gideon beside her. The men also exchanged silent greetings.

Willow couldn't stand any more of this. She turned and spoke to Gideon. "I'm heading back to the store to finish the books."

Gid frowned. "I want to hear the answers to the questions."

"Stay. I'll be fine. I've only to walk along the boardwalk. I think I can manage that without you by my side."

Gid touched her arm. "Please? Give me just a few minutes. Your father will likely want to introduce you to the new buyer. And with so many trains about to depart, there are a lot of strangers in town."

She sighed. That was true enough. She nodded, and Gideon seemed to ease. "Thank you."

Willow settled in for the rounds of questions, but she kept her attention fixed on her clasped hands because the man beside Papa kept looking at her in a most disconcerting way that had her stomach in knots.

Eden Houston inhaled courage and exhaled fear—at least, that was what she tried to tell herself. She stood at the rear of the crowd with one hand pressed to her roiling middle and studied the back of Adam's head.

He still had that curl of hair at the crown of his head that insisted on sweeping in the wrong direction, but, if anything, his shoulders seemed broader than when she'd seen him last. He was darker too. He must be spending a lot of time in the sun lately, judging by his tan and the sun-lightened tips of his curls. He never had been good about remembering to wear his hat. She used to tease him that one day he'd come home with his brains all cooked.

He hadn't seen her yet. She'd purposely been keeping behind him because she didn't want their first meeting in over two years to be in a crowd. Truth was, she hadn't figured on him no longer having an office.

She'd taken a risk earlier and gulped down a meal in a nearby diner, afraid that Adam might walk in at any moment. When she'd discreetly asked the proprietress about any churches in town, she'd learned that Adam had given up his church to a new man and would be leaving town on the next wagon train.

Just as he'd said in that last letter.

She hadn't planned to join him.

After they'd lost their son and he'd seemed content to carry on as usual, she'd been livid. She'd crawled into the bed her exasperated parents had provided for her and not come out except for the most basic of necessities for two weeks. And then she'd only risen because her father, bless him, had told her she would get up or he would dump her onto the floor. After that, she'd sat in the rocking chair, staring out the window in the sitting room for most of each day, simply trying to make right of her world. But no thoughts or imaginings could make life right ever again.

She'd known she was acting like a spoiled child, yet she hadn't been able to find the gumption to change her behavior.

Adam had come to call daily, and, heartless as it was, she'd turned him away each time, refusing to see him.

Then, one day he hadn't come to the house like usual.

She wasn't sure what she'd expected him to do about her repeated rejections, but hieing off to the west as they'd originally planned hadn't even crossed her mind.

She'd waited in her rocking chair, half-heartedly snapping the beans mother had set in her lap, wondering what the delay could be. Of course, she hadn't planned to admit him, so she wasn't even sure why she'd noticed his tardiness. After a while, she'd grown worried. Worried enough that she'd risen from her chair and gone onto the porch to see if he might be coming up the lane. She'd sat in the sun on the porch for thirty minutes before realizing he likely wouldn't come that day. Or the next. Or the next.

And then he'd arrived with a wagon all packed for the trip west and expected her to join him as they'd planned! So much anger had surged through her that she'd gritted out that she wished him all the best and then slammed the door to her room. She could still remember the slump of his shoulders as he'd stood in her parents' living room with his hat in one hand.

She hadn't expected him to leave. She'd thought he would stay. Change his mind. Give her time to adjust, and then they could go back to life as it used to be. To happier times.

But he hadn't come again after that.

A few weeks later, his first letter had arrived.

He'd told her he would never love anyone else but that he had to follow where God was leading him. He said it was breaking his heart, her rejection and turning her back on what they both knew the Lord had called them to. And so, he'd decided to follow his—their—call. Letters came weekly after that—long letters filled with nothing . . . but everything.

At first, angry that he'd dared to move on without her, she'd refused to even read them. But Mother forced her to sit and listen while she read. Slowly, her pique faded, and her heart began to chastise her for her own part in their separation. For allowing grief and despair to make her a prisoner. For refusing to continue living life.

And then, one day, the sermon at church had been about taking every thought captive, and she'd realized that she hadn't been exercising any control over her despondent thoughts. She'd prayed and asked God for the strength, and now, here she stood, knees trembling like a newborn foal. Her heart remained shattered, but she at least felt somewhat resigned to continue living now.

At the center of the circled crowd, the wagon master said, "I've asked Parson Houston, who will be joining us on our trip to say a prayer for us today." The wagon master stepped to one side, swinging an arm in invitation for Adam to step up beside him.

Panic zipped through her! She wasn't ready to face him. It certainly wouldn't do to shock him with her presence while he stood helpless in front of a crowd! She thought about bolting, but that would surely draw his attention. Instead, she eased to one side and hid behind the rather large bonnet of the woman in front of her—but not before she got a quick look at her husband's face.

She couldn't help a sharp intake of breath as her heart thumped hard in her chest. This handsome man was still her husband, and just one glimpse of his face filled her with regret for the way she'd treated him. He'd been grieving too!

"Father, we come before You today to ask Your blessing on our trip west."

The sound of his tenor swept into her and settled into all the cracked places like the balm of a familiar pathway after a long trip into the unknown.

A sob escaped before she could suppress it.

The man beside her glanced sideways.

She bowed her head and folded her hands. "Lord, forgive me," she whispered. *I don't know how I let myself get so low as to make such a mess of things or if he will even truly want me back. His letters have said all along that he does, but I know that might not be exactly how he feels. He's a good man, and of course, he would say that. Please go before me. Prepare Adam's heart for our meeting. Please, don't ever let me betray him like I did again. Give me the joy of Your strength. Give me the hope of Your goodness. Give me the motivation of Your Holy Spirit.*

With her prayer finished, she tuned in to the silence all around her. The crowd was disbursing. With a start, she lifted her head—and looked right into her husband's gray eyes.

"Eden!" His voice emerged, hardly more than a breath.

Chapter 4

Willow walked with Gideon toward where Papa, Declan, and the stranger stood talking—likely about the news of the Donation Land Act extension from the way they hovered over the newspaper they'd somehow gotten ahold of.

Papa glanced up and waved the paper. "Willow! Darling, come and meet Mr. Harrington." He clapped the man beside him on the shoulder and directed the conversation with the folded paper like a bandmaster. "Mr. Harrington, may I present my daughter, Willow Chancellor. And this man beside her is Gideon Riley. He'll be traveling with us to Oregon."

Mr. Harrington took her hand and bowed over it, lingering too long for propriety. "Miss. I have to admit, overwhelmed by your beauty as I am, I'm honestly sorry to be staying behind."

Willow smiled, but again that curl of unease swept through her as she tugged for the release of her hand. She certainly would not be sad to leave him behind.

Hoyt transferred his attention smoothly to Gideon, stretching out his hand. "Mr. Riley, was it? Forgive me if I overstepped." The slight smirk on his lips proved he didn't care a whit about whether he'd offended Gideon.

Willow swallowed. The man obviously didn't know Gideon at all if he thought he might be interested in her.

Gideon shook his hand. "No forgiveness necessary." He said the words, but they came out stone cold and no smile of polite greeting graced his lips.

Willow felt her jaw go a little slack. What had gotten into him today? She'd never seen him treat someone so coldly before.

He turned to offer her his arm. "Shall I escort you back to the store?"

Willow started to agree when Papa brushed him off. "Willow, I'd like you to stay with me, please. There are a few fellow passengers I'd like to introduce you to and then we'll take Mr. Harrington to the store. You can likely answer some of his questions about our suppliers better than I can. Gideon, see you at dinner? I think we'll all join you at Felicity's Diner this evening for a meal."

Gideon stepped back, lips pinched into a line. "Sounds good. I'll see you all then."

His gaze flicked off Mr. Harrington and landed on her, then he strode away, easing through the crowd to stop at Micah's side.

"Come, Willow." Papa drew her attention. "I want you to meet, Mr. Cranston, our wagon master, and then, I assure you, Mr. Harrington, we'll go right to the store and sign that final paperwork." Papa tapped him on the arm with the newspaper.

When they reached Mr. Cranston's side, Papa handed over the paper. "Thank you for allowing me to read the news for myself. Very encouraging. May I present my daughter, Willow, who will be traveling with me."

Mr. Cranston clasped his hands behind his back and gave her a little bow along with a once-over. "Miss Willow. A pleasure to make your acquaintance. I do hope you plan to have good sturdy boots and a good-sized bonnet for the trip?"

Willow felt her face heat. It was most improper for a stranger to speak of her wardrobe. Why was it that older people seemed to think it all right to dispense with propriety?

"Forgive me," he hurried to add. "But I've seen people need to turn back for the lack of forethought on small things just like that. We will be crossing a vast stretch of land with no towns and the few mercantiles that we do pass are always suffering for provisions. I only mean to caution against want of necessities."

"Never fear," Papa assured him. "I've been reading every article and pamphlet I can get my hands on. I think we are well-provisioned and Willow will be properly kitted out for the trip."

Mr. Cranston gave another sketch of a bow. "Very well. Until launch day, then, Miss Chancellor." With that, he turned his focus to the next people waiting to speak to him.

Willow felt a bit put out by the whole conversation. She tossed a frown over her shoulder.

Papa took her by the arm. "Never mind him. Let's get Mr. Harrington to the store and show him around, shall we?"

As they walked, the men made small talk that Willow ignored while trying to tamp down her despair over a trip that she didn't want to take in the first place.

Her one consolation . . . She glanced over her shoulder to where Gideon still stood, smiling now, as he pumped Micah's hand with seemingly great joy. What could that be about? The Donation Land Act reversal, perhaps? But they'd already shared their joy about that.

"Watch out, Willow!"

Papa's call of alarm came just in time to help her avoid the watering trough she'd almost run into.

Feeling her embarrassment in her cheeks, she hoisted two fistfuls of her skirts to follow Papa and Mr. Harrington up the steps to the store.

Goodness, her falling upside down in a watering trough would have been news that traveled faster than the renewal of land donations!

Corbin Donahue held the door for the Chancellors like he felt a proper gentleman would. He gave Willow his most charming smile as she passed, and it was no hardship whatsoever. She had blue eyes a man could drown in and curves that made a man contemplate what no proper gentleman would.

He bit back a grin. No one had ever accused him of being a proper gentleman.

She swept past without giving him even a glance, however.

Hmmm. A challenge. He liked a challenge.

Battening down his anticipation at the hurdle before him, he followed them into the dingy interior of the mercantile. One glance shored up his thankfulness that his business wasn't in merchandise. Though, as stores went, he supposed, this one was in pretty good shape. The rows of items were neat and organized and clean.

Boring.

No risk, adventure, or thrill of the hunt.

He adjusted his satin necktie and tried to look interested when Mr. Chancellor beamed at him and swept a proud gesture to the store.

"Here you are. This, of course, is the main room of the store. You'll find that we stock all the wanted necessities along with many additional luxuries that people in town can only find in our store! Come, come! I'll show you around."

From the corner of his eye, he saw Willow flip over the "open" sign on the front door and slip behind the counter. She bent her head over a set of books.

Mr. Chancellor cleared his throat and Corbin pulled his attention back to the man. Only the paperwork to sign and he'd get paid. Then he could be on his way to Oregon. But . . . with the renewal of the land act, he'd get twice the amount of land if he arrived with a wife. Of course he had money to buy land, but starting out with free acreage would be better. Then he could use more of his money for building a house.

As they strode down the hall with Mr. Chancellor babbling something about showing him the storeroom, his mind drifted to Willow once more.

Of course, he hadn't planned to go west with this first wagon train. He needed some time to get himself set up. And it would raise suspicions if he claimed to have sold the store again so quickly as to join a wagon train in two weeks. Maybe he should just try to find a different woman to woo.

But . . . He glanced back toward Willow, bent over those books, her long neck exposed by the tilt of her head. Where else would he ever find a woman as fine as that one?

He could figure this out. As soon as he signed over the paperwork to Grant Moore and got paid, he'd be free and clear to do whatever he wanted. He'd have to put his mind to conjuring up a plan.

What would it take to get Willow to feel that she owed him a debt?

His gaze landed on her father.

And he bit back a triumphant smile as an idea presented itself, fully formed.

Tamsyn Acheson took a deep breath, willing herself to breathe through her pain as she stepped from the boardwalk into the Independence mercantile. People bustled, bumping and clamoring to have their voices heard above one another. Tamsyn's heart sank. There was no way she would escape this pandemonium without being jostled a time or two, but . . . She tossed a glance over her shoulder to the wagon.

Edison stood beside it, arms folded, face placid.

Tamsyn swallowed. Thankfully, today he seemed quiet and cooperative. She motioned for him to remain where he was, then pressed onward. She inched past two women who doddled over a row of canned goods. One of the women bent to examine a jar of fruit, bumping Tamsyn's back with her parasol handle.

Agony flamed. Tamsyn flinched and a solitary whimper escaped. She hoped her tight-pressed lips melded the sound with the noise filling the room. Gritting her teeth, she navigated to the far side of the store and paused near a display of soap cakes. Fewer people congregated there. Picking up a bar, she closed her eyes, pressed it to her nose, and inhaled slowly, willing down the threatening tears.

Mmmm. Orange blossom, perhaps? Whatever the scent, it was lovely, soft, and floral.

Edison hadn't had a good night last night, and she'd paid the price. She was nervous over whether she could still pull this plan off. What if they got a few days down the trail and Edi went into one of his fits? Would the wagon master expel them from the train? At the meeting a few minutes ago, one of his rules had been that there would be no toleration of violence toward other members of the wagon train. Of course she ought to have known that would be a rule. And most of the time Edi was fine. But if something set him off . . .

She placed the soap back on the table and caressed it with a fingertip. She really shouldn't spend the money for something so extravagant.

After Mother had said she couldn't handle Edi anymore and he had to go, what else was Tamsyn supposed to do? She couldn't leave her mentally challenged brother to face the world on his own. He would be killed sooner than later because of his penchant for fits of rage born of his frustration when he couldn't accomplish some task or another.

Last night it had been that he wanted to tie his own boots. And when she'd tried to help him, he'd backhanded her shoulder, sending her crashing into the hub of their wagon wheel.

She simply needed to get him to Oregon. Get them some of this land—what a boon that the Donation Land Act had been renewed!—and then give him a set of daily tasks that he could accomplish with ease. Even on the way west, giving him the task of driving the wagon would keep him content. It was all the other moments when he wasn't driving that concerned her.

But once they reached Oregon, life would settle into a routine. She would get some sheep and spin her wool, and they would somehow survive on her earnings.

God would provide. She firmly believed that. She only wished that, somehow, He would help her figure out how to soothe Edi's temper when needed.

She rolled her shoulder in an attempt to ease the ache in her back, and glanced around.

The pretty redheaded woman smiled at her from behind the counter at the front of the store. "Is there anything I can help you find?"

Tamsyn shook her head. "No. Thank you. I was just . . . taking it all in." She forced a smile and on second thought, added the bar of soap to her basket, and then made herself move, so as not to draw any more undue attention.

She trailed the pad of her finger along the front edge of a shelf holding a jar of buttons and spools of thread. When would she next see a mercantile? She sniffed. When would she next have the money to shop in a mercantile? She had spent most of the money she had to supply their wagon with the most modest of supplies. But she couldn't skimp on food or Edi would get grumpy and irritable.

Blowing out a breath, she hooked her basket over one arm and began adding a few things.

She would be leaving everything familiar, and yet . . . What care had she for anything left behind? Ma and Pa had worked hard with her brother all these years and then had finally given up on him. Pa had fallen into drink and Ma had been set to drive Edi miles away and leave him to fend for himself.

This was her only option.

Thank goodness she'd been setting some money by from the eggs and cream she took to the mercantile in town each week or she and Edi would have been in a real bind.

God? Are You seeing me down here? Lost and broken and weary?

It was the right thing to stick with her brother. She harbored no doubt about that. But the years stretched before her long and dark. Edi had cost her.

Cost her the hope of one day having a family of her own.

Cost her daily peace of mind.

But she owed him. His plight, after all, was her fault.

Tamsyn absentmindedly twisted the gold ring on her thumb as she watched the two matrons leave with their colorful jars of fruit. One held a jar of cherries up as they exited the building and the sun glinted through red juices, making Tamsyn's mouth water.

On impulse she added a jar of cherries to her basket. She could only afford the one. But maybe it would give her a moment of peace on one of Edi's particularly rough nights. Cherry pie was his favorite.

Again, she twisted the ring.

Remembering the sense of betrayal she'd felt the night Ma practically chased them from the property, drove her fingernails into one palm. She'd hoped Ma might change her mind.

But hope was woven of illusions and dreams. It was an emotion better left untouched. If she didn't allow herself hope, she couldn't be crushed. If she didn't dwell on her longing for love, the loneliness that crept upon her in the wee hours of the night felt less sharp.

But today, with the launch of the wagon train only a couple weeks away, she felt nostalgic. Lonely. A bit scared, if she were honest.

Hard as it was to survive here, she had no desire to try to survive with Edi out there abandoned in the middle of the wilderness.

Lord, if this isn't meant to be, please prevent us from going from the start. I need Your wisdom. I'm going to be Edi's sole caregiver and I don't want to get us into a bad situation.

Ma may have been bitter to be stuck with a son who required so much emotional tending, but at least she'd carried the burden some of the time. Now it would be all up to Tamsyn.

And today, that thought weighed her down. It didn't help that she'd hardly been able to sleep last night for the pain in her back. Of course, Edi had been immediately sorrowful when he'd seen that he'd hurt her. He'd rushed over, hauled her up with his brute strength, and forced her into a fierce embrace, which hadn't helped.

She blinked and added a new strop to her basket.

Today's emotions surprised and frustrated her. She pushed them back down where they belonged. Hidden. Tucked out of sight.

If the Lord allowed Edi and her to continue, they *would* make this trip. And she would be strong no matter what Edi or the trail handed out to her. She'd been adapting and learning to deal with Edi's whims all her life. She would make it through this too.

And no more whimpering about it.

Throwing back her shoulders, she added a new razor and at the last moment a small snare and a fish trap, then approached the front counter.

The woman smiled at her. It was all at once welcoming and full of friendship. "Hello, again. Didn't I see you at the meeting for the Caesar Cranston wagon train?"

Tamsyn nodded. "Yes. My brother and I will be joining that train." Thankfully, Edi had been in a compliant mood when they'd met the wagon master and his second, Mr. Hawkeye. Edi had nodded to all the questions as she'd instructed him to do, and they had been given permission to join. Tamsyn hadn't realized how much she'd worried about that first hurdle until they were walking away.

"We are going to join too. I'm Willow, by the way. Willow Chancellor."

"Tamsyn Acheson."

"Well, it's a pleasure to meet you. I'm looking forward to getting to know you better over the next few months."

Though Tamsyn sensed that Willow meant the words wholeheartedly, sadness filled her eyes when she swept a glance around the interior of the store.

"Your husband got a yearning for Oregon?" Tamsyn surprised herself by asking.

Willow laughed. "Oh, I'm not married! It's my father. I only recently—this morning, actually—found out that we would be going. I'm admittedly a bit torn at the prospect. But . . . What is life without a little adventure, right?" She grinned and thrust a fist above her head like she was ready to take on the challenge with fervor.

Tamsyn couldn't help but return her smile. What she wouldn't give to have that girl's intrepid personality.

Another customer approached behind her, and she quickly counted out what she owed. "Well, I'll look forward to chatting with you again soon."

And she would, too. It surprised her how connected she felt to this woman after such a short conversation. Maybe her loneliness really was getting to her.

At a loss for what else to say, she took up her things and started toward the door. She winced, feeling like she'd ended that conversation awkwardly. Should she have said more? Maybe invited the girl to her fire for tea and biscuits sometime before they took off?

No. Not that.

The fewer people who met Edi prior to launch day, the better it would be for her. The last thing she wanted was for Edi to get her kicked out of the wagon train ere it had even left—unless that was what God wanted, which she hoped it wasn't.

She reached for the handle, but the door swung outward before she took hold of it. The bell above it jangled as a man, broad and tall, stepped into the opening. His jacket, cut of supple brown leather and lined with fur, hung from a frame head-and-shoulders above her own.

Tamsyn glanced up and felt her eyes widen. He was one of the scouts from the wagon train! For half a second, they remained toe to toe with her looking up at him, and then she dropped her chin. Her gaze snagged on the button straining to remain closed in the middle of his chest.

Don't draw attention to yourself.

Tamsyn dutifully kept her gaze glued to the button and dropped a curtsy. "Pardon me."

The scout retreated to the boardwalk. "Ma'am." He lifted his hat from his head and swept it in a gesture that indicated she was free to pass.

Gaze still lowered, she stepped into the doorway.

"I'm the one should beg your pardon."

It was the smooth tenor of his voice that elicited her disobedience. She had to tip her chin up a good way to see into his face, unlike with Edi who stood nearly eye to eye with her.

His hair, dark and wavy, hung a touch on the long side, especially noticeable as it swooped toward a pair of warm-pecan-colored eyes— one of which ticked slightly, as if he were a bit perturbed at the length of time she was taking to get out of his way but was too much of a gentleman to say so.

But something about the man's calm scrutiny reached deep inside her and lit a candle in a place that had been dark for a very long time. She eased out a breath.

And just like that, she snapped back to attention and tossed a quick scan up and down the street. Her heart dropped as she noted Edi. He remained by their wagon, but paced short steps back and forth, a sure sign that he was starting to get impatient.

A flame of fear burgeoned in her chest. The last thing she needed was for this man to witness Edi having a fit of temper.

Lifting her skirts, she murmured a hasty "Thank you" and swept past the scout. She hurried down the boardwalk toward her twin, who stomped one foot as she approached.

"Gone too long!" His brows slumped low over the bridge of his nose. "Edi hot."

"I'm sorry. Let's drive the wagon into some shade and get you a drink. That will help you cool down."

"Hungry too!" He yanked the basket from her so hard that it momentarily snagged on her arm.

"Ow, Edi, slow down, please." She rubbed at the place where she would likely have another bruise by tomorrow. "I can make lunch early."

"Good." He thumped the basket into the back of their covered wagon and stomped toward the front seat.

She hurried along her side to climb aboard before he could start off without her, but even at that, he'd slapped the reins to the horses' backs before she made it even halfway up to the seat.

"Edi!" Off balance, she bit back a cry, scrabbling for something to grasp hold of. She was in for it now. As she leaned to grab the back frame of the wagon seat, she glanced past her brother and, to her dread, found that the scout had remained outside the doorway.

And now, he was charging toward them.

Chapter 5

As the woman hurried down the mercantile steps, Striker Moss stared after her, unable to think for a moment why he'd come to the mercantile. One second, he'd been standing there enjoying the blue eyes and tawny porcelain features of the beautiful brunette, and the next she'd seemed to shrink into herself. He let the door go, and remained where he stood, turning his hat through his fingers.

She rushed toward a man with broad shoulders and curly brown hair similar to her own. He wore a dirty white shirt that stretched across his shoulders near to capacity. Perhaps it was the anger in the man's stance that kept Striker where he stood. They'd been in the crowd at the meeting a few minutes ago and there had been something odd about the way the couple refused to meet anyone's gazes and how they had hurried away promptly as soon as Cranston gave them his approval.

It might be good for him to pay attention to what happened here. One bad apple, and all that . . .

The woman spoke a few words, though with all the wagons and people and horses and caterwauling going on in Independence today, he couldn't make out what she said. The man yanked the basket from her so roughly that her arm got caught!

Striker narrowed his eyes as she rubbed the spot just below her elbow and said something in a placating manor.

The burly man didn't seem to want to hear what she had to say. After tossing the basket into the back of the wagon, he stomped toward the front. The woman quickly fisted her skirt and dashed along the other side but had to pause for a carriage passing in the street.

Before she could even climb all the way onto the wagon bench, the cad started driving!

Striker caught a flash of panic in the woman's eyes as she scrambled for a handhold.

"Hey!" Striker lurched off the porch and ran to leap onto the running board beside the driver's seat. He grabbed the reins. "Whoa!" He spoke firmly to the team and yanked the horses to a halt. "What are you thinking!" He glowered at the man.

And to his surprise, the man melted into a blubbering crouch, and frantically began scooting away from him. "I'm sorry. Don't hit me. I not mean to hurt Tamsyn!" He lifted one arm to protect his head as if Striker might bludgeon him with his fist.

Shocked, Striker whipped his gaze to the woman, who remained sprawled only halfway on the bench across the way. Her eyes fell closed, and despair etched her features.

Striker swallowed. This was not as it seemed.

He raised his palms, continuing to balance on the running board. "I'm not going to hurt you. But you have to give—Tammy, is it?—time to climb up before you drive off."

She looked across the bench at him again. Her eyes were a blue that leaned toward the color of the northern lights he'd seen when he and Jer made that trek into Canada three years ago. She blinked and worked to get a leg up to the floorboards.

"Let me come around and help you."

"No." She continued to flounder. "I'm fine. I just . . ." Finally, she settled herself onto the seat and adjusted her skirt. "There. See?" She forced a smile. "And it's Tamsyn. Edison was just in a little too much of a hurry is all. Isn't that right, Edi?" She patted the man's knee.

He seemed to uncurl himself and lower his arms. But he kept his gaze fastened to his lap as he nodded. "Hungry."

The woman angled Striker a glance.

He couldn't let this go. He narrowed his eyes to let her know he was serious when he said, "We need to talk."

Her shoulders drooped and she tucked her lip between her teeth. "Okay. But can we do it later? If you come by our wagon this evening, I'll offer you some stew. Then we can talk after."

He really should make her talk to him now, but one glance at the agitated man beside her made him realize now was probably not the best time. He hoped he hadn't made it worse. He returned his focus to her. "Are you safe?"

She smoothed her skirts. "Yes. Of course. Quite safe."

He had his doubts but, giving her a nod, he dropped down to the street. "All right then. How about I come by around six?"

Her brow furrowed. But then she gave a quick dip of her chin. "Yes, six will be fine."

He lifted a hand, still unsure whether he should be letting her drive off with her . . . what was the man to her? Surely not husband? "I'll see you tonight then."

She gave another crisp nod and then nudged the man. "All right, Edi. We can go now. Just take it easy this time."

As Striker watched them go, he slowly backed toward the mercantile porch.

Tamsyn.

An unusual name. But he liked it. It seemed to suit her.

He gave himself a shake. *Bullets.* That was why he was here. Bullets and coffee and hard-tack, and Jeremiah's special order of liniment.

He shoved the image of the troubled couple from his mind, pushed back into the mercantile, and strode toward the counter.

He dropped his hat onto the wood, propped himself against his palms, arms locked, and waited for the proprietress to finish with the duo of ladies near the dress goods. His gaze landed on a bolt of turquoise-blue silk the exact color of that woman's eyes.

Tamsyn.

Tamsyn what?

And he hadn't caught the name of the man. Wait, no . . . She'd said it. Edison. She'd called him Edi, though. They would be nothing but trouble on a trek west, and that was certain.

If it weren't for the woman's eyes, he could wish they'd only paused near today's meeting out of curiosity. Except he distinctly remembered hearing Cranston give them his approval to join the train.

He scrubbed one cheek against his shoulder. On a wagon train through the middle of hostile territory? That couple would be nothing but a detriment. Nothing but a peck of trouble with a capital T based on the short interaction he just had with them.

Yet . . . his eyes dropped closed. The despair in her expression when she'd seen him approaching . . . Well, he couldn't harbor a soft spot for every woman experiencing a hard place in life. And yet . . .

He blinked away the vision of her disappointed posture.

"May I help you?" The shop mistress approached with a smile.

It was only a few moments before he was leaving the store with his purchases. Jeremiah would be pleased that his foul-smelling rub had come in on time.

But they had those extra cattle to round up—Caesar's way of planning ahead for lean times, which was smart.

And he still needed to talk to Caesar to get a little more information about Tamsyn and Edi before he made it to their fire by six. Also, he'd only halfway been paying attention to Caesar's conversation with them. Maybe it hadn't been what he thought it to be at the time.

Please, God.

He suddenly realized he had no idea where they were camped. Not near the other wagons that had begun to gather on the west end of the field for the Cranston train, he felt certain.

A woman as beautiful as Tamsyn was memorable. He would definitely remember if he'd seen her before. She'd captured his attention at the meeting, of course, but he'd thought she was married to the man beside her. But now?

He wasn't so sure.

What he was sure of was the fact that they simply could not join the wagon train. There was too much danger in the man's instability.

Willow felt a little piece of her heart shatter as she watched Papa and Mr. Harrington shake hands after signing the papers down the counter a ways. The agreement apparently allowed her and Papa to stay in the store until the morning of their wagon train's launch and then Mr. Harrington would take over.

Mr. Harrington doffed his hat in her direction and then took his leave.

With a sigh, she walked over to flip the sign to "closed" a little earlier than usual. She had a lot of sorting and packing to do in the next two weeks. And she hadn't even found time to think about the proper way to pack a wagon. When Mercy arrived last year, she'd taught her a whole lot about how organization smoothed a day's routine, and Willow had determined from then on to practice the trait that seemed so elusive to her. In the wagon, there would be things that they needed once in a while that they wouldn't need on a regular basis, so those items needed to be accessible, but out of the way.

Oh, this whole thing was squeezing her head with such an ache.

As she strode past Papa, he lifted the paperwork and blew on the fresh signatures. "Wonderful! We're off on a new adventure, dearest!" He fanned a stack of bills with a smile. "I do hope you're not terribly vexed to be heading off to Oregon?"

His question reminded her that Gideon had said she ought to ask him his reasons for wanting to go to Oregon, but she wasn't sure she could face the answer at the moment. Nor did she want to dampen his mood.

Instead, she forced a stiff smile that she hoped looked genuine. "I'm always happy to be with you, Papa." She needed air. "I'm just going to go for a walk." She started toward the back door.

Papa hurried to say, "That's fine, but could you get Declan's room set up for Mr. Harrington to stay in until we leave? I told him he could stay there starting tonight until we are out of the building."

Willow froze. She wasn't one to be impertinent, she truly wasn't, but Papa expected her to not only prepare and pack for a six-month journey in the next two weeks, but also now house a guest?

Since she had her back to him and he wouldn't see her irritation, she drew in a slow breath through her flared nostrils. "Yes, Papa."

Before he could say more, she hurried through their apartment at the rear of the store and right out the back door. Skirts hoisted enough to give her feet room to move, she reached a run by the time she passed the barn and hit the gravel path toward the creek at a full-out sprint. Rage threatened to explode at any moment.

She ran until she couldn't get enough air to run another step and then she froze on the bank of the creek and growled a feral bellow that allowed her to release her frustration but wouldn't travel back to the town and raise an alarm. It felt so good that she did it again, a little louder this time, fists balled and the tendons in her neck straining.

Gravel crunched on the path behind her.

She spun. "Gideon." She slapped one hand at the tangle of curls that had come loose from her bun to dangle in her vision like a taunt, and pivoted back to look over the creek once more. She took a calming breath. Then another.

Of course he'd followed her. She should have thought that the men might be in the barn packing the remainder of Micah's wagon.

Working to tuck the curl back into its proper place, she tossed him a glance over her shoulder. He barely looked to be breathing hard and she was gulping air so rapidly that she started to feel dizzy. "I'm fine. You didn't need to follow me."

Why, oh why, was everything spinning? When the creekbank seemed to dip from beneath her foot, she took a bracing step, but misjudged and planted her foot on a stone that turned beneath her boot and rolled down the embankment. "Oh!"

Her arms flailed, doing a poor job of helping her maintain her balance. She was going into the creek!

And then Gid's warm hand snaked around her waist and yanked her against his firm chest. He turned her into him and pressed one broad gentle hand against the back of her head. "Breathe, Wil. Just breathe. Slow and easy."

She began sobbing before she even realized what was happening. Deep, wracking sobs that took the strength from her legs and would have left her in a heap on the ground if it weren't for Gid's arms.

She felt his lips press into the hair above her ear. "Shhh, it's all right. Everything will be all right." The warm brush of his breath caressed her ear and the side of her neck.

Pull yourself together! She took a bracing, shuddering breath. Then another.

Blinked. Sniffed.

His shirt soaked up her tears on one side and she swiped the pads of her fingers over her cheek on the other. "Sorry."

"You've naught to be sorry for."

"I don't normally fall apart like this."

"I know."

She felt a tremor cascade from her shoulders to her ankles. "It's done. Papa signed over the store. And now I'm to prepare a room for Mr. Harrington, so I'd best get back." Despite saying the words, she didn't move from the comforting circle of Gid's arms.

Something rumbled in Gid's chest. "What room?" There was a note of irritation in his voice that she didn't often hear.

Did he think Papa was giving the new owner one of their rooms upstairs? Hoping to reassure him, she hurried to say, "None of your rooms upstairs. The room Declan has been staying in. Declan has been sleeping nights near Micah's cattle in a small tent for a few days now, anyhow."

Gideon eased his hands to her shoulders and set her back from him. "Yes, I know, and that's what I was afraid of. Do me a favor and lock your door at night. Something about that man raises the hair on the back of my neck."

Willow rubbed at the moisture still coating her fingers. "I'll not say that I disagree with you. But I think it's just the strange circumstances. I was disposed to dislike him before I ever met him."

Gid frowned as his gaze drifted over the landscape. "Maybe. I'm not so sure, however." The frown was still in place when he lowered his attention to her, once more. "You going to be all right?"

Willow stepped back, realizing her reprieve was over. This paradise of security and comfort in Gideon's arms would likely never come her way again. Why did that thought cut like a razor when she felt so determined to put the man from her mind?

She rubbed her fingertips together again. "Yes. Thank you. I'm fine. You didn't have to—" She'd already said that. "Sorry I . . ." She didn't have any words of explanation for all the agitated emotions swirling inside her, so she simply ended with a shrug.

His frown eased. "Everyone needs to get away from it all sometimes. Just, next time . . . don't go off unescorted, please? There are a lot of strangers coming into town now, as I already said."

Why were her fingers so fidgety? "Yes. I know. I'll try to be more careful if there is a next time." She gave him a self-deprecating smirk.

Suddenly Gid's chin jerked up. "Do you smell that?" He spun to look back toward the town.

Willow followed his gaze to where they could see a black roil of smoke belching into the sky. "No!" She lifted her skirt and started back toward town at a sprint. "Is that a fire?"

Gid ran behind her. "Hurry! It looks like it's near the store! Joel and Avram are upstairs!"

Chapter 6

Eden wasn't sure what she'd expected from Adam after not seeing him for nearly two years, but having him practically ignore her hadn't even crossed her mind.

At the end of the meeting, he'd gaped at her and gasped her name, then she'd seen that telltale bulge in the muscles of his jaw—a sure sign that he was angry. Oh, he was a gentleman and had offered her his arm and then escorted her to this room where he boarded in the hotel that stood almost directly across the street from the diner she'd eaten in earlier.

Then he'd said, "I'm sorry to do this, but I'm supposed to officiate a funeral in thirty minutes. I have to go." And without another word he'd turned and left her standing in the middle of the room.

Weary from her long day of travel, she'd crawled onto the bed and taken a nap, expecting that he would return before she woke.

But now, the sun hung low enough in the sky that it dipped below the rooftop of the building next door—a mercantile if she remembered correctly—and Adam still hadn't returned.

Eden paced to the window and flipped back the muslin curtain. Did he plan to keep her imprisoned here until he was well on his way to Oregon without her?

Her lips tilted at the thought. She deserved nothing less, she supposed.

Adam's room lay at the front corner of the hotel. The window she stood at faced the street, but the one to her right looked down on the alley between the boardinghouse and—yes, she'd been correct—Chancellor's Mercantile next door. A sign hanging in the side window of the store supplied the name.

Adam's room had grown stuffy with the afternoon sun beating in, so she lifted the sash and propped it open with a short stick lying on the windowsill that was likely meant for that exact purpose.

The scent of pot roast and potatoes wafted on the welcome breeze and her stomach growled so loudly that she slapped her palm over it. Adam might not be thrilled to have her back in his life, but she'd more than somewhat expected that, and it didn't mean she needed to starve herself.

Decision made, she lowered the window back into place, and gathered her shawl from the chair where she'd tossed it earlier. A movement out the side window caught her eye as she swung it on. She stepped nearer and glanced down to see what it was.

Below her, a man walked through the alley, heading toward the back of the buildings. She couldn't make out his features, or even the color of his hair, because he wore a black hat and the shadows in the alleyway were quite dark now. She caught a glimmer of light glinting off something near his cuff as he passed the farthest window of the mercantile and then he turned the corner to walk behind the store. As he did, a match flared and he bent over it.

Lighting a cigarette, most likely.

Perhaps the alley was just a cut-through locals used.

At any rate, darkness was falling fast and if she wanted to get some dinner, she'd better hustle.

At the bottom of the stairs, she moved through the small entry lit by milk glass oil lamps and passed the unoccupied desk to step onto the boardwalk out front. She drew in a long breath, and her stomach growled again at the scent of the pot roast that wafted even stronger here on the street than it had up in the room.

As she crossed the street, she tucked her shawl close and angled a glance toward the sky. *Well, Lord, I didn't get such a warm reception, did I?* Despite having expected a cool welcome, she found herself rather more hurt than she'd anticipated.

Even as she moved into the diner and asked for a table for one, love for Adam swelled in her chest. How could she have mistreated him so?

She hoped he wasn't going to punish her for the rest of her life.

At a table near the window someone gasped. "Fire!"

Within seconds, everyone in the diner spilled onto the boardwalk. Smoke whipped on the whim of air currents at the back of the mercantile!

She clutched her shawl tight at her throat, one image prominent in her mind.

The man turning the corner only moments earlier, his face lit by the golden glow of a match!

Micah and Mercy were working with Gideon to move the rest of Micah's supplies when Gideon, who was hauling a crate of canned goods, suddenly set the crate down and ran out the door, calling, "Willow?"

They both turned to the propped-open back doors of the barn to watch Willow sprinting down the trail toward the creek with Gideon hot on her heels.

Mercy lifted her apron to dab at the moisture on her forehead. "I don't think it was right of Wayne to keep this trip from her. She needed more time to prepare, both emotionally and—" she swept a gesture toward the wagon they were packing "—logistically."

Micah transferred the crate in his hands into the new wagon. "She'll come around, but I can't say that I disagree with you."

For several minutes they continued to transfer crates and boxes from one wagon to the other.

Only a few crates remained when Micah's head snapped up. "Do you smell smoke?"

Mercy looked toward the mercantile and felt her eyes widen as she saw flames hungrily scooting along the back wall of the store near the corner. "Micah! The boys!" She snatched up her skirts and was already sprinting.

The boys had returned from school a couple of hours ago, and Micah had told them they could read quietly in their rooms upstairs!

Mattox scrambled from beneath the wagon, and she heard his claws clacking on the ground behind her.

Micah surged past her. "Mattox stay! Get water, Mercy!"

Mercy darted after him. "Micah you can't—" But she was too late.

He barked, "I mean it, Mercy!" as he yanked open the back door of the store and dove inside.

Mattox whimpered, spun in an agitated circle, and looked up at her.

Defeat washed through her as she eyed the conflagration. Would anyone be able to make it out? She must do her part!

"Come on, boy." Mercy retraced her steps and lurched into the tack room. She grabbed up two buckets—it would be a paltry amount of water in the face of such devouring flames, and the creek suddenly seemed very far away.

She ran with Mattox loping at her side, praying as she did so. "Dear, Lord. Dear, Lord. Dear, Lord!" They were the only words she could think to say.

One thought plagued her. How had a fire of such magnitude started so quickly?

Micah dashed through the Chancellors' apartment yelling for anyone inside to get out. He banged open the bedroom door and thankfully saw no one.

The roar of the flames crackled, bursting through the wall behind him. Smoke eddied against the ceiling like ferocious storm clouds.

He crouched low and scrambled through the store. Thankfully he didn't see Wayne. Not standing behind the counter, or any of the shoulder-height shelves. He must have gone out already!

Gratefulness surged as he took the stairs to the second floor three at a time. Smoke hung heavy and blinding in the stairwell. "Boys!" He coughed as he burst into the room he shared with his son and Gideon.

Empty.

His heart fell. "Boys!?"

The smoke stung, and tears streamed from his eyes. Combined with the smoke, he could hardly make out Mercy's door across the hall. He found it more by feel than sight and flung it open.

Both boys huddled on the bed in the far corner!

Micah fell to his knees in relief. But the open door was allowing boiling billows of smoke to come in.

Tears streaked Avram's cheeks and Joel had him wrapped in a hug.

Micah stretched out his arms. "It's okay. Come here, boys." He motioned them toward him.

Both boys scrambled off the bed and fell against his shoulders.

Micah only took a second to reassure himself that both were okay, and then he set them from him. He pegged his son with a look even as he hefted Avram into his arms. "Joel, I need you to be brave, son. There's a fire, but we are going to get out of here. You just cling tight to my hand and follow me and try to hold your breath and not breathe in too much smoke, okay?"

Joel nodded, but he was already coughing, and moisture now glistened on each of his cheeks.

Micah felt a surge of pride at how brave he'd been until he arrived. "We need to be fast. Hold on tight." Micah rushed out of the room, half hauling Joel behind him.

He froze, heart falling.

A wall of angry orange climbed the stairwell.

Chapter 7

Dusk hung on the nigh side of dark as Adam wearily rode back into town from the funeral he'd conducted at a ranch a few miles away. It was unfortunate, the timing of Eden's arrival—even though it set his heart to hammering with a hope he hadn't thought to feel ever again this side of heaven.

Still, he'd been so shocked to see her and afraid of saying the wrong thing, something that might send her running right back east again, that he probably hadn't handled the surprise very well. But he'd already been pressed for time due to the wagon train meeting and had been on his way to the livery to fetch his mount when he'd looked up and seen Eden. There really hadn't been time for small talk.

Now all the questions he'd been forced to suppress for lack of time bubbled to the surface. How had she gotten here? Who escorted her? When had she gotten here? More importantly, what was she doing here?

Dear Lord, please don't let me get my hopes up only to have them crushed again. Help me to love her like You would want me to love her.

The whole ride back to town, he'd been telling himself to proceed with caution. Her reasons for being here might not be what he hoped.

At the livery he stripped his saddle and gave his horse a quick rubdown. He forked him some hay and put a measure of oats in his bucket and then hurried toward the hotel along the rapidly darkening street.

But he was only partway there when he saw a crowd milling out front of the mercantile.

And then his gaze lifted to the sky above the building. Sparks were flying in every direction! "Dear Lord, have mercy!"

He dashed toward the chaos.

He hadn't seen smoke on his ride into town, though it had been nearly dark. But he hadn't smelled the smoke either, so however this fire started, it must have blazed up fast!

He scooted to a stop on the street next to the gathering crowd. The town's merchants were running in this direction with buckets and every sort of jar and container. But the inferno already engulfed the back of the store and was creeping along the sides of the building toward the front.

"Did everyone get out?"

A woman next to him waggled her head, unsure. "The sign on the door reads 'closed.'" But even as she said it, the main door of the mercantile burst open.

The man who'd been with Wayne Chancellor at the wagon train meeting backed out dragging Wayne by his armpits.

As his heels thumped down the steps in front of the mercantile, Wayne coughed and sputtered.

Thank the Lord he was breathing!

Adam rushed toward them. "Is anyone else in there?"

The newcomer eased Wayne to rest on the street and squatted by him, doing plenty of coughing of his own. He shook his head and waved his hat before his face. "I don't think so. Does anyone live upstairs?"

Adam's gaze shot to the second story. Smoke blackened the sky above. Through the large window of the mercantile he could see crackling orange flames where he knew the stairs should be. He swallowed. He didn't want to think about what might have happened to anyone who'd been up there. Micah, Mercy, Gideon, the boys . . .

Lord, please don't let anything happen to any of them. Send Your angels to protect everyone from injury. He clapped the newcomer on the shoulder. "Thanks for getting Wayne out."

Several men rushed up to gather Wayne and carry him farther from the building.

The orange glow wavered eerily on the hotel next door. The clapboards smoked, and flames burst to life!

Eden!

"Everyone get water on the hotel next door!" Adam yelled.

Besides Eden, other people were inside! Had they all heard the clamor and evacuated? Doubtful. Some of the rooms didn't even have windows facing this direction.

Adam hit the boardwalk in front of the building at a full sprint, shoving the man who tried to stop him out of his way. "My wife is in there!"

The lobby remained empty, thank goodness. "Out! Everybody out! Fire!" He yelled down the hall, hoping beyond hope that anyone in here heard him.

His first priority was Eden and then he'd start on the third floor and check every room. But when he crashed into his room on the second floor, expecting to find Eden, she wasn't there.

His heart thrashed in confusion—happy that she wasn't here, but . . . Had she left him again? Maybe his inability to find the right words earlier had sent her straight back east? No. Not this late at night. But . . . where was she?

He shot a glance toward the burning mercantile he could see across the alley. Surely she hadn't gone into the mercantile to try to help? That would be so like her. Fear threatened to collapse him to his knees. "Lord . . ." Nothing else would come to mind. He felt frozen with indecision. And then he realized she might just as well have gone upstairs to help.

He burst up the stairs to the next floor. His mouth went dry when he saw no sign of Eden, but he couldn't do anything about her just yet. He started banging on doors. "Out! Fire. Anyone in here?"

A few doors opened and those who had called it an early night blinked sleepily at him. "Out! There's a fire." He pointed to the eerie dancing glow where the light from the fire next door now spilled through the window at the end of the hall.

All eyes widened in panic, and most everyone hurried to do as he'd said.

But on the end closest to the danger, a little old lady turned and tottered back into her room. "Ma'am! No! You can't—" He worked to angle his body through the crush of people now surging toward the stairwell behind him.

Finally past the crowd, he ran the rest of the way down the hall and didn't even bother to knock. He burst into the old lady's room.

"Why of all the—" Eyes stretched wide in shock, she clasped her hands to the high part of her chest where he could see that she'd managed to undo two of the buttons on the high collar of her full-length dressing gown. The woman snatched up her cane and swung it at him.

"Ma'am—" Her cane connected with his arm. "Ow!" He ducked another swing as he rubbed at the spot. "With all due respect, ma'am. There's no time for you to dress." He snatched the stick and held it while he planted a shoulder into her middle and swung her onto his shoulder.

"Young man, you put me down this instant! I must dress first!" Her fists went to work on his back. At least it wasn't her cane. He was tempted to toss it—and maybe her—but she might need it when he got her to the street.

"Trust me, everyone will understand the state of your undress."

After that, she thankfully went limp.

On the first floor he hurried her to the boardwalk and passed her off to a man who was directing traffic away from the buildings. "Don't let her go back inside."

The woman glowered at him and grabbed the top of her gown to hold it closed.

"Right this way, ma'am," the stranger said.

Adam could still hear the woman's protests as he dashed back inside to make sure the building was emptied. To his left he could already see flames licking at the interior wall of the hotel's lobby.

He turned right and yanked open the first-floor door, and ran down the hall banging on all the doors. "Fire. Out!"

All these rooms seemed empty. *Thank You, Lord.*

He dashed back down the hall. The lobby door had swung shut behind him. He grabbed the doorknob. "Ah!" He snatched his hand back from the searing pain and backed away wide-eyed.

He'd gotten everyone out—except himself!

Striker Moss had done his scouting and discovered that the names Tamsyn and Edison Acheson had indeed been added to the travel roster by Caesar.

He'd also asked around and learned that they'd been parking their wagon on the north side of the large field outside of town for several days now.

He'd just swung into his saddle to head that way when he heard a cry from down the street. "Fire!"

That couldn't be good. He clicked to his horse and directed him that way at a trot.

"We need water! Form a brigade!" someone yelled.

Striker swung down and hitched his horse to the rail in front of the diner across the street from all the smoke.

A blond woman in the diner's doorway already handed buckets and mixing bowls out to anyone who would take one. She was obviously getting them from someone inside because every time she pivoted back into the diner, she reappeared with another container.

People scooped water from the watering troughs up and down the street.

Jeremiah appeared out of the smoke with two buckets in his hands. He slung the water against the side of the building, but the flames were so hungry it had little effect.

"I'll take one of those." Striker thanked the woman for the bucket and fell into line at the end of the closest brigade.

Ahead of him, the parson who'd prayed over their journey at the meeting yelled for them to transfer their attentions to the hotel next door, and then Striker saw the man dive through the hotel door, likely to help people get out.

He turned and spoke to the man behind him. "This store is lost. Focus on the hotel!" Even as he said it, he saw tongues of fire beginning to dance on the clapboards.

They were doing their best, but as rapidly as those flames were spreading, it didn't look like they were going to be able to save either building.

Mercy had only made it partway to the creek, when she'd met Gideon and Willow charging her way. She thrust the buckets at Gideon. "We need water. It's the store!"

Mattox barked as though urging them to hurry.

Gideon took the buckets and reversed course toward the creek.

"Papa!" Willow cried, freezing Gid in his tracks as Willow tried to surge past Mercy.

"No! Willow!" Mercy grabbed her and held on. "Micah went in. Micah's in there. Don't worry! He'll make sure Wayne gets out."

Willow seemed to relax at that.

Gid gave her a nod of thanks and continued his sprint toward the water.

After only a moment however, Willow tried to evade Mercy's grasp. "I have to make sure!"

But Mercy held firm. "The best thing we can do is keep clear heads! The boys are in there too!" The last words emerged on a sob.

Mattox whined and pressed his snout into her palm. She stroked his head absentmindedly.

Thankfully, her emotion seemed to have gotten through to Willow. She stilled and threw one arm around Mercy's shoulders, staring at the engulfing flames. "How did this happen? I was just in there a few minutes ago."

"I know. Me too. I don't know what happened." She took Willow's hand and tugged her toward the barn. "We're going to need more water. We have to hurry."

Her knees were barely strong enough to hold her upright. "Avram. Joel. Dear Lord, my boys. Please. Please." Her thoughts were jumbled, and she couldn't seem to pray in full sentences.

Behind her she heard Willow uttering similar prayers of desperation.

Mercy pushed Mattox toward his spot beneath the wagon. "Mattox lay down! Stay." He hesitated for only the briefest of moments before he moved to do as she'd said. She'd never been more grateful for the dog's obedience. "Good boy." She hated to leave him, but here he would be sheltered from falling cinders.

She and Willow each grabbed up one of the last two buckets in the tack room and rushed out.

Gideon was almost back with his two full ones when they careened onto the trail. He continued past them with only a nod of acknowledgement. Frustration etched his jaw into a hard line.

Mercy knew just how he felt. This was too slow. It wouldn't be enough.

She forced herself to stay on track and do the job before her. She babbled nonsensical reassurances to Willow as they both dipped bucketfuls from the creek and hurried back toward the store.

The return trip was harder, trying not to spill any of the precious drops of water. But by the time they returned, Gideon had tossed his empty buckets aside and stood with his hands on his hips, shaking his head.

Mercy questioned him with her eyes as she handed him her bucket. To her surprise, Gideon heaved the water onto the roof of the barn instead of onto the fire at the back of the mercantile.

"Gid!" Willow protested.

He took her bucket with a shake of his head. "It's no use. It's too hot. My two buckets didn't even slow the flames. These two buildings are done for." He wagged a finger between the mercantile and the hotel next door, then tossed Willow's water onto the barn roof as well. "I'll wet the barn roof to keep it from catching flame. Why don't you two head around front." His gaze landed on Willow. "I bet Wayne is out front, worried about where you are." He swung his head for Mercy to lead the way. "Likely Micah too."

At that, Mercy snatched Willow's hand. "Come on. Let's go find them."

But Willow hesitated, searching Gideon's face. "Promise you won't go in?"

He nodded.

Only then did Willow allow Mercy to lead her away.

The heat in the nearest alley was too hot to bear, so they dashed on past two more buildings and up that alley, spilling out onto the street behind a milling crowd that had gathered to watch the disaster.

When the fire started, Eden had been ready to dash onto the street to see how she could help, but the owner of the diner grabbed her arm and told her to stand in the doorway and hand out the containers she brought to her. She'd been happy for something to do and handed out buckets and serving bowls to anyone willing to battle the blaze. But she'd nearly abandoned her post when she'd seen Adam bring an older woman to the door of the hotel and then rush back in.

And he hadn't yet emerged!

Now, she ran onto the street, splashing through the rivulets of mud streaming down the roadbed, and ran toward the hotel.

"Whoa, ma'am. I'm right sorry, but I cain't let you go runnin' o'er there."

The man's grasp held her firm, and she spun to see him with the handles of two full buckets in his other hand. Sweat dripped from his dark forehead, and she realized he must be one of the runners sprinting to the creek to aid the brigade, which was mostly getting a slow trickle of water from the pump down the street now that all the troughs were empty. With a second glance, she realized he was one of the scouts introduced at the meeting earlier.

Desperation clawed at her throat as she divided a glance between the fully-engulfed hotel and the kind gray-blue eyes of the man holding her arm. "Please. My husband went into that hotel to get people and I haven't seen him come out again."

The wide eyes leveled on her were a striking contrast to smooth golden pecan skin. He bounced his scrutiny between her and the building that was almost completely engulfed in flames, and she could see the truth in his eyes. Anyone who hadn't yet come out, wasn't going to.

Sorrow nearly took the strength from her legs. Especially when she noticed that even the brigade had now turned their efforts to wetting down the nearby buildings, instead of putting out the fires.

"Please." Even she could hear the hopelessness in her voice. "I know it's asking a lot. I don't want to risk your life . . . Please just let me try to find him. I owe him that much."

"Ma'am, you listen now. Listen real good. You swear you'll stay right here—" he released her long enough to tap a finger toward the street "—and I'll go in and see what might be done." He yanked off his bandana and thrust it into one of the buckets, bringing it up and wringing the water from it.

Tears swelled to blur Eden's vision. "Thank you. Yes. I'll stay." As the man tied the bandana around his face and started across the street, she reached to touch his arm. "Please, be careful."

He tugged the brim of his hat, water glistening on his brown skin. "Yes'm."

Despite the bustle all around her, Eden's feet felt glued to the street. She watched as the man whose name she could not remember sprinted through the melee. He went to the side of the hotel farthest from the encroaching flames, and kicked in one of the windows, reaming out the glass with the hard leather of his boot.

And then he disappeared into the column of smoke pouring out the new opening.

Eden swallowed.

Please Lord, don't let me have just sent that man to his death.

Chapter 8

Adam retreated from the doorknob that now started to glow red and the choking cloud of smoke shooting beneath the door. He fought down the terror hammering against the inside of his sternum, squeezing his lungs, dulling his thoughts. *Lord . . .* He wanted to pray, but no coherent words came to mind.

Had Eden come all this way only to collect the charred bones of her husband from the rubble of a burned-down hotel?

Holding his breath, he cradled his burnt hand to his chest and searched for an escape. But all around him the smoke hung so thick, he could hardly even see.

He retreated two hurried steps and tripped over something that had fallen in the hallway. He crashed to his knees, catching himself with both hands. He felt the skin over his burn give way with a sharp slice of pain.

His body rebelled and gasped.

Pain seared his lungs and the choking coughs that followed made it even worse. His mind screamed for him to stand, but his muscles refused to obey. Heat penetrated the soles of his boots! He dragged himself with one elbow and tried not to choke on his own breath.

A Bible verse penetrated his mind.

When you walk through the fire, you shall not be burned, nor shall the flame scorch you.

The reminder of the words Isaiah had penned scores of years in the past was like a shower of water washing his mind of the freezing panic.

Thank You, Lord.

From somewhere he heard the crash of shattering glass.

He lifted his head and felt a blessed blast of air on his face and for the briefest of moments, the smoke in the hallway cleared just enough for him to see down to the end.

A man stood in the smoke with a bandana over his face. "This way!" he called, already running toward Adam.

Adam scrambled forward on all fours, once more holding his breath, ignoring lungs that begged for air, ignoring the black spots trying to blind him, ignoring the sharp agony pulsing in his palm.

A strong arm wrapped around him and hauled him to his feet. Adam had never been so thankful to lean on the strength of another. The man half-led half-carried him into the last room down the hall and to the window. Glass lay shattered all over the floor. That must have been the sound he'd heard a moment ago.

Behind them, he could hear the crackle of flames devouring dry wood and plaster.

"Hurry!" His rescuer yelled.

They reached the window.

"Help me with him!"

Hands reached in to grab him and yank him out. He turned to help the man who'd saved him but saw that he'd already climbed out. His face remained hidden by the bandana and his hat.

And then Adam stumbled onto the street away from the main column of smoke and dragged in a blessed lungful of mostly smoke-free air. Then another. And then a coughing fit bent him double.

"Adam!" Eden's running footsteps accompanied her cry and then her arms were around him. "Thank You. Oh, thank You, Jesus!"

And even through his choking coughs and the relief rushing through him, Adam had the presence of mind to cry out the same prayer. But his prayer had less to do with his recent salvation from the flames and more to do with his wife's arms being around him for the first time in a very long time.

Willow followed Mercy onto the teeming street, unable to tamp down the dread rising to choke her throat. This wasn't right. What could have started this fire? They were always careful with lamps, lanterns, and candles!

Who knew the building could ignite so fast!?

Papa. Please, please.

Where was he?

The crowd milled, too thick to see through. She was too short. Even if he was out here, she'd never find him until things calmed down.

And then a loud crash drew her attention up to the porch of the mercantile. The double doors burst open and through the smoke two men emerged, one dragging the other by the pits of his arms!

"Papa!" Willow surged forward, but arms held her back.

"Stay back, lass."

Several men hurried forward to help.

Mr. Harrington released Papa and stumbled to one side, coughing.

What was he doing back in the store? Had he returned early to see if she'd gotten his room ready? She brushed the questions aside. She couldn't worry about him right now.

Several men stepped forward to carry Papa, and Willow scuttled after them as they crossed to the diner's porch. They laid him out on the boardwalk. Papa's arm flopped to one side.

Heart squeezing in dread, Willow refused to give that image a foothold. She fell to her knees by his side and pushed his hair back from his face. "Papa?"

He sputtered a weak cough.

"Someone bring water!" Willow feared that in her panic, her words sounded less than kind. "Please. Please, someone bring me water." She never took her eyes off Papa's soot-smeared face. Even his whiskers were mostly black!

Someone set a bucket beside her, and she scooped up a handful. "Here, Papa. Open your mouth. A little water, hmmm?"

Weakly he parted his lips, and Willow dripped a few drops into his mouth between her knuckles.

Papa swallowed, coughed, then swallowed again. "Gid-eon?" he rasped.

Willow spoke to the closest man. "Can you please fetch Gideon? At the barn." She pointed behind the store and felt satisfied to see the man hurry to do as she'd asked. She wasn't sure why Papa wanted Gid. She was only relieved to have him alive and talking.

She turned her focus back to Papa. "He's coming. Are you burnt? Hurting anywhere?"

He shook his head weakly. "No. Just—" He coughed again weakly and waved a hand. "S-smoke." Tears streamed from the corners of his irritated eyes.

Willow squeezed his shoulder. "The smoke will clear, Papa. It will clear. Just rest and breathe."

As soon as Mr. Chancellor was laid out on the diner's porch, Mercy, thankful that he seemed to be breathing, turned her attention to those milling on the street. She still hadn't seen Micah and the boys! Panic threatened to take her to her knees, but then she'd be of no use to anyone!

She grabbed the arm of a man with dark hair and turned him, only to see that it wasn't Micah. "Sorry. Have you seen a man with two boys? All have curly hair?"

The man shook his head. "Sorry, miss."

She dashed another few steps, searching faces as she went. "God, please save Micah and the boys. Please, don't—" She couldn't bring herself to finish that sentence and was left with only, "Please. Please. Please."

Her breaths came in short hard puffs.

She'd nearly reached the end of the crowd which milled in front of the hotel, and still hadn't found them!

Parson Houston was there, however, bent double in the middle of the street with one hand propped against his knee and the other curled against himself. A blond woman that Mercy didn't recognize hovered nearby.

A man with kind blue eyes stood next to them—one of the scouts who would accompany their wagon train. His expression turned to concern the moment he looked at her. "Ma'am? There somethin' I can help you with?"

She spun to search the street in all directions again. "I can't find— I'm looking for my—a man and two boys." She described them again. Her vision blurred even as she registered the parson straightening.

"Mercy?"

He sounded rough, causing her to turn to him. Golden orange light glistened off the parson's sweat-dampened skin. He looked almost as bad as Mr. Chancellor had looked when that other man dragged him out of the store a moment ago. "Are you okay?"

Beside him, the blond woman frowned slightly at her. Could she be his wife? He'd spoken of her but had never told anyone she was coming.

He brushed away her concern. "What's this you say about Micah?"

Her terrified gaze transferred to the store. Lifted to the second story which was nearly consumed toward the back, but looked almost normal along the front—other than the smoke that roiled out of the open downstairs door. "The boys were upstairs. He went in to get them."

"Dear Lord, have mercy."

She doubted the parson had meant for her to hear the dread that filled the words.

The scout pointed to a window in the peak of the roof. "Up there, ma'am!"

Thinking he was only asking where they were in the building, Mercy nodded, feeling all her despair rise to suffocate her.

"Lookee there, ma'am. You see?" Sheer joy rang in the scout's voice.

Wait! Was that movement at the glass?

The window shattered outward! Several kicks cleared the remaining shards and then a blanket draped over the jagged shards that remained.

Mercy covered her mouth, rapidly blinking away tears of joy. But anxiety still squeezed her chest. It had to be Micah. But . . . Had he found both boys?

One long leg thrust through! Micah climbed onto the roof of the porch holding Avram in his arms and then turned to help Joel through the opening.

"Thank You, Jesus!" Mercy lifted her skirt and dashed through the crowd.

Behind her she heard the scout's deep voice command, "Somebody get a ladder now. Help them boys!"

Micah and the boys scooted carefully to the edge of the low-pitched roof, all of them coughing. Avram wrapped his arms around Micah's neck and cried into his shoulder.

Mercy pressed the fingers of both hands alongside her nose and couldn't bring herself to look away from the beautiful sight of her family perched on the edge of that roof.

A ladder was quickly fetched from behind the diner and propped against the shingles. Micah swung Joel onto it first, and he started down, feeling slowly, one foot at a time, for the next wrung down.

Flames crackled at the opening of the window!

"Hurry!" Mercy urged.

Micah swept Avram onto his back, ensured that he had a good grip, and then swung a foot onto the ladder.

Mercy grabbed Joel off the second to the bottom rung and hugged him tight. "I'm so glad you are all right!"

Joel squirmed and tried to wriggle free, but she held onto him, watching Micah descend.

With his voice muffled in her shoulder, Joel quipped, "Could breathe easier in all the smoke."

Mercy laughed and settled him on the street, roughing a hand through his hair. "Sorry if I squeezed you too hard, I'm just—so happy!" She said the last words as she lifted Avram from Micah's back and gave him the same treatment she'd given Joel.

Avram wasn't as embarrassed by her display of overjoyed affection. He wrapped his arms around her and sobbed against her neck. "Mr. Micah saved me, Mama."

"I know, sweetheart. I know." She soothed a hand over his back. "It's all right now. You're safe."

"We lost our book!" he sobbed.

"It's okay, we'll get you a new one."

Micah stood on the ground now, one hand resting on Joel's shoulder as he smiled softly at the sight of Avram in her arms. Soot covered his features, making the blue of his eyes stand out even more than it usually did. His gaze drilled into hers and she saw relief there, but also a bit of wonder.

Wonder, indeed! God had spared their lives!

Mercy clung to his gaze over her son's shoulder.

The scout urged everyone to step back from the buildings which would collapse within the next few minutes. They complied, but Mercy did so more by feel than anything because she couldn't take her eyes off the beautiful sight of Micah standing before her whole and unharmed.

He'd sacrificed himself to save their sons! As they crossed the street, she searched him from head to foot, still soothing a hand over Avram's back.

He smiled, spread his arms, and spun in a circle so she could see he was unsinged.

They paused in the shadows of the alley between the diner and the building next door.

Mercy lowered to her haunches and settled Avram on his feet. She reached to take Joel's hand. "How about you boys. Nothing hurting? No burns?"

Both shook their heads.

"Good." Mercy rose to her feet with a sharp nod. "Then we're going to be fine because we are all together." She wouldn't dwell on the fact that they'd all lost all the clothing they owned except what they currently wore and the few things that were already packed into the wagon in the barn.

Micah stepped back reluctantly and swung his hat toward the brigade that continued to sling water on the nearby buildings. So far, it appeared they were going to save all the buildings in town but the two. "I should go help." He gave her an apologetic wince.

Before she even realized what she was doing, Mercy stepped forward and grabbed his arm. "No." She tugged him around to face her. "You should kiss me." She rose on her tiptoes, wrapped her arms around his neck, and pressed her lips to his with all the gratefulness, joy, thankfulness, and awareness of God's blessing bursting inside her.

It only took him half a moment to recover from his surprise, and then his arms wrapped around her, and he kissed her in return.

Mercy heard the thump of his hat hitting the ground near their feet, felt the broad strength of his hands spread against her back as he drew her against him, and tasted the salt of her own joyous tears as her lips melded with his.

Her thumbs stroked a caress against the stubble of his jaw as her lips danced with his, silky and smooth. She couldn't withhold a sigh of bliss.

Embarrassed by her impulsiveness, she might have pulled back, but this kiss . . . Sakes alive! She could hardly fathom how wonderful it was.

There was no crushing punishment in this kiss. No fear. No assault by a man wanting to dominate her.

Only tender love, pleasure, and, like Micah said, the wonder of such intimacy with another.

Micah's kiss was restrained. Patient. Gentle.

So she lingered—savored each sweeping caress of his lips over hers. Relished the warmth of his hands against her back.

"Pa? Is she allowed to do that?"

Joel's incredulous voice penetrated the fog of her passion and made her drop back to her heels with a shy chuckle. Keeping her attention on her clasped hands, she swept her tongue over her lips. The taste of smoke and salt had never filled her with such a heady sensation.

Micah's low laugh filled her with warmth and held no embarrassment whatsoever. He reached out and snagged her arm to stop her from retreating another step. He pulled her in tight and tucked her head against his collarbone. "She most certainly is, son. I haven't had a chance to tell you yet, but Ms. Adler has agreed to be my wife and your ma."

"She has?!" Joel's voice squeaked.

She felt Micah nod above her head. "What do you think of that?"

Mercy didn't leave Micah's arms, but pulled back enough to see the boys' responses.

Joel grabbed Avram by both arms and jumped them in a circle. "We're gonna be brothers!"

Avram's nose crinkled, even though he bounced with as much enthusiasm as Joel. "What's brothers?"

Joel stopped and his little face scrunched into a pinch of concentration. "It means we always stand up for each other when other kids are mean and that sometimes we fight over toys, right Pa?"

Micah's warm laugh rumbled in his chest, and Mercy relished the vibration of it beneath her hand. She took in the orange glow glistening in the dark stubble of his jaw, and reflecting in his eyes that were shadowed by the darkness now as he peered down at her. "I guess that sounds about right, son." He offered a wink—that feral reflection disappearing for one brief moment before it reappeared again.

Mercy tucked one side of her lip between her teeth. "I'm sorry I kissed you like that. I just—"

He held up one of his broad fingers and then settled it against her lips. His gaze never left hers as he said, "Hey, Joel?"

"Yes, Pa?"

"Why don't you take Avram around to sit on the front porch of the diner. But don't move from there, understand? You both stay there until your ma or I come get you."

"Yes, sir."

Mercy's heart pounded. He'd said "your ma" like it was the most natural thing in the world. Tears burgeoned in her eyes as happiness swelled inside her.

Micah must have caught sight of her tears in the light from the fire, because he said, "Hey, what's this now?" He cupped her cheeks and leaned his forehead against hers. "Don't cry."

She shook her head, suddenly unable to speak.

"We're all fine. The good Lord watched over us."

She nodded. "I'm just so happy and—"

Across the street the front wall of the mercantile collapsed in on itself, sending a spray of sparks into the night sky.

"Oh, this is all such a muddle."

Micah urged her face back toward his. "I'll thank the Lord every day for this fire because it broke through your barriers."

Heat that had absolutely nothing to do with the fire shot through her cheeks. "I probably shouldn't have—"

Micah shook his head and tapped her mouth with one finger. "Don't ever apologize for kissing me. In fact—" he grinned "—you can go ahead and kiss me like that any time you want to."

Mercy smacked him gently. "Oh, Micah, I was so happy to see you all come out of that window. I came this close to falling apart." Her finger and thumb revealed only the sparest of space between them.

Micah took her hand and kissed her fingers. "I might have to conjure other ways to make it look like I'm near death, then."

She laughed, and slapped his chest a little harder this time. "Don't you dare."

He tilted his head and settled into his heels, with his hands laced at her back. "I love you, Mercy Adler."

She dipped her head, tucking her lip between her teeth. After a moment she offered, "I could tell. It was . . . nice."

"Only nice, huh?" A chuckle escaped him. "I guess we need more practice to get to amazing."

She laughed, still unable to meet his gaze. He hadn't said he enjoyed it.

Micah touched her chin, nudging her to look at him. A small furrow trenched his brow as though he were trying to discern her thoughts. "I don't want you to feel pressured by that. A kiss is always meant to be enjoyed by both parties." His thumb stroked the dip beneath her lower lip.

"And did you?" She blurted the question before she lost her courage. "Enjoy it? Because you can tell me if you didn't, and I will . . . try to do better."

His frown smoothed as though he'd finally understood what was bothering her. "I don't ever want you to feel like you have to do anything to please me, understand? You don't have to kiss me in any way other than what feels natural to you. I did enjoy it and I will enjoy it because of my love for you. Not because either of us—" he rolled a hand through the air "—performed perfectly."

Renewed love for him surged through her. What a wonder she felt every time she considered what God had helped her escape and the love he'd given her along the way.

Happiness lifted her to her tiptoes again. But she stopped short. "Maybe we could practice some more right now?"

Micah laughed and gave her a firm, lingering kiss. Then he stepped back and pressed the pad of his thumb over his lower lip. "Unless the boys are here to interrupt, I think that's about all the practicing we ought to do until we've said our vows." He tilted her a smile. "You aren't going to change your mind about that, are you?"

She shook her head. Suddenly her eyes widened, and she darted a look to where the store and their rooms had once stood. "As long as you don't mind marrying me in—" she swept a gesture to her dirty blouse and muddy skirt "—this."

Micah tugged her in for one more short peck. "You could wear a gunny sack and I'd still marry you."

She smiled, but her gaze traveled to the smoldering ash heap that had been the store once more. "Where are we all going to sleep tonight?"

Micah squeezed her hand. "I'll get that figured out. See to the boys? They're probably hungry. I'm going to see if I can find Gideon and the Chancellors and we'll come up with a plan."

Mercy pointed toward the diner's porch. "Mr. Chancellor and Willow were on the porch the last I saw."

"Well . . ." Micah stretched a hand toward her, and she slipped her fingers between his. "Seems like we're headed in the same direction then. I think I like that."

He smiled down at her, and despite all the chaos reigning around them, Mercy somehow felt like all was right in her world.

Chapter 9

Eden took Adam's good hand and led him to the porch of the building beyond the hotel.

He didn't fight her—only continued to stare toward the conflagration with a blank look in his eyes. Someone set a lantern beside them, and Eden gave the man a nod of thanks.

"Adam? Are you all right?" She reached for the hand he kept cradled against his chest. A gasp escaped her. "Oh, Adam!" Most of the skin had been torn away from his palm, and large blisters covered the pads of each knuckle.

He seemed to come to himself then. He straightened. "Grabbed a doorknob. Thought I was done for, Eden."

She touched his cheek in the briefest of caresses. "But the good Lord was not done with you."

He cut her a sharp look as though he might be surprised by her proclamation.

She would have loved to linger over the touch, but maybe it was what had him giving her such a narrow-eyed look. Or maybe it was something else altogether?

She withdrew her hand.

Who was the woman on the street a moment ago? Was she something to Adam? How much had her selfishness cost her? She didn't even know her own husband's acquaintances. Eden swallowed. Her one consolation was that the woman had seemed to be looking for a different man and Adam said her name like she might be a friend but nothing more.

Taking up the lantern, she raised it to study his palm in better light. Her stomach churned as she gently cradled his broad hand. "This needs to be tended to by a doctor. Is there one in town?"

When he didn't respond right away, she lifted him a look and stilled.

His gaze lingered soft and warm on her features. He swallowed. "It's good to see you again, Eden."

"It is? I mean—yes, I'm happy to see you again too, but I wasn't so sure you'd be happy to see . . . me."

He reached with his good hand to take her own and stood gingerly to his feet. "Bring the lantern and we'll see if we can find Doc in all this hubbub." His words emerged gritty and soft.

And as Eden did as he'd bade and followed him down the street, her heart dipped in her chest because she realized just what a rift she'd created between herself and the man she loved with all her heart.

And the pain of it was nearly tearing her in two.

Willow swallowed down the panic rising in her chest. She must remain calm. Keep her composure. Be here for Papa.

She'd been so relieved when Mr. Harrington brought him out alive, but now . . . Something wasn't right. Papa's breaths sounded like he was sucking them through ticking soaked in water, each one labored and rattling.

Willow rested on her knees beside him, sitting back against her ankles. She held his hand where it rested on his chest which barely rose and fell. But her focus remained fastened to their store that had just collapsed into a heap of rubble. Everything they'd owned . . . All of it, gone.

The first wall of the hotel collapsed in on itself and Willow followed a drifting fiery red spark all the way to the street where it died in a muddy puddle.

Snuffed out like all sensation.

She felt nothing. How could she feel such absence of emotion in the face of such tragedy?

Movement beside her drew her attention.

Gideon fell to his knees by Papa's head. His shoulder bumped hers as he leaned forward so he would be in Papa's line of vision. "Wayne?" He scrutinized her prostrate father with uncertainty. "Someone said you wanted to speak with me?"

Papa roused enough to open his eyes and blink slowly at Gideon. Then he worked to free his hand from Willow's grasp and reached toward Gid.

Brow furrowing in surprise, Gid flicked a glance at her and then back to Papa's hand which he took. "I'm right here, Wayne. What do you need?"

Papa stretched his other hand to Willow, and she gave it, still feeling distant as though she were watching from a far-off place. Papa pressed her hand over his heart and then pressed Gideon's on top of hers. He rested both of his hands atop theirs. His gaze settled on Gideon, his eyes barely slit now. "Remember . . . your . . . promise."

Gid shook his head. "You're going to be fine. We've sent for the doc. He's—"

Papa gave a short sharp shake of his head. "Remember!"

Gideon hesitated for a moment but then hung his head in seeming resignation. "I will, sir."

Papa's gaze swung to hers.

Willow forced a smile. "Do you need anything, Papa? Water? Maybe that will help clear your throat?" She offered the words by rote. There seemed to be no hope to allay the emptiness inside her.

Papa's face turned soft. He tilted his head toward her. Squeezed her hand where it still rested on his chest. "You're strong. Remember . . . you can . . . do all things . . . through Christ . . . who strengthens."

Willow nodded. "I know, Papa. Don't worry about me. You just concentrate on breathing until Doc gets here." Her words were spuriously bright for how hollow she felt.

Papa nodded. Smiled. "Love . . . you."

"I love you too, Papa. The doctor is almost here." She wasn't sure that was true. It seemed like ages since she'd heard someone call for a message to be sent to him.

Papa's gaze drifted back to Gideon's. Weakly, he lifted a hand and motioned him closer.

Papa whispered something that Willow couldn't quite make out. All she could hear was the air rattling at the back of Papa's throat.

Gid leaned back and gave a nod. "I will, sir."

With that, Papa pressed their hands gently against each other again and eased out a long breath.

He didn't inhale.

"Papa?" Willow felt dismay swell inside her. "Papa?" Her voice broke.

Gideon gently swept his thumb over her fingers before he eased back and withdrew his hand to prop it against his thigh, but Willow remained where she sat for the longest time. She watched Papa's chest, willing him to draw another breath, willing herself to feel movement beneath her hand. Surely Papa would sit up at any moment and give her that sly smile of his. But his ribs did not expand, his eyes did not flutter, and his lips did not move.

Willow snatched her hand back into her lap with sudden distress. But just as quickly as the emotion arose, it disappeared. A bleak void filled her.

She focused once more on the ash heaps across the street. On the soot-streaked faces of friends looking down at her in shock.

Mercy stood there, her face full of sorrow and compassion. Micah, beside her, had his arms folded and a frown on his face as he studied the ruins across the road. Parson Houston had one hand curled against his chest and a blond woman that Willow didn't know stood beside him. The woman's eyes were a bit wide, and tears shimmered on her lower lids.

And then Willow's gaze landed on Gideon. He remained kneeling beside her, his assessment searching as though to see what her response might be. He didn't say a word, but when she moved to stand, he leapt quickly to his feet and reached down to help her up.

She started toward the porch steps, but then froze, realizing she could not go home—in fact, had no place to go. She clasped her hands in front of herself, unsure what to do next.

If only she could think through all the hollowness ringing inside her.

Gideon couldn't help but realize how small Willow was as he took her hand and helped her to her feet.

Before this, with vibrant energy spilling from her every pore, he'd never thought of her as small. Boisterous, energetic, full of life. Yes. All those things. Even earlier when he'd held her out by the creek, he hadn't thought of her as small.

But now she looked pale, gaunt, and lifeless. And it emphasized her tiny physique.

He blinked away the memory of her in his arms. It had been a long time since he held a woman tenderly in his arms, was all. But now Wayne had asked . . .

With a shake of his head, he forced the thoughts away. Tomorrow would have enough trouble of its own.

Caesar Cranston, their wagon master, stepped out of the crowd and paused at the bottom of the diner's steps. "It is my understanding that several of you who have lost your homes were to be part of our wagon train. Anyone who needs a bed is invited to join us on the west side of town near the Kansas River. We've some tents and will make do for tonight until y'all can get things sorted come morning."

Gid gave him a nod of thanks.

Willow still hadn't moved, so he touched her elbow. "Let's go inside and sit for a moment. I need to talk to you."

Her expression remained blank. "What did he say at the last?"

Gid shifted his hat through his fingers. She wasn't going to like it. "That's partly what I need to talk to you about. But, not here, hmm? Inside?"

With her arms wrapped around herself, she glanced toward the empty space that had been the store. The barn stood behind it, clearly visible. Thankfully, he'd saved it from being ignited by a spark.

He wished he could offer her a jacket, but all he had was his buckskin shirt. And he doubted she would want to don it, dirty and damp as it was.

He settled a hand against her back, hoping to urge her to move. She was as pale as the moon rising in the distance and needed to get off her feet. Thankfully, she heeded his prodding, and when they stepped into the diner, gratefulness filled him when Felicity bustled ahead of them to set a steaming teapot onto a table. She gave Gid a nod. "I'll bring soup."

He thanked her and pulled out a chair for Willow, then took the chair across the table.

Remember your promise.

As Wayne's words drifted through his memory, Gid felt like his throat might clamp off all air. Yes, late last fall he'd promised Wayne that if anything happened to him, he would watch out for Willow. He remembered the man's words as if they'd had that conversation yesterday. *I've quite honestly been afraid for my life since this started.* Willow's uncle, Grant Moore, who had married Wayne's sister and was the owner of Moore Brewing, had fallen on financial difficulty and wanted Wayne to split the proceeds from the store with him. He'd claimed it was money due his wife, even though Wayne's father had specifically given him the store.

He couldn't help but wonder about the cause of this fire that had sprung up so quickly. Was Grant Moore behind it? Tomorrow, Gideon would go to the law in town with what he knew.

In the meantime, there was his promise to Wayne.

Make her happy.

What in the world had made him agree to that? Surely, he was the last person on earth who could truly make Willow happy. Certainly not anytime soon.

No matter that he admired her pluck and zest for life, no matter that he'd once told Wayne it would be easy to love someone like her . . . She deserved someone younger. Someone who wasn't still grieving his deceased wife and unborn child. Someone who wasn't so world-weary. And yet, how could he keep his promise to Wayne, if he didn't marry her? And what was he going to do if she wouldn't have him? After all, only this morning he'd assured her that her father wasn't in any danger.

Once, maybe she would have been thrilled to receive his attentions. But her interest in him had long since seemed to have waned. And now . . .

Trying to ignore the shaking in his hand, he poured tea into the cup before her and added a generous scoop of honey from the jar on the table. It would be weak, but at least she would get something hot into her.

She still stared blankly out the windows toward the store.

"Willow?"

With a slow pivot, she refocused on him. Her eyes remained dry, something that puzzled him considering her tendency to run in a high emotional state. He wouldn't have been surprised if she'd fallen into a heap of sobbing distress, nor even if she'd flown into a temper, but this distant blank stare was something he wasn't prepared for.

He righted his own cup and poured for himself, resisting a wince. What he wouldn't give for good strong coffee. He eschewed honey for his own cup.

How was he going to tell her what Wayne had asked of him so soon after all she'd lost?

He opened his mouth, but all that came out was, "Drink a little tea, would you? I think you need the warmth, if nothing else."

Absentmindedly, she lifted the cup to her lips and took a mincing sip. But then she plunked it back into its saucer. "My stomach isn't right."

Gid took a bracing gulp of his own tea and grimaced at the searing blandness of it. Tea was bad enough, watery tea even worse. He should have let it steep longer.

Felicity bustled up and placed steaming bowls of chicken soup before them and a basket of rolls in the middle of the table.

Willow offered a smile that didn't reach her eyes. "Thank you, Felicity. You didn't have to go to the trouble."

Felicity squeezed her shoulder. "No trouble. None at all."

Gideon caught the glisten of tears on the older woman's cheeks as she spun back toward the kitchen and hurried off.

Willow eyed her soup with the barest hint of a furrow on her brow.

Gid lifted his own spoon. "Just a few sips."

Her frown grew. "Papa would say a blessing."

"Yes. Let's do that." He certainly needed God's help. He bowed his head and thanked God for the food, also asking that He give them wisdom for the days ahead.

He felt gratified to see Willow lift her spoon and sip some broth, but even then, she took only a few tiny sips.

He set into his own soup with grim determination. This wasn't the right time to say anything to her. The wagon train wasn't leaving for a couple of weeks. At least they had that buffer of time for her to adjust to her new reality. For tonight he simply needed to find her a place to rest because she seemed in no state of mind to hear him. Tomorrow or the next day would be soon enough.

And yet, by then she might remember . . .

Micah, Mercy, and the boys joined them at their table.

Micah touched Willow's shoulder as he sank into the chair next to hers. "I'm very sorry for your loss. Your father was . . . Well, we owe a lot to him and will forever be grateful for how he took us on last fall, even knowing we didn't have all the experience we should. He taught me—us—so much over these last months. He was a good, good man."

Gideon couldn't have agreed more with that sentiment.

Willow murmured agreement, her gaze fixed to her soup bowl. "Thank you. Yes, he was."

As Felicity arrived with soup for Micah, Mercy, and the boys, Micah leaned to the side and cleared his throat. "We've moved him to the church for now."

Gideon studied the woman across the table. Would the news bring the flood of emotion he'd been expecting?

Only a quick tick of a furrow pinched her brow. "Thank you for helping with that."

Gideon poked at a noodle with his spoon, feeling the weight of his concern for Willow crushing his heart.

Micah looked at him then. "I spoke to Cranston, and he's got room for all of us. Mercy and Willow can be in one tent, and you and I will have the boys with us."

Gideon nodded. "Okay."

They all ate in silence after that.

But Gideon couldn't suppress his dread over the conversation he needed to have with Willow. Maybe he would be able to come up with a solution to Wayne's request to protect Willow without having to do the obvious.

He sighed and dropped his spoon into his empty bowl. Who was he kidding? There was only one acceptable solution. He had to marry her. The problem was, he didn't think he could keep both promises to the man who'd been such a mentor to him. Marrying him wouldn't restore her happiness—especially not when she remembered that he'd only this morning reassured her that he didn't think Wayne was in any danger. Sure, she was in shock now. But she would remember. And when she did, he would be in for the brunt of her temper.

Still, there wasn't any other solution that he could see. He certainly couldn't leave her here and keep his promise. He would simply have to convince her. He just needed to come to terms with it himself. She had found him attractive once, so maybe . . .

He let his gaze settle on her. It wasn't that he wasn't attracted to her.

His wife, Verona, had been a sturdy woman who captured his heart with her kindness and steadiness—pretty, yes, especially when she smiled.

But Willow . . . One glance at her arrested a man's attention. From her fiery red hair and porcelain skin to her slender, graceful frame, she was all woman in a way that could make a man's mouth dry.

He'd seen the way that Harrington scoundrel watched her earlier. He was only one example. Willow could have any man she wanted.

He swallowed and pushed his spoon at a bit of broth in the bottom of his bowl.

Taking her to wife would be no punishment other than the principal of it. He didn't want a wife who didn't want him. Nor did he want Willow forced to take a husband because she had no other options—no matter how attractive he found her.

And yet . . . here they were and what other options did either of them have?

His stomach grumbled and he snatched up one of the rolls from the basket Felicity had brought.

This was no good. No good at all.

Chapter 10

Corbin Donahue paced in the darkness outside the diner, calling himself every sort of fool.

The old man should have lived! He'd gotten him out in time!

One thing he could say for the delay . . . It had certainly made the rescue look legitimate.

How could the old man have been so weak? The rescue should have put Wayne and Willow in his debt!

Now?

He must think.

How was he going to salvage this?

First, he had to get out of town immediately. Men like Grant Moore would not take kindly to a recent acquisition burning to the ground before they could even take possession of it. He'd taken the paperwork straight to him yesterday and received the remainder of his payment. And then he'd returned to the store to put the second part of his plan in motion.

But now, a thought struck him. If he fled town, Grant would likely come after him. It would be better if he cut the man off at the pass by visiting him. Too late to do that tonight, but first thing in the morning, he would take care of it. He needed a good story. Plenty of time to come up with one.

He glanced to where he could still see the smoking ruins of the mercantile and hotel. He honestly hadn't expected the store to go up so fast. He'd never had that happen before. He'd always had more time. Of course, the last building he'd ignited had been made of brick and it had taken some doing to get it to burn—he'd been aided only because of the timber bracing and the wooden roof and interior paneling. He ought to have figured that a building made of timber and clapboard would go up faster than a brownstone.

That was what he got for planning on the fly.

He'd rushed in to tell Wayne and Willow that the store was on fire and rescue them but found that Willow had already left.

Then the old man had insisted on fetching something from behind the counter. Corbin told him to hurry, but Wayne had a hard time finding it, and finally, Corbin joined him behind the counter. Wayne had been on his knees, frantically searching all the cubbies for something.

"I'll help you find it. What is it?" he'd asked, falling on his knees beside the man.

Wayne coughed. He motioned with his finger and thumb about three inches apart. "A metal box. Silver."

Corbin set to scooping out the contents of the cubbies. The first contained receipts. The second, quills and an ink pot that spilled all over his hand. The third, several spools of string. They'd still been searching when he'd heard footsteps that Wayne must not have heard. He'd waited a moment and then peered above the counter to see boots disappearing up the stairs across the way. He hadn't dared call out a warning. That must have been the man who escaped onto the roof with the two boys only moments after he'd brought Wayne onto the street. He shuddered to think that he might have killed two boys. He was glad not to have that burden on his conscience.

But at the time, he hadn't known the man was going after children. He'd thought he must be trying to save personal possessions, and he hadn't wanted Wayne trying anything heroic and dying in the process, so he'd kept quiet.

Finally, Wayne had given an exultant cry and thrust a hand above his head. "Got it." He shoved the small silver box into his coat pocket.

By the time they'd stood, Corbin had been shocked to see the wall of flame galloping toward them from the back. They'd barely had time to get out!

He still couldn't fathom what had done the old man in. He hadn't even been singed!

Irritating!

His death put all sorts of complications in Corbin's path.

Now he was going to have to come up with an entirely new plan. He hated having a good plan wasted!

His gaze snagged on the church steeple, standing in contrast to the gray smoky sky behind it. Earlier, he'd seen the men take Wayne's body in there.

What had the man searched for so insistently? Whatever it was, it had cost him his life.

It only took Corbin a few minutes to reach the church. He climbed the steps to the darkened porch and scrutinized the street in both directions. No one in sight. He tried the handle. It turned easily beneath his grip.

He found Wayne laid out on a blanket to one side of the entry.

Without striking a light, Corbin quickly felt of the man's coat pockets. There.

He withdrew the small silver box and transferred it to his own pocket. He would examine it later in the light.

Satisfied, he eased back into the darkness that enveloped the porch.

Corbin shuffled his feet and eyed Grant's door with dread as he worked up the courage to knock. It was early, but he didn't want to miss any of the goings-on at the wagon train and he needed to get back there so he could speak to the wagon master about buying in on Wayne's position in the train.

Be confident. Be firm. Be the man other men fear.

He gave himself a nod and stepped forward to pound his fist firmly against Moore's door. He was mid-knock when his gaze caught on his sleeve's cuff. His cufflink! It wasn't there! Where had he lost it?

His heart hammered as he quickly checked the other arm. The other one remained attached to his sleeve, thank goodness. This pair of links had been a gift from his grandfather. Pure silver inlaid with mother-of-pearl, they were important to him. But more than that, they were unique.

He wracked his mind. He felt certain he'd been wearing them when he'd signed the contract with Wayne Chancellor. He remembered one catching on the edge of the counter as he signed the documents.

A cold wash of horror flooded over him. Had he lost it in the fire? Think!

But wait, everyone knew he'd been in the building that day and also that he'd been in there when he rescued Wayne. So even if it was somehow found in the fire, it wouldn't incriminate him. His only loss then, was missing part of the gift from his grandfather. The man had been everything that Corbin aspired to, and he'd been proud of Corbin. In fact, he'd set up his first job—well, the first job where he'd killed someone to fulfill a contract.

Corbin tugged his coat sleeve down to hide the missing jewelry. Disappointing, but not a tragedy like he'd first feared. There would be no finding it now. The ashes were still too hot even if he could go poking through them without looking suspicious.

Irritation washing through him, he pounded on the door again.

It took a few moments for it to creak open and for Grant Moore to poke his head around the side of it.

His eyes widened briefly, and then they pinched into narrow slits. "What are you doing here?" He seemed anything but happy to see Corbin on his porch. That was clear.

Corbin thrust his chin in the air. "Why did you burn down the building you'd only just purchased? I'm wondering if I should go to the sheriff with what I know."

Grant's mouth went slack. "I didn't— What are you talking about? I thought you started it!"

Corbin huffed, keeping his voice gruff and firm. "I told you yesterday that I get paid based on my reputation. It would do me no good to burn down a recent acquisition, which is what brings me here. You've damaged my reputation, and you owe me."

"Listen now . . ." Grant sputtered. "I had nothing to do with that fire!" He pointed a finger. "Get off my porch!"

Corbin thinned his lips and tilted him a glower. "I'm not going anywhere until we settle this. Now invite me inside like a gentleman."

Grant looked aghast. "My family is in here," he hissed. "And if anything happens to them, and I mean anything, you'll wish you'd never met me. No. You can't come inside."

Relief washed through him. He'd succeeded in getting the man to wish him gone. "I don't want to hurt your family. That's not how a good reputation is made." He gave the man a pointed look. "If I didn't start that fire, and you didn't start it, what do you think happened?"

Grant shook his head in bafflement. "I suppose that it could have been an accident?"

Corbin shifted a step closer. Time to close this deal. "We may never find out, but I need you to know that if I ever discover that it was you, I will be back."

The older man turned a little pale beneath the flush on his cheeks. "It wasn't me! I wanted that store. Now it will cost me hundreds to rebuild and restock!"

Time to ease up. Corbin stepped back. "All right then. I believe you. And I might even be able to help you with some of the funds you'll need to rebuild."

Grant quirked a brow. "How?"

"I want to buy Chancellor's wagon and all the supplies and the oxen. I'll give you five hundred dollars."

"That's only half of what it's worth!"

"It's more than you're going to get from anyone else at this late notice. And it will give you money to rebuild." Corbin held his breath. He had more money, and Grant knew it. He'd been paid four times that for the job he'd done for the man. Would he go for it?

Grant lifted his chin. "Six hundred."

Relieved, Corbin thrust out a hand. The price was half of what he would have paid if the man had been better at haggling. "I'll take it."

Moore's lips pressed into a thin line as he reached past the door to shake his hand. Corbin dug the money out of his poke and thrust it through the crack. And with that, the deal was concluded.

He walked away with relief coursing through him. His reputation would remain intact, and Moore would turn his attention elsewhere to look for a cause of the fire.

It was all that he could have asked for.

Now he just had to convince Cranston to give him Chancellor's spot.

Willow woke the next morning, surprised that she'd finally fallen asleep. She and Mercy had been given a tent next to Micah and Gideon's. Thankfully, Mercy kept her condolences to a minimum and fell asleep soon after they laid down.

Willow stared into the darkness for the longest time, simply trying to process the fact that Papa was gone. She still hadn't managed to settle the reality of it in her mind. And one thought tormented her. Yesterday Gideon told her she ought to talk to her father about why he was selling and heading to Oregon. She'd had the chance and not taken it.

But most troubling of all? Gideon assured her that he didn't think Papa was in any danger!

And now Papa was dead.

She squirmed but couldn't escape the painful stab from that thought.

A question lingered . . . Had the fire been set on purpose? Had Papa—the store—been purposefully targeted?

It seemed incomprehensible, and yet . . . the store had gone up so fast! Had Gideon known something that he hadn't told her?

Her pulse rushed so fast that she could hear it whipping like a windstorm in her ears!

Papa had always been there for her. After they'd lost Mama, he had been her center, her constant encourager, a stalwart support. He'd worked hard but always made time for her. He'd provided well and loved wonderfully.

She rolled to her side and curled in on herself.

Could she survive without him?

If your strength seems uncertain, remember that the Lord's is not. Had it really only been this morning that Gideon had said those words to her? They'd seemed so palatable at the time. Now she wasn't even sure she understood what they meant.

Those were the thoughts that kept swirling through her mind until, at some point, when the light was already brushing the tent above her with a blush of dawn, she must have dozed off.

Now Mercy was not in the tent, and Willow sat up, dread rising in her. If only she could simply fall into the oblivion of sleep where Papa could still come to her in her dreams. If only she could live in that space forever and never have to face the reality of missing him.

But that wasn't possible.

And with each waking breath, her anger grew. Gideon had some explaining to do! Not only about Papa being in danger, but . . . Papa had said, "Remember your promise." What had Gideon promised? And what had Papa whispered to him at the last?

More importantly, did he know if Papa had been murdered? The very thought made her want to retreat into herself. But if it were true, the sheriff ought to know!

She pushed back the blanket and searched for her shoes. There at the end of the pallet—not even a pallet, really, just a blanket spread on grass. She thrust her feet into the boots and caught the acrid scent of smoke on her dark-blue dress—the only item of clothing she owned now.

But that paled in comparison to the loss of dear Papa.

Lord, what am I going to do?

She pinned up her hair as she contemplated.

She could rebuild. But . . . she thought of Papa's dream to build in Oregon. Maybe that would be better, and yet . . . she had no income. She would need to visit the bank and see what savings might remain to her in Papa's account. But first . . .

She emerged with hands fisted to find Gideon seated on a log by a fire with his back to her. Her eyes narrowed, but his saving grace lay in the fact that Micah and Mercy sat on a log to his left. The boys to his right. The wagon master, Caesar Cranston, stood nearby, too. And poor Mr. Harrington, who had lost the store he'd only just purchased from Papa. He sat on a log across the fire with his elbows pressed onto his knees, hands clasped, and head hanging as though all the burdens of the world had descended upon him.

Willow envisioned the stack of dollar bills Papa happily fanned yesterday—the stake that would have gotten them a new start in Oregon. Burnt now, along with everything else.

The group seemed to be mid-conversation—further reasons that her questions for Gideon would have to wait.

". . . nothing left on the shelves," Micah was saying to Mr. Cranston.

Caesar frowned and leaned to one side to spit a stream of tobacco, then sucked on his lower lip, deep in thought. "Might indeed be better for us to pull out early then."

"What's happening?" Willow folded her arms against the morning chill, wishing she wore something more substantial than her thin dress.

Mr. Harrington's head snapped up. His gaze settled on her, and Willow felt something squirm inside her. Why, despite all he'd risked to save Papa, did one glance from the man raise goose flesh on her arms? Surely, she must have misjudged the man at the meeting the other day. A lecher wouldn't have risked his life to save a practical stranger!

She forced herself to give him a nod and a smile of greeting if only as a way of thanking him for trying to save Papa. Yet something inside her still recoiled at the searching look he gave her.

Perhaps it was only the remainder of Gideon's cautioning words spoken near the creek yesterday, or simply her dislike of Papa's wanting to sell the store in the first place.

After another spare nod, she focused on the ground near her feet.

Gid leapt up and stepped over the log to hurry toward her. She couldn't seem to prevent the glower she leveled on him. His footsteps faltered, but after only a moment, he ducked into her shelter and returned with one of the blankets, which he draped around her shoulders.

"Thank you." She swallowed away her anger with him for now. "What's happening?" She took a few steps closer to the fire's warmth to distance herself from the man she wanted to rail at. Sadly for her, he kept pace with her.

The group at the fire exchanged glances.

Gideon finally spoke from beside her. "We went to the other mercantile in town this morning to pick up some cloth and a few other necessities that we all lost. It seems that one of the other wagon masters encouraged all his people to quickly take what they needed, and the store had very few of the items we required."

Willow felt her lips squeeze into a grim line. "Wright never did stock his store like he ought. Pa talked to him often about being more organized to keep his profits up."

Gideon nodded. "Anyhow, Cranston thinks we should all leave sooner than planned so as to beat the rest of this year's wagon trains to Fort Kearny, where we can hopefully restock some necessities." Willow's gaze drifted to the oxen in the distance and Gideon must have read her thoughts because he hurried to add, "It's been warm enough that the grass should be adequate for the teams."

Cranston shuffled his feet. He studied something in the grass before him. "I'm sorry to say, Miss Chancellor, but I won't be able to allow you to join us on this wagon train." He peered up at her. Spat another shot of tobacco that made Willow's stomach curl.

"What?" Gideon, Micah, and Mercy all asked the question at the same time.

Cranston frowned and poked at a stone beneath his toe. "No women unaccompanied by a male relative. It causes too much hassle amongst the single fellas. There might be another wagon train that will take you, but as I said, not this one." He pegged Micah with a look. "I know you and I already had this discussion."

Micah scrubbed his jaw and concentrated on the ground between his feet.

But Mercy stood. Her gaze narrowed on Micah, and she plunked her hands on her hips. "Is that why?"

Micah looked up, brows raised as though in surprise, but Willow detected a bit of dread tightening his features. "Why what?"

"You know very well! Why you asked me to marry you!"

Despite the sadness cloaking her, Willow felt a tiny spark of joy poke through. Micah asked Mercy to marry him? That was wonderful! Except . . . Willow divided a glance between the two.

The narrow glare Mercy fixed on Micah brought to mind the blade of a guillotine about to fall.

Micah raised his hands. "Just calm down now, Mercy. No, it's—"

"Calm down?" Mercy stiffened. "Did you actually just say that to me, Micah Morran?" She hefted two handfuls of her skirts and spun to walk away from the fire, shooting over her shoulder. "Boys stay here!"

Oh, dear.

Micah hung his head and massaged the back of his neck for a brief moment before pressing his hands to his knees and rising. "If you'll excuse me, I'll be back shortly. For what it's worth, I vote we do leave early." He strode quickly in Mercy's direction. Mattox, Micah's huge black dog, trotted ahead of him and thrust his snout into Mercy's hand, begging for a rub. Mercy complied, but it didn't ease the anger in her expression. The couple paused on the banks of the river, and Willow tore her gaze away from the tension in the lines of their shoulders.

She hoped they would work things out between them.

Joel and Avram exchanged a look. Joel arched his brows, swung his legs, and poked the long stick in his hands into the flames, lips pressed together tightly.

Willow guessed that he didn't like Mercy speaking to his pa in such a manner.

Avram frowned in his mother's direction with concern pinching his lips.

Since Mr. Harrington and the boys seemed content near the fire, Willow realized her questions for Gideon would still need to wait.

She sighed. She wasn't sure she could summon the strength to confront him at this point anyhow.

Okay, what then?

She first needed a necessary, and then she needed to see about Papa. She would have to visit the minister and see about a spot in the church cemetery. After that . . . well, it seemed that at least one of her questions had been resolved. If Cranston wasn't going to allow her to travel, she must figure out a way to rebuild here.

Except . . . the realization hit her like a punch.

Papa had sold the store to Mr. Harrington only yesterday. She had no land on which to rebuild.

Her gaze collided with that of the man beside her.

Gideon frowned down at her. "We need to talk."

Yes, they did, but she would lose control if they started that conversation right now. Besides, she wasn't sure she felt clearheaded enough for it. She could still hear her pulse rushing in her ears.

Why did it feel as though every thought had to be dragged out of a miry clay? She blinked slowly and looked around.

The necessary at the back of the store . . . that was the first stop. She would take inventory in the barn and feed the chickens. That much, at least, she could do. After that, the bank. Then she would force herself to go see the minister. She would rather Parson Adam performed the ceremony since he had been such good friends with Papa. Hopefully, the new minister wouldn't mind.

She removed the blanket from around her shoulders and set to folding it. "What time is it?" She placed the blanket back into the mouth of the tent.

Gideon tugged a small pocket watch from inside his shirt pocket. He clicked it open. "Eight forty-five."

Willow nodded. The bank wouldn't open for another fifteen minutes—maybe thirty if Mr. Chase arrived late this morning. Plenty of time to get a few things taken care of at the store.

Her stomach curled, threatening to empty. It might have followed through on the threat if it weren't already so empty from her lack of food the day before.

She no longer had a store. No property. Nothing that remained to her except for the dirty clothes she wore.

Dew soaked into her boots and hem as she started across the field toward town, leaving the men at the fire behind.

"Where are you going?" Gid hurried after her.

"I am going to feed the chickens and then I'm going to the church to . . ." She cleared her throat, unable to finish that sentence. "After that, I need to visit the bank to see whether Mr. Chase will be able to help me buy and rebuild here in town."

Gideon kept pace beside her. "Willow, can you please slow down for a minute?"

She froze and whirled to face him. "You told me he wasn't in danger!" The words burst out before she had time to rethink them. Her fists clenched so tight that she could feel her fingernails biting into her palms.

Gideon's eyes fell closed. "I know. And yes, I know the fire could have been set purposefully, but we don't know anything for certain, Willow."

She had to look away from the sorrow in the gaze he lowered to her.

They were in the middle of the field now, with town on one end and wagon encampments closer to the other. In the distance, back by the fire, she saw Mr. Harrington and Mr. Cranston shake hands. What could that be all about?

Gid was right, of course. There was no way of knowing how or why the fire had started. It was irrational of her to blame him. She forced herself to relax and pressed one hand to her forehead. "I just wish I knew what caused it or why it started."

"I know."

The softness of his words made her want to throw herself into his arms once again and lean into his strength. She sealed her lips tight and took a step back. She would not begin crying, or she would never stop.

When he didn't move but only continued to quietly look down at her, she knew she needed to make her escape. "Listen, Gideon, it has been a pleasure to know you all. But if Mr. Cranston won't allow me to join the wagon train, I have to get started on surviving here. I wish you all the best and hope the good Lord watches over you." She looked toward town, unable to meet the blue of his gaze as she said, "I will miss you all."

She may never know what Papa had asked of him, but she'd just have to live with that. She started walking once more.

But the warmth of Gideon's fingers settled around her elbow. "Please wait."

Willow swallowed down the emotions begging to explode. She still couldn't look at him. "What is it?"

When he released her, the absence of his touch raised a hollowness inside her.

He remained silent for so long that she finally glanced his way.

He rubbed a finger against his temple. Opened his mouth. Closed it. Frowned. Scratched at his temple again. Then blurted, "Marry me?"

For one long moment, Willow simply stared at him. And then a dry bark of laughter caught her unaware. Without a word, she pivoted toward town and double-timed her steps.

She couldn't think on that request too long or her betraying heart would have her running back to him and begging him to let her say yes. Gideon was a gentleman and the epitome of kindness itself. But she knew that the last thing he wanted was a relationship with her. He'd made that plain—why even the way he'd struggled to voice the proposal revealed his aversion.

No, she wouldn't punish him—or herself—simply because she'd fallen on hard times. If she said yes, his punishment would arise from being stuck with a woman he didn't love—hers would stem from loving a husband who would never love her in return.

She hurried to the pile of burnt rubble that had once been the store and around back and into the privy.

When she stepped out a few moments later, the door squealed its normal protest. Gideon stood across the yard near the barn, his hands propped against his hips and his face angled to the sky as though he might be praying. She washed her hands and face in the bucket that they kept by the privy and dried them on the scrap of now smoky toweling.

Anger beginning to rise, she slung the towel back over the little bar Papa had fixed to the side of the privy and marched toward Gideon.

With his chin still raised, he lowered his gaze to search her face. Her narrowed eyes must have captured his attention because his chin slowly lowered, and he caught his lower lip between his teeth. "It was your father's request."

Her squint scrunched so tight now that she could barely see through the slits of her eyes. Her hands settled on her hips. "Truly? Papa's last request was that you sacrifice everything to marry a woman you don't want?"

"I didn't say it was his last request, and that's not true." Despite the declaration, he didn't sound convinced.

She lifted her chin. "Isn't it?"

He surprised her by stepping right into her space, so close that his legs brushed her skirt. His eyes glittered blue fire as he leaned over her. "And what if I told you that your beauty captivated me from the first day I laid eyes on you?"

She stepped back from the shocking allure of those words. She whirled to search out the bank. Mr. Chase always built a fire first thing for the coffee that he kept on the stove all day. Drat. No smoke trailed from the bank's chimney yet. "Don't pander to me, Gid."

"Willow . . . I know I'm too old and not your ideal husband, but—"

She spun back to face him so quickly that she must have startled him into silence. She'd never thought of him as too old. Whatever had given him that idea? "On the contrary, I've never thought of you as too old or less than ideal." She clamped her teeth against the side of her tongue to keep from blurting more. Whatever made her confess that? If she wasn't careful, in a moment, she'd be blathering how much she admired him. She blew out a breath. "That, however, does not mean that we can marry. And now, I truly must bid you farewell and wish you safe travels."

She took a step but then hesitated and glanced over her shoulder. "Why did Papa want to go to Oregon?"

Gideon swallowed. "That's partly what I need to talk to you about."

"So?"

"Not here. Let's find someplace . . . more sheltered." He touched her elbow. "I'm concerned you might be in danger here."

"What? Why?" She glanced around. No one was even in sight, much less paying them any attention.

Gid released a sharp breath. "That's also partly what I need to talk to you about." He motioned. "How about in the barn?"

"Fine. I need to feed the chickens anyhow."

Once they were in the barn, she stepped through the side door into the chicken coop and slung some grain to the happily clucking oblivious critters. After she retreated into the interior once more, she dusted her hands and pinned Gid with a look. "Well?"

"I think your uncle might have had something to do with the fire."

Willow's jaw slipped for a beat. "Uncle Grant? Whatever do you mean?"

"I mean, he wanted your father to start giving him half of the store's profits. I mean, he didn't want to pay for any of the labor to keep the store going. I mean, he made threats strong enough that Wayne came to me last fall and extracted a promise that I would take care of you if anything happened to him."

Anger, hot and sure, flared. Willow's hand shot out and connected with Gideon's cheek. A loud *crack* reverberated off the stalls, and though Gideon looked stunned, her slap also didn't appear to have hurt him much.

She felt the sting of shame shoot from her palm to her core. She rubbed her thumb into the hollow of her hand. "I'm sorry. That was uncalled for. It's just . . . you knew that, and yet yesterday you told me he wasn't in any danger."

He thrust a finger toward the smoldering ruins out the barn door. "Would you have suspected your uncle capable of such a thing?"

Willow's shoulders slumped, even as she shook her head.

"Well, neither did I." He hesitated, staring at the rubble for a long moment. "And now I have to live with that." His narrowed eyes pinned her once more. "But one of your father's last requests was that I keep you safe. And that's what I intend to do."

One of . . . "You keep saying that like you are trying to avoid telling me something. What is it?"

He shook his head. "It's nothing. Can we please address the issue of your uncle?"

Willow felt as though too many pictures were flashing in her mind. So many that they all melded into a seamless blur. "But Uncle Grant would never . . ." The words trailed away as she realized they lacked conviction. Uncle Grant might never hurt her, but many times she'd seen a spark of animosity in him directed toward Papa. But murder?! Surely, he wouldn't go that far. "It makes no sense. Why would he burn the place to the ground if he wanted Papa to split the proceeds with him?"

Gideon frowned. "Yesterday, your father sold the store to Hoyt Harrington."

Willow's gaze drifted out the barn doors to the heap of ash. She envisioned Papa blowing on the signatures when she'd left him. Had Uncle Grant been trying to destroy evidence of the sale? But why wouldn't he have simply offered to buy the new owner out? He certainly had the money.

"It's only supposition, of course," Gid amended. "I don't think we'll ever have proof."

She pressed one hand to her forehead. "This is too much to even comprehend. I really can't— I can't even— And you're going to be gone, and I'm . . ." Heat swept through her face. How easy it would be to say yes to his proposal at this moment.

She didn't want to stay. There were too many happy memories to haunt her here. In fact, this land rightfully belonged to Mr. Harrington, and she wouldn't fight him about that. But she had to make a living somehow.

Gideon stepped closer. Reached out and hooked his first finger around her pinky. "I meant what I said, Willow." He spoke softly. "Marry me." He tilted his head and pleaded with his eyes.

Willow swallowed and willed herself not to focus on the wonder of his broad thumb stroking over her knuckles. She would marry him in a heartbeat if she thought he really wanted her. But she wouldn't saddle him—or herself—with a pity marriage.

She snatched her hand from his, pivoted on one heel, and left him there, only remembering that he'd said she might be in danger when she was already halfway to the church.

A shiver shimmied along her neck. She glanced back, half expecting to see some looming specter of danger, but all she saw was Gideon, keeping pace with her a few steps back.

Anger and relief vied for preeminence. Fine, if he wanted to follow her around all day, she didn't have the power to stop him. It wasn't like he would be here any longer after the wagon train pulled out. At least she would feel safe for this one last day.

She really needed to figure out what was going on.

She faced forward in time to see the new parson striding up the church steps.

Had she done the right thing in denying Gid's proposal? It was too late to change her mind now, she supposed.

With a sigh, she hurried up the church steps. "Good morning, Parson Miles."

Chapter 11

Mercy glowered at Micah as he strode to join her. The feeling of betrayal grew stronger with each beat of her heart.

The hurt in his gaze was the only thing that kept her from lighting into him again. She forced herself to remain calm. "Did you talk to him? To Mr. Cranston? Before you asked me to marry you?"

Micah stepped close enough to take her hand. The warmth of his fingers settling against hers took a measure of her anger. She closed her eyes and drew in a long, steadying breath.

And when she opened them, Micah stepped even closer, raising her hand to settle it against the beat of his heart. He slipped his hands to her waist and urged her closer. "How many times did that" —he swallowed, seeming to discard several inappropriate words— "man, tell you lies about how no one else would ever love you?"

She blinked at the unexpected understanding filling his gaze.

He lifted one finger to trace gentle strokes against her chin. "I already wanted to marry you, Mercy. I love you. And you are more precious to me than almost anything else in this world other than our boys. I wanted to give you time. Time to heal. Time to make sure you feel the same way about me. But yes, yesterday I did speak to Cranston, and he did tell me he wouldn't allow single women to join the caravan.

But all that did was hurry my proposal. A proposal," he emphasized, "that I *wanted* to offer."

Mercy felt like a fool. She had mistreated him in front of others—this man who had been nothing but kindness and patience itself, this man whom she loved—whose very touch was even now filling her with a longing for more. "I'm sorry, Micah. I shouldn't have . . . spoken to you like that, especially not in front of others."

"I forgive you." Micah leaned close and settled his lips against her forehead. Then he drew her against his chest.

She relished the strength and security of his arms about her and the smoky scent of him as his voice rumbled above her head.

"People who have been abused are a little like tenderized meat, to my way of thinking."

She frowned but held her silence, knowing he would explain.

"They were hammered and hammered and hammered until they were raw and bruised and broken, not only in body but also in spirit. Those wounds take time to heal, and sometimes all it takes is the smallest of jabs to revive all the pain." He pressed a kiss just above her ear. "So, I'm sorry for being one of those jabs this time. I'll try to do better at being open with you about my reasoning."

Mercy closed her eyes and thanked God once again for this wonderful, understanding man He had brought to her. "It's not your fault, Micah. You're right that Herst used to taunt me with how no one would ever love me."

A tremor worked through Micah, and his hand settled gently against the back of her head. "He was a liar." His voice emerged gruff.

She hurried to finish. "But I know now that's not true. I should have taken stock before flying off the handle." She eased back and looked up at him.

He bent his head and brushed his lips over hers in a way that made her wish they were not in such a public place. But almost before the kiss had begun, he pulled away. "We'll both try to do better next time."

She nodded.

A glint of mischief lit his eyes. "So what do you say to a sunset wedding?"

"Tonight?" she gasped.

He nodded. "Tonight. I have a feeling Cranston will want to take off first thing in the morning. Especially since he's itching to beat the stampede."

Mercy felt her eyes widen. Heat washed her face. But they'd just stood here and said they would try to be more honest with each other. "Micah . . . Those blows you spoke of. Herst was, well, I'm not sure if I'll be ready to . . ."

Micah bent and captured her gaze. "The only reason for the rush is so you'll have the protection of my name. There's no expectation on my part for anything beyond that."

She released a breath of tension. "But I don't want to disappoint—"

He silenced her by sweeping a curl from her forehead behind her ear. "Remember what I said last night? You are not going to disappoint me. Love is longsuffering and kind, Mercy. It does not seek its own good, but only the good of others."

The last of her tension eased out as she settled more comfortably against him. She gazed into the striking blue of his eyes. "What did I ever do to deserve a wonderful man like you?"

He grinned and tilted his head as though he'd just been struck by a thought. "I am pretty great, aren't I?"

A bark of laughter escaped as she stepped back and thumped his chest. "That you are, Micah Morran. That you are."

"So, sunset?"

She pressed her lips together and nodded. "Sunset."

He grinned, and Mercy wondered how he had the power to make her emotions do such an about-face in such a short amount of time.

She eyed the river. Would she have time to wash before this evening? The privacy to do so? Maybe she and Willow could stand guard for each other. With the sun beating down as it was, it wouldn't take long at all for their dresses to dry.

She turned and saw Willow marching toward town with Gideon hot on her heels.

She smiled. Maybe in a couple of hours, then. She had a feeling that Willow and Gideon would be standing beside her and Micah repeating their own vows at sunset.

Corbin had been slumped near the fire all morning, trying to come up with a story. Thankfully, the wagon master hadn't hesitated when he'd offered to pay for the spot opened up by Chancellor's passing, so that was one trouble off his mind.

Now, he had to figure out how to convince Willow to become his wife. Because he not only wanted the wagon stocked with supplies that her uncle had sold him, but he also wanted more land in Oregon.

And maybe it was also the competitor in him—because he'd seen the way Riley looked at her this morning and would love to see the man taken down a peg or two.

Other than those reasons, she would be a pretty picture on his arm in the Oregon Territory. A man might even run for governor with a woman of her beauty and poise at his side. Even though she hadn't been happy with her father for selling the store, she'd been charming and polite when they'd first met, so she could also be a thespian when she needed to be.

In politics, that would be a boon.

She'd also proved she was smart by helping her father run their store all these years. He'd seen her balancing the books yesterday, so she could help a man run his campaign finances, couldn't she? And way out in the west, there wouldn't be that much oversight, so if a few funds were misappropriated, who would be the wiser?

Lastly, who was he kidding? What man wouldn't want to marry such a dainty and beautiful woman? Just the sight of her lit a fire in a man's bones.

One side of his mouth quirked up. His charm had worked on plenty of women up to this point. There was no reason to think she would shun his proposal.

He'd wanted to talk to her when she first emerged from her tent, but Riley had been there, and then they'd gone off together. But Riley could trail after her all he wanted. It would be all for naught.

Corbin had a plan, and it was a good one, thanks to his retrieval of the box that had been in her father's pocket.

He twisted the compartmentalized ring on his finger, staring in the direction that Willow and Riley had disappeared a few minutes earlier.

He couldn't do anything right away because too many tragedies happening right on top of each other would raise suspicions, but Gideon Riley wasn't going to make it all the way to Oregon.

Corbin bit back a smile. It would give him something to look forward to.

For now . . . He rose to his feet. It was time he moseyed into town and found Willow.

After speaking to the minister and setting Papa's service for four o'clock that afternoon, Willow headed to the bank. She could feel Gideon's gaze drilling into her back the whole way down the street but did her best to ignore him.

She felt prepared to hear from Mr. Chase that Papa didn't have any savings to speak of. After all, he'd often spoken of how the Lord always provided just enough.

What she wasn't prepared for was to find Uncle Grant just inside the door, leaving the bank. A chill zipped down her spine at the coldness in his eyes when they fell on her.

"Willow." He said it flat with absolutely no affection.

"Uncle Grant. Good to see you." Had he detected the tremor in her words? She stepped to one side.

He gave her a nod and started to brush past but then stopped. "Wanted to let you know that I sold your pa's wagon to the man who's taking his place in the wagon train. Also—" he reached to squeeze her arm "—I'm glad you weren't hurt in the fire." He ducked his head as he released her.

Had that been guilt in his eyes?

Without another word, he continued on his way. The bell above the door jangled as he headed out.

Both hands fisted into tight knots. Not even a whisper of condolence about Papa. And he hadn't even asked if she needed anything from the wagon! How had she not realized what a low man her uncle was all these years?

Only after he walked away did she realize that he'd taken it upon himself to sell something that belonged to her! And was keeping the money for himself, it seemed!

Willow turned to Mr. Chase, who eyed her with decided sympathy in his expression.

She stepped up to the counter. "Mr. Chase, I'm here about Papa's account. I'm wondering if there might have been any money in our savings?"

Mr. Chase shuffled his feet and avoided eye contact as she dropped her gloves onto the counter. "I'm sorry, but much as it pains me to say this, the account was in the name of the store. And your uncle just finished transferring the meager funds that were in the account to his own."

Confusion set her spine ramrod straight. "What? How could he do that?"

Mr. Chase seemed to be flummoxed as he stuttered, "Why, why he had paperwork indicating that your father sold him the store and all assets pertaining to it, including what was left in the bank account."

Willow felt her jaw go slack as she tried to make sense of that. "But how is that possible? Just yesterday, Papa sold the store to Mr. Harring . . . ton."

Willow clutched at the counter to stop the room from whirling as the truth hit her. Then giving herself a mental shake, she put her trembling hands to smoothing her skirt. "Never mind, Mr. Chase. I wish you all the best." With that, she whirled and rushed onto the porch, but then froze. She had no idea what to do now.

"What did you find out?"

Gideon's voice came from so close beside her that she spun to face him with a gasp.

He raised his palms. "Sorry. Didn't mean to startle you."

Willow fiddled with the collar at the base of her throat. "You'll never guess who was just in the bank with paperwork indicating he purchased our store!"

Gideon frowned in the direction of Uncle Grant's carriage that rolled down the street.

"Yes! That scoundrel Harrington must have been working for Uncle Grant!"

With a wince, Gideon took a step nearer. "I'm sorry Willow. I know that has to hurt that your uncle would have underhandedly subverted your father like that."

Willow waved a hand. "I don't suppose it matters. In fact, Papa may have sold the store to Uncle Grant if he'd only come and asked straight up. What's done is done."

But what was she going to do to survive? That was the question.

"My offer stands, Willow."

Her eyes fell closed. How was the man so adept at reading her mind?

Footsteps crunched on the street below the bank's porch. Willow glanced down and felt every muscle in her body tense as Hoyt Harrington paused, dividing a glance between Gideon and her.

She couldn't help but nudge her chin up slightly. And before she thought better of it, she blurted, "Mr. Harrington, were you working for my uncle when you purchased the store from my father?"

The scoundrel frowned and turned to watch Uncle Grant's carriage turn out of sight. His feet shuffled and he shifted his hat through his fingers. "I had no idea what kind of man he was when he hired me." He swept a hand around the back of his neck and peered up at her with seeming sincerity shining in his eyes. "You have to believe me, Willow. I was just doing a job. But then I met you and your father and well, you are good people. I had no idea he would resort to—" He stilled and waved a hand. "Well, never mind that. I've no proof."

Willow's eyes shot wide. She bounced a glance off Gideon then settled her scrutiny on Mr. Harrington, not wanting to miss anything. "You think Uncle Grant had something to do with the fire?"

Mr. Harrington's boots ground against the gravel beneath them. "Well now, I'm not sure. And I certainly have no evidence. I suppose that's something we'll have to leave for the authorities to investigate."

He took the steps up to the porch then and stopped beside her. He never took his gaze from her when he said, "Mr. Riley, if you wouldn't mind I would like to have a private word with Miss Willow."

Unease shot through Willow, and she took a step closer to Gideon, relieved to feel his shoulder bump hers. This disquiet that filled her was probably nothing. The man may indeed have been duped by Uncle Grant and was naught but a misused bystander in all this. Still, something in her revolted at being left alone with him. "Whatever you have to say to me can be said in front of Gid—er, Mr. Riley."

Mr. Harrington cleared his throat. "Very well." He held out his hand and at first all Willow noticed was the blackened tips of his fingers.

"What happened to your hand?"

He glanced down, continuing to hold out his palm. "In the store yesterday, I knocked over a pot of ink and it spilled on my hand."

Willow's gaze drifted to the small silver box and she took a sharp breath. A vague recollection of it from years ago filtered into her mind. She reached a trembling hand to take it.

The silver box, about the size of her hand, was engraved with a ballroom dance scene on the top, and each fluted panel around the sides depicted a domestic scene. The four silver, fluted feet finished the details with a touch of elegance. Mama used to keep it on her nightstand. She had put her ring in it when she scrubbed floors, gardened, or grubbed out the barn. But she always returned the ring to her finger the moment she'd washed up.

Willow opened the top to stare down at the red velvet that encased the silver wedding band which had once been her mother's. The ring blurred through the tears that suddenly filled her eyes. "Where did you get this?"

It was a treasure indeed, especially on this, the day after she'd lost everything that meant anything to her.

"It was what took us so long to get out of the store. Your father refused to leave until we found that. We were behind the counter for quite some time searching all the compartments. That was when I spilled the ink." Mr. Harrington took a step closer, angling a shoulder to block Gideon from their conversation as much as possible.

Gideon made a low sound at the back of his throat and retreated a couple of steps.

Mr. Harrington tilted his head and his gaze softened on her features. "Miss Willow, I believe I have a solution to your current dilemma."

Oh no! Willow swallowed and took a step back.

But he stepped with her, clapping his hat to his chest. His brown eyes were solemn as he looked down at her. "Allow me to make up for my mistake in working for your uncle. And to offer my assistance to help you get to Oregon. Do me the honor of becoming my wife?"

Willow blinked. Angled her head to study the water barrel across the street in front of the livery. Her head spun. My, this was all a muddle.

She had nothing and no one. And no place left here in Independence. Uncle Grant might rebuild the store, but how long would that take? And there was no guarantee that he would give her the job.

She felt eyes on her and glanced past Mr. Harrington to find that Gideon had moved to a position where he could see her and now stood watching her in that quiet way of his with his hands propped against his hips and his blue eyes filled with concern.

She swallowed.

She didn't want Gideon to marry her out of pity, but being married to him would be infinitely preferable to being married to Mr. Harrington. No doubt, Mr. Harrington's charm had turned many a lady's head, but for her, it only caused her great unease.

She retreated one step and then shuffled sideways to bring her closer to Gideon once more. "I'm sorry to inform you, Mr. Harrington, that Mr. Riley has already asked me to be his wife, and I have agreed."

Beside her, she heard Gid release a sharp breath.

Whether from relief or regret, she wasn't quite sure.

Chapter 12

Gideon could hardly believe his ears. Relief washed through him, and he stepped forward to rest one hand against Willow's back. He didn't miss the decided animosity that sprang into Harrington's narrowed eyes.

Ignoring the man, Gideon reached for the ring box in Willow's hands. He studied the silver band intricately engraved with tiny leaves. "It's beautiful. Your mother's?"

Willow nodded. "I haven't seen it for years. I didn't even know that Papa kept it."

Gideon turned a look on Mr. Harrington. "We thank you, Harrington, for bringing this to us at this time. I know that Willow will appreciate being able to wear her mother's wedding ring as her own." He hoped the man would take the words for the dismissal they were.

Oh, but Harrington didn't like it—not one bit. A muscle ticked at the outer corner of one of his eyes, and his lips were pressed so tight they were almost white. But he was a self-possessed man—Gid could say that of him, at least. After a moment, he stepped back, gave Willow a slight bow, and offered his farewells.

Willow watched as he stalked back toward the encampment. Then she turned to face him. "Gid, you really don't have to marry me if you don't want to."

Gid swallowed, wishing he could reassure her that she had nothing to worry about, but he wasn't sure. He found her attractive. That was true enough. But he was old enough now to realize that a good marriage needed so much more than just attraction between two people to make it work. And yet he was also old enough to realize that any two people who wanted to make a relationship work, could do so if they worked at it.

The question he needed to answer for himself was . . . did he want to? Because relationship inevitably required risk.

The last thought struck him square in the chest.

That was it. The reason he'd resisted his attraction to her for so long.

Because with love came the potential for loss, hurt, and sorrow. He'd experienced too much grief already in his short life, and he had no desire to ever walk through that valley again.

He tamped his wants back into submission with firm resolve.

He could both protect his heart and keep his word to Wayne. What he felt for her wasn't yet on the level of what he'd shared with Verona, and these circumstances were different, and he would be careful to guard his heart. He didn't allow himself to linger on that concern.

He stepped closer to her, feeling satisfied to note that she held her place instead of retreating as she had with Harrington. He stroked a stray curl of her hair back from her brow. "I want to. I'm not trying to say it will be easy for us. We'll have a lot to come to terms with between us, but with God's help, we'll work through it."

He heard her swallow as she turned her face to study a wagon passing on the street. "Very well. I'll marry you, and thank you to boot, for giving me your name when you didn't have to."

He could have argued that it was required of him, but he knew hearing it wouldn't reassure her, so he held his silence on that matter, saying instead, "Tonight, then? I'll arrange it with Parson Houston if that is agreeable to you?"

She was fiddling with her collar again. "Yes. Yes. That's fine, I suppose, but I don't . . ." Her hands fell to her sides, and then she motioned to her dress with helpless frustration. "This is all I have to wear."

"You look fine." At her sharp look, he amended more softly. "Better than fine." He reminded himself of his resolve to keep his distance and refrained from telling her that he would find her beautiful even if she was wearing mourning garments.

Her shoulders sagged. "Very well. If you've the time to accompany me, I'd like to visit the sheriff and then gather some wildflowers for Papa's . . . grave."

"Of course."

Gideon strode beside her toward the sheriff's office, keeping an eye on the surrounding streets in case Willow might still be in danger. The fire didn't make sense. Why would her uncle go to all the trouble of disguising his purchase of the store only to burn it down the very day he acquired it?

He was missing something. He just couldn't put his finger on it.

She must have forgotten about going to see the lawman, for instead of heading to the jailhouse, she turned down the street. As he followed her into a field near the Missouri River on the north side of town, he shoved down all his doubts and concerns for the future, their age difference, and whether he could keep himself from loving her. He simply wanted to protect her from whatever had happened here. And getting her out of town was surely a good way to do that, right?

Tamsyn had just gotten Edison settled with a bowl of oats when Striker Moss and his companion, a man whose name she could not recall but who she remembered seeing at the meeting, strode up to their wagon.

Here it came then. *Lord, help me to trust You no matter what they say.*

She swallowed and dried her hands on her apron. She supposed it had been too good to be true that he hadn't tracked her down yesterday.

What with the fire in town and all, it would explain the delay. But now, dread clawed inside of her at the prospect of being so close and yet being denied passage to Oregon.

Despite the longing to beg for his accommodation, she forced calm and politeness. With a dip of her knees, she said, "Good day."

Both men paused on the other side of the fire with their hats pressed to their chests.

Mr. Moss gave her a nod. "Morning, miss."

Tamsyn refused to let her despair close her eyes. The way he emphasized "miss" let her know he had done a little digging into their past, not that she had tried to hide the fact that Edison was her brother.

She gestured to the pot keeping warm at the edge of the fire. "May I offer you some oats?"

Her stomach rumbled, and she hoped they hadn't been able to hear it from where they stood. If both of these brawny men wanted a serving there wouldn't be any left for her.

The men exchanged glances, and the one whose name she didn't remember gave a short shake of his head.

Striker turned back to her. "No. Thank you, ma'am." He nudged his hat at the man beside him. "This here is Jeremiah Jackson."

"Miss." Jeremiah gave a sketch of a bow. His features were quite striking with that dark skin contrasted with the slash of white teeth and those soft eyes that seemed able to look right through her. There was a kindness in the man's expression that was missing from his companion's.

"Pleased to meet you, Mr. Jackson."

His smile widened. "Just Jer to my friends, miss."

From his seat on his rock near the fire, Edison grunted, "Oatmeal's good. You should try it."

Striker strode closer to him and gestured to the upturned log round that she'd placed there. He spoke to Edison but included her with a glance. "Mind if we have a seat?"

Edison only gave a shrug of one shoulder as he chewed noisily, and Tamsyn motioned that Mr. Moss was welcome to the log. She'd intended to have Edison chop it after he ate, but she supposed it would do just as well for a seat as anything.

To her surprise, instead of taking the seat for himself, Striker motioned for Jeremiah to sit. He strode to the few remaining pieces of a log that someone before her had thoughtfully sawed into rounds and hauled one closer to the fire.

He jutted his chin at the pot of oats as he sank down on the other side of Edison. "Please, don't let us stop you from eating your breakfast."

Tamsyn pressed her lips together. There was no chance she would sit here and eat in front of two strangers who may have come to kick her out of the wagon train. Nervousness had her stomach in such knots that she might not be able to swallow anyhow.

She'd heard the story about Mr. Cranston saying he would brook no unaccompanied women on his train. Would he consider Edison to be company enough? More to the point, would Mr. Moss? Because he now knew of her brother's challenges.

"I'm fine." She sank onto her own rock across the fire from Edison, leaving Striker to her right and Mr. Jackson to her left. "How may I help you?" She pressed her palms tight in her lap.

If she and Edi were forced to stay behind, would she be able to find work here in Independence? Her gaze involuntarily drifted to the town.

Striker cleared his throat, drawing her gaze back to him. He sat hunched over his knees on the seat that was much too short for his long legs. His forearms rested against his thighs and his hands were clasped before him, but his direct brown gaze remained pinned on her. "I'm sorry I didn't keep my word and stop by last evening. By the time we got the fire dealt with in town, it was late, and I didn't want to disturb you."

She nodded, willing down another roil of tension. "I understand. I hope everyone is okay?"

Neither man seemed to want to meet her gaze.

"I'm afraid not." Striker's brow tucked into a quick furrow, and he prodded a pebble with the toe of his boot. "The owner of the mercantile didn't make it."

Tamsyn twisted toward him. "Surely not Willow?"

He shook his head with quick reassurance. "She's fine. It was her father."

Sorrow swelled with surprising swiftness. Had the woman enjoyed a good relationship with her father? She and Edi had not, yet she still would grieve if she learned of her father's passing. He may have left them years past, but that didn't mean she didn't love him. Yet, how much harder it must be for a woman whose father had likely been close to her for their shared work at the mercantile?

Realizing the silence had stretched, she offered, "I'm so very sorry to hear that." Once again, her gaze drifted toward the town. Smoke continued to wisp in twisty curls from the ashes of the two buildings that had burned.

Her stomach rumbled again—even more loudly this time. She felt heat sweep through her cheeks.

"You know, those oats, they smell mighty fine." Mr. Jackson rose, hooked the lid off the pot, and hung it from the metal bar she'd positioned for that task. He then ladled a bowl and the nutty scent drifted on the breeze.

Despite her despair over going hungry today, she was thankful to see that he'd felt comfortable enough to change his mind. She motioned to a canning jar on the tailgate of her wagon. "You'll find a spoon in that jar, Mr. Jackson."

The man nodded quietly and went to fetch one.

All the while she felt Mr. Moss's scrutiny as surely as she would have were she a bluebell and he a botanist.

She narrowed her eyes at him, growing weary of the delay. "I suppose you're here to tell me that we can't join the wagon train?"

He drew in a long, slow breath, his focus transferring to Edison before returning to her.

Before Mr. Moss could reply, Mr. Jackson appeared by her side. He bent and thrust the bowl at her.

Surprised, she glanced up at him.

His eyes were a perfect match for the sky just before dusk, and they were full of kindness now as he smiled down at her. "Please go on and eat, miss. You ain't gonna offend neither ol' Strike there nor myself by breaking your fast." He held the bowl closer.

"Thank you." She accepted it from him.

With a nod, he stepped around her and moved toward his seat once more.

When her stomach grumbled yet again, Tamsyn smiled her embarrassment. "I'm sorry. I didn't break my fast yet today because, well, I needed to check the snares and butcher a rabbit. Then Edi—" She broke off and thrust a bite of oats into her mouth before she could blather about how he had gone into a fit because he couldn't find his favorite shirt, and she'd had to help him look for it. By that time, she'd needed to feed Edi lest his hunger raise his temper even further.

"You're right I am here about your passage with our train."

Halfway down onto his seat, Jeremiah froze and daggered a sharp glance across the fire at Mr. Moss.

Tamsyn paused with her spoon partway to her mouth. It was the way Mr. Jackson seemed to be giving his friend a warning that birthed a minuscule shard of hope.

As though telling his friend to calm down, Mr. Moss raised his palms.

Jeremiah released a sharp sigh and sank the remainder of the way into his seat. He rubbed his broad brown palms against his knees.

Mr. Moss turned his scrutiny back on her, and Tamsyn shoved her spoon into her mouth so fast that it clicked against her teeth. She swiped at her lips, feeling humiliation shoot through her.

She plunked the spoon back into the bowl and set it on a rock by the fire, hunger nowhere near abated, yet unwilling to risk further degradation. "Please just come out with it, Mr. Moss."

He drew in a deep breath and eased it out slowly, studying her the whole time. "It's not a simple thing, Miss Acheson. Out on the trail, there are dangers that sometimes require quick responses—obedient responses." He sat straighter, twisted in her direction, and stretched his legs out before folding his arms over his chest.

The man's scrutiny could practically bore holes. Was he waiting for a response? She'd just opened her mouth when he continued.

"I admit that my first inclination was to deny your passage. But Jeremiah has urged me to ask you a few questions before we make our decision. Can I count on you to answer truthfully?"

Tamsyn's chin notched up before she thought better of it. "I'm a Christian woman, Mr. Moss. I always endeavor to honesty."

His eyes narrowed. "And yet, you made no mention of your brother's . . . incapacity when you applied to join this train."

She pursed her lips and sucked on the inside of her lower one. "Fine. I suppose that was less than honest. You are correct. But . . ."

His brows lifted at her hesitation. "But?"

"I believe he will be fine. After a long day of work, he is usually weary and sleeps hard." He also sometimes grew irritable, but she merely had to coax him to lie down and he would almost inevitably be out until she woke him the next morning.

"'Believe' is not very convincing if you'll forgive my saying so."

Tamsyn flicked her fingers at a bit of ash that had drifted to her knee. "I admit that he sometimes forgets the manners I've tried to instill in him. However, he's never—" She broke off. Saying he'd never hurt her wasn't quite true. In fact, she could still feel the effects of his recent temper. "He's always repentant and docile for days afterward. And he's never hurt anyone but me."

That was true enough. Not even Ma. She had a feeling that constantly hearing from Ma how his infirmity was all Tamsyn's fault had raised some animosity in Edi toward her. And how could she blame him?

She hadn't thought it possible, but Mr. Moss's gaze seemed to sharpen. "He hurts you?"

Raising one palm, she met his gaze, holding steady. "Never purposefully. But he's . . . strong. That said, I've always been able to get through to him."

Mr. Moss scrubbed his fingers over his jaw and glanced across the fire at his fellow scout. Jeremiah only held his hands toward the warmth of the blaze and nodded as though encouraging him to continue.

"And yesterday?" The brown of Mr. Moss's eyes churned like the waters of a tumultuous creek in spring runoff. "What would you have done if I hadn't been there? If you'd fallen, your legs could have been crushed beneath the wheels of the wagon."

Edison shifted, face downcast. "Sorry. Edi so sorry."

Tamsyn rose and skirted the fire to take his empty bowl and rest a gentle hand on his shoulder. "I know, Edi." She moved to the pot and ladled more oats into his bowl. With a glower in Mr. Moss's direction, she returned and pressed the bowl into Edi's hands once more. "I wouldn't have fallen off. I'm strong."

His gaze swept her from head to toe, and his jaw jutted to one side as though he doubted her assessment. "Your skirt could have caught in the spokes." He lurched to his feet and set to pacing, one hand scooping through his hair and pausing to grip the back of his neck. "Any number of things could have happened."

Tamsyn smoothed her hands over the front of her skirt. "Outbursts like the one you witnessed yesterday are very rare. I can't promise you they won't happen. What I can promise is that they won't be directed at anyone but me and that I will do my best to keep my brother in line."

The man stopped pacing to pause before her.

Tamsyn swallowed. Had she noticed yesterday just how tall and broad he was? He'd been wearing that large coat. Maybe she'd assumed it made him seem larger than he actually was. But she'd been wrong. Why, one of the huge, strong hands propped against his hips could just about crush her skull.

"Why do you want to go to Oregon?" His lips thinned as though he were irritated to even be having this conversation.

Tamsyn stood her ground, but she couldn't stop a sigh from slipping free. "My father left us when Edi and I were no more than children. And Ma helped us as long as she could. But a few months ago, she was—" Tamsyn pressed her palms tight and willed herself to hold it together. She tilted a nod toward the wagon. "May I speak to you over there, perhaps?"

His gaze darted to Edi, who was once more chomping down oats, and his expression seemed to soften. "Yes. Of course."

"I'll be right back, Edi. Mind your manners, hmm?"

Edi nodded, remaining fully concentrated on his bowl.

Tamsyn felt Mr. Moss's presence behind her as she strode to the other side of their wagon as surely as she would have felt a stalking cougar. Trying to will down her irritation with this entire situation, she stopped and spun to face the man.

He stood at the end of the wagon with one shoulder propped against the bed. The look he leveled on her was almost stern, but at least he held his silence and let her find the best place to continue. She cleared her throat. "Edi and I are twins. When we were born, my cord was wrapped around his throat. My mother often . . . *emphasized* to him that it was my fault that he was . . . not right."

Mr. Moss's brow sank into a row of deep furrows. "I'm sorry to hear that."

Tamsyn tangled her fidgeting fingers into a clasp before her. "A couple of months ago, Mother decided that Edi was old enough to make his way on his own in this world. She planned to . . ." Tamsyn swallowed. "Drive him to a town several miles away and drop him off. When I told her that was unacceptable, she chased me off too." Tamsyn studied the grass near her feet. "Since then, Edi and I have been on our own. You asked why we wanted to go to Oregon. Why I wanted to go to Oregon. Well, if I'm honest, it's really the Oregon Donation

Land Act. One hundred and sixty acres this year for Edi if we can get there. It would make a big difference for us."

Mr. Moss folded his arms and seemed to settle into his heels. "So you've been taking care of your brother? On your own?"

Tamsyn spread her hands. "He has no one else." She hoped her words didn't sound like she felt burdened by the task.

The man's sharp gaze made her feel like skewered game roasting above a fire. "I can see how you think that getting to Oregon would make a difference for you, but Oregon is not a kind frontier. It would be better for you to stay in a town near civilization where there are people who can help you."

Feeling her hopes deflate, Tamsyn forced herself to draw a slow breath. "And just who do you suppose would give a single woman like me a job, Mr. Moss? And who would watch Edi while I worked all day trying to make a living for us?"

His arms loosened, but his hands came to rest on his hips again. The furrow was still firmly entrenched on his brow. "Can you sew?"

Tamsyn sighed. As though she hadn't already thought of every possible job she could do with Edi underfoot. "Independence already has several seamstresses, Mr. Moss. But, yes, of course I can sew." She tamped down the anger starting to rise inside her. "I can also bake. But Independence has two bakeries. I could tutor children. In fact, I tried that back home. But no family wanted to send their children to our house in case what Edi has is contagious. Which, of course, is patently ridiculous, but that is the way of the world. I'm also quite a hand with herbs and medicine, but again . . . the baseless fear." She forced her shoulders to relax. "If you can name it, then I have probably tried it. The thing is . . . Edi is good with animals. He's good with regular tasks that need to be done every day. If we had some land that we could farm, I could give him regular chores to do each morning at a specific time, and he would do them. If we had some land, we could raise animals, and I could card wool and sell it. We could plant and raise our own food. It would solve a lot of our problems."

"Raise a site of problems too, I reckon."

Tamsyn met him gaze for gaze. "In this world, we will have trouble, Mr. Moss. But we are told to take heart, for Jesus has overcome the world. In Him, we may have peace." She wouldn't mention how much she doubted her ability to live out that principle. She had tried often, after all, and always seemed to be tromped back down into despair.

She swallowed and forced herself to say the next words. "No matter your decision, I know that the Lord will be with Edi and me." *Please, Lord. You will, won't You?* "Whether we must remain here or whether you allow us to join you on your way to Oregon, the Lord will see us through, even if we must take the trail to Oregon by ourselves."

He stiffened. "Surely you wouldn't attempt such a hopeless feat."

Ah! A hopeless feat. Something she might be able to accomplish! Tamsyn grew weary of this conversation. "You say it would be hopeless, however, I have been underestimated all my life, Mr. Moss. I must do what is necessary to take care of my brother. It is my understanding that the trail to Oregon is now quite visible across the prairie and that we would not have a difficult time finding our way." Her heart hammered in her chest. *Please, Lord, don't let him make me back my words.*

Mr. Moss turned away from her and paced a couple of steps. He paused and scooped a hand through his unruly hair, then pivoted to face her once more and plunked his fists onto his hips.

He stared at her for such a long moment that she grew uneasy, broke eye contact, and focused on her fidgeting fingers for a moment before bouncing her focus back to him. *Please, Lord. Please, Lord. Please, Lord.*

Finally, he glanced down and kicked at a clump of grass near his boot. His lips worked in and out as though he were deep in thought. He glanced at her wagon. "You have all the required supplies?"

Tamsyn willed down the hope rising lest it make a fool of her. "Yes. We passed all of Mr. Cranston's requirements. He already asked me that yesterday."

Mr. Moss blew out a sharp breath as though he might have hoped that she would say no. "Alright then, I won't raise my concerns to Cranston. You and your brother may join the wagon train. But please, Miss Acheson, do not make me regret this decision."

Such relief washed through her that she took a bracing step to counter the sudden weakness in her knees. "If you have any regrets on this trip, Mr. Moss, it will not be on my account."

He narrowed his eyes for a moment, and she saw the quick flick of a glance that he tossed toward the fire that they could not see on the other side of the wagon. She knew that Edi had just crossed his mind.

And my, how she hoped that Edi would not give Mr. Moss cause to regret allowing them to join the wagon train.

Chapter 13

Eden sat alone near the fire that Adam must have started at some point this morning before leaving their encampment. The evening before, he had thankfully allowed the doctor to bandage his burnt hand, and then he had brought her to his wagon, which was already packed and ready for the trip to Oregon.

It had been late by the time they arrived at the wagon, and she could tell Adam was in a great deal of pain. He'd shown her to the pallet in the wagon, had taken one blanket, and retreated to sleep on the grass underneath—much to her consternation. But despite her pleas for him to stay, he'd refused.

Eden poked a stick into the fire, despairing that her mistakes might haunt their marriage for the rest of their lives. This morning, she woke quite early, but Adam had already been gone by the time she stepped out of the wagon.

She wanted to refuse the tears of loneliness, but they snuck up on her unbidden. She knew this wasn't a mistake, returning to her husband's side. What she didn't know was how long it was going to take him to forgive her.

"Eden?" Adam appeared by the fire with a brace of hares hanging from a string in his hands.

She turned from him and dashed her fingers beneath her eyes.

He moved to stand beside her. His gaze swept from her eyes to the fingers she swiped on her skirt and back again. "I went to fetch some meat. Figured it might be good if we roasted a couple of days' worth so that you didn't have to do so much cooking on the first day or two." He stepped over to set the game on a rock.

She frowned at him. "First day or two?"

"Right." He roughed his fingers through that shock of unruly blond hair. "I just got the word. Because of the fire, we're going to leave early and try to beat most folks to Fort Kearny. I just heard the word myself a few minutes ago."

"I see." She didn't meet his gaze. There had been a time when he would have lingered with her in their bed, waiting till she woke to let her know where he was going. He might have kissed her awake with his lips pressed to her cheek. Maybe even tucked her close and—

She spun away.

The poor fluffy creatures looked pitiful, draped over the rock as they were. She worried the inside of her lip. How did one go about preparing hare? That was honestly one dish she could say she was certain she'd never tried. Back home when she was growing up, Miss Molly, their cook, had always prepared the meals. As the daughter of a doctor, she'd had a life of privilege, she supposed. When she'd married Adam, they'd had many a good laugh in the early days over her ineptitude in the kitchen, until finally, one day, she'd gone running to Molly, who had taught her the basics of how to cook—pancakes, rice, and fried chicken. By Friday of that week, poor Adam had seemed fit to be tied when she'd served him chicken and rice yet again. But he'd kindly deemed it her best meal yet. Eden had promptly run back to Molly on Monday morning. That week she'd learned how to make bacon, eggs, and a delicious salad dressing.

Over the years, she'd grown to be a good cook, even if she did say so herself, but . . . The butcher had always handed her a piece of meat, ready to be cooked.

She crinkled her nose at the prospect of the task before her.

Adam stepped up beside her again, and she could feel him watching her. From the corner of her eye, she saw him tilt his head.

"I'm sorry I wasn't here when you woke this morning. I thought you'd sleep later like you used to do."

Eden withheld a sniff and hoped tears wouldn't betray her again. It was one thing to sleep late in the quiet of your own home when there was nothing in particular that needed tending. Quite another to try to sleep with the loud bustling of the camp clanging just outside her canvas partition. "It's fine. You're busy, I know and I . . . surprised you yesterday."

To say the least.

She glanced down at his bandaged hand. "How are you this morning?"

He waved away her concern. "I'm fine."

She pivoted to face him and for a long moment they simply looked at one another. Eden wished she could tell what he was thinking. Did he wish she hadn't come? Wish that she'd allowed him to get on with his life? He'd said it was good to see her, but he *would* say that because he was a good man.

His focus roved to her hairline, drifted across her cheeks, and settled on her lips.

The camp bustle seemed to still and then blur into the distance. She waited. Hoped. Begged with her heart and eyes for him to come closer. Held her breath.

His throat worked, and he quick-stepped to one side and scrubbed the side of his first finger over his lips as though to erase the thought of kissing her. "I'd, ah, I'd best get moving. There's a lot to do today if we are going to pull out tomorrow."

Once again, Eden despaired over the rift she'd trenched between them.

The rabbits . . .

"Adam?"

"Yeah?" His voice emerged rough, gravelly with emotion. She knew him well enough to remember that sound.

"I don't—"

"Parson Houston?"

A tall man with a shock of black curly hair stopped by their fire. His blue eyes twinkled, and a smile stretched his lips.

"Micah. Good morning." Adam shook his hand. "Allow me to introduce you to my wife, Eden. Eden, this is my friend, Micah Morran."

Micah's brows shot up for the briefest of moments before he snatched off his hat. "Ma'am. It's a pleasure to meet you."

Eden offered him a curtsy. "And you as well, Mr. Morran."

"If you'll forgive me for interrupting..." He returned his attention to Adam, and his face once more broke into a broad grin. "Mercy has agreed to marry me."

"Well!" Adam thrust out a hand, and the men shook with enthusiasm this time. "Congratulations. I'm not surprised."

Micah laughed. "I think I am."

The sound of Adam's deep humor filled Eden with a contentment that she hadn't felt in a very long while.

"We wondered, well, with the wagon train pulling out come morning. We wondered if you'd be available to perform a service for us this evening? We thought around sunset."

"That sounds wonderful. Where at?"

Micah seemed perplexed. He stared around the bustling field blankly. "I don't rightly know yet." He laughed again.

"Well, come on." Adam clapped him on the shoulder. "Let's find Mercy and we'll pick you out a lovely spot."

With that, the two men hurried away.

Eden felt her shoulders droop as her gaze slipped to the hares. So much for telling Adam that she didn't know how to skin the poor little critters. She picked one up by a back leg and held it at arm's length, casting a critical eye over it.

How hard could it be? Something like taking off a coat, right?

Adam didn't need to be burdened with a wife who couldn't hold her own! She could do this!

She gave herself a bracing nod but then tossed a glance at the sky. "Lord? A little help here, please?"

"Need some help there?" A woman's amused voice spoke from the next campsite over.

Eden spun toward the sound, feeling grateful despite her embarrassment. "You don't by chance know how to skin and cook a rabbit, do you?"

The woman's chuckle rang melodic and low. She approached with her hand outstretched for the brace of hares. "My name is Tamsyn Acheson, what's yours?"

"Eden. Eden Houston. I'm the—" she swept a motion in Adam's wake "—minister's wife."

"Well, it's lovely to meet you, Eden." She swung a gesture toward her fire. "Come and join me for coffee, and I'll have my brother skin these for you. Then I'll show you how to spit them over the fire."

Eden released a breath of relief and angled a glance toward the sky. *Thank You.* To the woman she said, "You are a miracle sent directly from heaven."

Tamsyn laughed. "Well, I wouldn't go that far, but I'm happy to be of help."

Willow stood next to her father's grave, clutching a bouquet of lupin, foxglove, and purple loosestrife. Gideon had planted himself beside her, a stalwart silent support in the face of her grief. On her other side, Declan kept sniffing and shifting.

Across the gaping black hole that waited to swallow her dear papa, Parson Houston clutched his black Bible in both hands. He had read some scriptures and now spoke of all the ways that Papa had been a friend to him. He also invited others to share how Papa had impacted their lives.

She ought to speak. Ought to say what a wonderful father Papa had been to her. How he had been such a comfort after they'd lost Mama. But she was afraid that the emotions clogging her throat would choke off her words, so she remained where she stood.

She jolted a little in surprise when Gideon stepped forward and cleared his throat. "Wayne was a good and kind man. He gave my family and me an opportunity to better ourselves, and well, if it wasn't for him I don't know if Micah and I would have been able to make this trip west. He taught us a lot."

Across the circle of those gathered, Micah nodded.

Gideon continued. "He taught Micah and me everything he knew about wainwrighting, and I know we'll both be grateful to him for the rest of our lives for what he did for us when we were down on our luck." Gideon stepped to the casket that someone had hammered together. He leaned forward and laid Papa's hat atop the smooth lid, then pressed his hand to the wood beside it for a moment. After that, he turned to glance her way, twisting his own hat in his hands. He returned to her side but never broke eye contact.

In his blue eyes, all soft with concern, Willow found the strength that she'd been missing earlier.

She took a breath and stepped forward. "Papa was the best of fathers, especially after my mother died." A memory suddenly hit her, and she smiled. "I'll never forget the first morning after Mama passed, how Papa tried to cook breakfast for us. It was a simple meal. Just oatmeal and cold milk. But he got sidetracked with milking the cow, and the oatmeal burnt to the bottom of the pan." She couldn't help a laugh. "In fact, I think at least a good inch of that oatmeal was solid black. The kitchen was full of smoke when I came down to see about the smell." Willow pressed her lips together for a moment to gather herself. "He may have failed that first time, but he didn't give up. He went to Miss Felicity across the street." Her gaze landed on the diner's owner.

The woman gave her a misty-eyed smile. "He sure did. Took me near a month of Sundays to teach that man to fry an egg!"

Several around the group chuckled, Declan's laugh loudest of all.

Glad that they were remembering the good times and not only the tragedy that had taken dear Papa from her, Willow nodded. "After he learned to cook, he tried to learn to cut my hair. He stood there praying the whole time as he cut it, but apparently, the good Lord chose not to answer his prayers that day."

This time there were more than a few chuckles in the crowd.

She felt Gideon's scrutiny and glanced back to see him angling her a sideways smile. She pressed one hand to the back of her head and waggled her fingers. "I may have had a haircut so short that I passed for a boy for several weeks."

When the humor died down, Willow felt her own smile fade. The coffin was such a stark reminder of her new reality. She felt weakness to her very core. How could she go on?

She squeezed the next words through a tight throat. "There are no words to convey the depth of love I have in my heart for my dear papa. I can hardly fathom that I'll never get to hear his hearty laugh again or feel the warmth of his hand wrap around the back of my neck. But I'll forever be grateful that he taught me to trust in Jesus. And I have no doubt that Papa heard the Lord say, 'Well done, good and faithful servant.'"

It wasn't enough. There were so many stories to tell. So much of Papa's strength, humor, and faith to share, but she couldn't seem to say more just now.

Parson Houston gave her a gentle smile and a nod.

Returning the gesture, Willow stepped back by Gid's side.

Declan stepped forward then and spoke of how Papa had taken him in and treated him like a son when his own father abandoned him. How Papa had loved him and how he wished that he'd had one more opportunity to thank Papa for all he'd done.

Willow felt tears pricking the backs of her eyes and tuned out the words before they could make a blubbering mess of her.

The rest of the service faded into the background as she searched for the will to hold herself together. How had she gone from yesterday being so shocked and upset with Papa to today missing him with such an ache that it threatened to sap all her strength and drop her to the dirt right here in front of everyone?

She nudged her chin toward the sky. She would not. She swallowed against the acrid bite at the back of her tongue, and just as she had when Declan spoke a moment earlier, battened down the tears that threatened and forced a smile as she thanked each one who had come.

Men lowered the pine box into the hole, and Gideon coaxed her forward with a hand to her lower back, reminding her that she needed to throw the first handful of dirt.

She stepped forward and did so, breathing steadily in and out. She hated the feel of the grit on her palm and the solid thud of it against the box.

She stepped back and waited, breathing steadily in and out as Declan and several men filled in the hole. All the while, Gid remained steadfast by her side.

And then the task was done.

The hole was filled—mounded up like an unsightly brown scar marring the beautiful prairie grasses of the Independence cemetery.

As Willow stepped forward once more and laid the bouquet on Papa's grave, she heard Gideon talking to Parson Houston in quiet tones.

The men shook hands, but before they separated, the sheriff stepped up beside Gid.

Willow's head came up. She'd meant to go see the man earlier and had somehow forgotten in all the chaos and stress. Perhaps he'd come to see her? And yet it wasn't her the sheriff was looking at.

He stretched a hand to Gideon. "Thanks for coming by to see me earlier. Just wanted you to know that I've been to the site of the fires and had a look around. I'll be conducting interviews. And I will do my best to figure out what happened."

"I may have seen something."

To Willow's surprise, the parson's wife stepped forward.

She now fiddled with the lace at her collar as every eye in the group fixed on her. "There was a man who walked down the alley just before the fire started. As he turned at the end, he went toward the mercantile, and I saw a match flare. I thought he was lighting a cigarette. But . . . I've not been able to get that image out of my head."

Mr. Harrington stepped closer.

The sheriff frowned before he transferred his gaze back to the minister's wife. "Did you get a good look at him?"

The blond woman shook her head. "No. I'm sorry. He wore a black hat and a long black coat and I was on the second floor of the hotel looking down. I couldn't really see much."

Mr. Harrington gestured from his own long black coat across the fire to the ones worn by several other men who stood talking in clusters. "That could be anyone, I suppose, right, Sheriff?"

"It's certainly not much to go on . . ." The sheriff hooked his thumbs into his waistband. "However, it's a place to start. I'll ask around and see if anyone else saw anything." He did transfer his gaze to Willow then. "I'm very sorry about your father, Miss Chancellor. If I can, I'll send word to the territories when I know more."

Willow gave the expected nod but inwardly despaired. How long would that take? Would she ever learn what had happened at the store? What killed dear Papa? A chill slipped down her spine as she considered the parson's wife's words. Had someone purposefully set fire to the store? Why would someone do such a thing?

Whatever had happened, it very nearly killed five people. If Mr. Harrington hadn't gotten Papa out . . . and if Micah had been even a couple moments longer. She shuddered at the thought of what could have been lost.

Gideon stepped to her side, and she only then realized that the others had disbursed. So, it was time then.

She couldn't bring herself to meet his gaze.

She wasn't ready for this. Not the being married to Gideon part. She would have welcomed that under other circumstances, she supposed. Even now, if only she thought he wanted her, too.

It was the moving on. The leaving of everything familiar. The loss.

But . . . her gaze drifted to the town that no longer offered any shelter or income for her.

What other choice did she have?

Corbin had very nearly given himself away with a gasp when the parson's wife stepped forward and mentioned that she'd seen him. He'd been ready to bolt, felt a fist tightening around his throat, but then she'd said she hadn't caught a good glimpse of him.

Relief nearly stole the strength from his legs.

Enough had already gone wrong on this jaunt. The last thing he needed was one more hurdle to overcome.

But now, he pondered what to do about the parson's wife. Again, he couldn't do anything too soon, or suspicions would rise.

Irritation clawed through him.

There were too many cracks in this dam he was trying to hold together, and he needed to keep holding it together for at least another few weeks.

He took a calming breath and forced himself to walk nonchalantly with the rest of those gathered to the knoll where tonight's weddings would take place.

Bitter bile rose to coat the back of his tongue.

Riley and the parson's wife may have won for now, but their day would come.

Corbin smiled. Yes. Come sooner than they realized!

Chapter 14

W illow stood at the back of the small group gathered on a knoll overlooking a wide stretch of prairie. In the distance, a belt of deeper green likely meant water of some sort down in that ravine. Why had she and Papa never taken a day to explore there?

She clenched her teeth.

Too busy running the store, she supposed. Too busy keeping up with life's demands. And now . . . Papa had no more demands to keep up with.

Somehow, the sibilant swish of the grasses playing at the whim of the evening breeze comforted her—like the sounds of home.

She picked at the hem of her sleeve, trying not to think about how this home would soon be far away.

To the west, the sun sank into the horizon, casting bold and brassy hues against the sky, which arched above them like a brazen bowl turned upside down.

At the front of the gathering, Micah and Mercy stood shoulder to shoulder before Parson Houston. On either side of them, Avram and Joel tried to hold still as they'd likely been instructed, but both boys were having a hard time acting like grownups. They kept peering at each other behind the couple's backs and grinning like the imps they were. Mattox, the huge black dog who never strayed far from Micah, sprawled to one side.

Micah gripped Joel's head and gently turned him to face the parson. Then his broad brown hand splayed against Mercy's back as he smiled down at her, and she glanced up at her soon-to-be-husband with such awe and love in her eyes that it made Willow's heart ache.

Would she ever have that for herself?

She cast a glance to the man beside her. Did Gideon regret that Mercy had chosen Micah over him? From the smile playing on his lips as he watched the couple exchanging their vows, he didn't seem any too upset. Yet, she knew he'd fancied Mercy—at least for a while.

As though he'd felt her inspection, he suddenly swung his gaze her way. His smile faded as his expression turned serious. "Are you all right?" he whispered.

"Yes."

Lies. She didn't know if she would ever be all right again. With the toe of her boot, she prodded at a clump of grass.

Gideon leaned close, lowering his voice further. "You're certain? You don't have to do this, you know."

Tension tightened her brow even as the warmth of his breath fanned against her cheek and made her fully aware of how close he stood. Was he forgetting that Mr. Cranston had said she couldn't travel without a relative to escort her and that, thanks to her uncle, she had nothing left here either?

But maybe his questions had nothing to do with her . . .

"If you want to back out, Gid, I won't hold you to your proposal." She held her breath because much as she didn't want to be married to a man who didn't want her, she even more didn't want to be left to survive on her own.

He frowned and pegged her with a stern look. "That's not what I meant."

Willow pressed her lips together. Flicked a glance toward Micah and Mercy. Prodded at the grass again. "Do you regret that she turned you down?"

Surprise arched his brows. "Mercy?"

Willow raised him a look of exasperation. "Are there many other women I should know about?" Who else had he thought she'd been speaking of? His handsome countenance had attracted women far and wide, she felt sure.

Gid pulled a face. "Certainly not. Just Verona, who you already know about." He swept a hand around the back of his neck as he transferred his gaze to Mercy. "And Mercy was a passing fancy, yes. But . . . I think I felt sorry for her having to raise Av on her own and because of her history more than anything. I'm honestly very happy that she's found her place with Micah."

Willow swallowed. Just like he felt sorry for her because she'd lost everything? What would happen a few months down the road if he came across another helpless woman who needed his assistance? Would he then label Willow as a "passing fancy"?

"I don't want you to regret marrying me, Gid." The whispered words popped free before she reconsidered.

Several men in the crowd whooped loudly, and Willow glanced toward the front to see that Micah had dipped Mercy low and was kissing her soundly. Mattox barked and frolicked around them. The boys laughed, and Joel hid behind his hands, peeking between his fingers.

Despite her circumstances, Willow couldn't stop a smile. When she glanced to the side, it was to find Gideon's serious gaze still pinned on her.

He swallowed, looking a little guilty, like she might have caught him staring. He turned his focus to Micah and Mercy. "If I do have regrets it won't be because I chose to marry you, I can assure you that, Willow Girl."

Her heart tripped over the endearment even as her mind screamed, *More lies.* At least they weren't coming from her own lips this time.

Before she could form a reply, Parson Houston bellowed, "Let's have a round of applause for the happy couple!"

Micah ushered Mercy, the boys, and the dog toward where they stood. Willow smiled, hoping it didn't look too strained. She really was happy for Micah and Mercy.

When the applause died down, the parson continued. "And now, we'll celebrate with Gideon and Willow. Come on up here, you two!"

A question still lingered in Gideon's eyes.

Willow sighed and motioned for him to lead the way. There was nothing for it right now but to follow through.

Gid shook his head and swept a gesture for her to go first. "After you."

Willow moistened her lips and took a step, but Mercy waylaid her. "Willow, wait." She thrust her bouquet into Willow's hands with a big grin and a squeeze to her shoulder. "Every bride should have flowers."

"Thank you." The words were automatic, but as she stared down at the bouquet, she felt her stomach twist into a tight knot. It was the same array of wildflowers that she'd just laid on Papa's grave. Could she, all in one day, bury her father and enter a marriage of convenience with the same flowers in her hands?

"Willow?" Gideon's soft question came from just behind her.

She lifted her gaze to find too many pairs of concerned eyes watching her. It wouldn't do. Not at all. She must hold herself together. She put one foot in front of the other. "Yes. Sorry."

Somehow, she managed to keep going until she paused at the front of the crowd before the minister. Gideon came to a stop, so close that his shoulder brushed hers, but he seemed content to clasp his hands behind his back as he settled more comfortably into a broad stance.

Parson Houston smiled. "Good evening to you both."

Willow wished she could have a glass of water but gave him a dip of her chin. She gripped the flowers tight, suddenly so thankful to have something to hold on to.

Since she was a child, she had dreamed of a beautiful wedding in the Independence church, of happiness and joy as she spoke her vows, of a man who loved and cherished her—a man who brought her gifts when she felt low, treated her to evenings at the theater, or picnics by the river, just because.

Never in her craziest imaginings had she considered that she might marry a man out of necessity nor that he would marry her out of mere duty.

"Willow?" Parson Houston made a pointed sound.

She blinked. A glance at Gideon showed he, too, watched her with his lower lip tucked between his teeth and a concerned furrow on his brow. She'd missed something.

"I'm sorry." She winced at Parson Houston. "Can you please repeat that?"

The parson gave her a nod of understanding. "Do you take this man to be your husband?"

"Yes. I mean . . . I do."

Beside her, Gideon released a breath.

He, too, answered in the affirmative when the parson directed the question at him.

After that, Willow forced herself to pay attention. She gave her responses in all the right places, wishing she could slow the march of her heart that threatened to overwhelm her. She offered her hand when she was told to and felt the cool metal of the ring Gideon slipped onto her finger. She stared absentmindedly at the silver band, feeling the absence of dear Papa—and Mama too—most keenly in that moment.

Suddenly the parson said, "Gideon, you may kiss your bride!"

Willow fumbled the bouquet and almost dropped it. As Gideon turned to her, she took a bracing gulp of air.

His hands settled gently against her arms. "Easy, Willow Girl," he murmured as he leaned past the flowers she clutched before her like a breastplate of armor. His lips grazed hers so softly that she might have dreamed it, and then he eased back just far enough to look down at her. A smile crinkled the corners of his eyes. And then he retreated, offering her his arm.

The parson introduced them as "Mr. and Mrs. Gideon Riley," and after a few hearty hugs and handshakes of congratulations, the crowd began to disburse, leaving her with her new husband.

Dear Lord.

What had she done? She wasn't strong enough to maintain this façade.

Gideon watched Willow's face as the crowd disbursed. Nearly as pale as the clouds floating on the horizon, she kept darting glances this way and that as though searching for an escape. She didn't seem to want to look his direction at all.

Concern rose in his chest. Not only for Willow's well-being, but for their future.

She was definitely not acting like herself. Had she even shed one tear since her father's passing? Not that he'd seen.

Everything in him wanted to ease her distress, however, he felt certain that if he tried to draw her closer it would only heighten her unease.

And with dusk now heavy upon them, there was the situation of their sleeping arrangements. He'd only the one bed in the front of his wagon, and he had no desire to sleep on the hard ground all the way to Oregon—not to mention the bugs that came with that—yet he also didn't want to burden Willow with one more concern.

Still, he remembered his father instilling that he ought to always begin as he intended to proceed. And since he had determined not to fall for the woman, what could it hurt to share a bed? Their union was now sanctioned, after all, in the eyes of God.

Willow would have to get used to him sooner or later. They might as well start now. They would be sleeping. Nothing . . . more. He would just keep his emotions out of it.

He swallowed away the memory of her soft lips beneath his as she'd stood practically frozen in place before the congregation a moment ago.

Whether Willow knew it or not, she needed him now more than ever. A gentle touch had always done wonders to ease Verona's distress. And Willow certainly needed grounding in this moment.

Swallowing away his hesitation, he stepped forward and took her hand, lacing his fingers through hers.

She shot him a wide-eyed glance and stepped to the side, but he held onto her gently. He tipped his head toward town. "Let's eat dinner at Felicity's, and then we'd best settle in. We've an early start tomorrow. Cranston wants to pull out as soon as the sun lightens the sky enough for us to see."

He hadn't thought it possible, but her eyes grew even larger. "I'm not hungry. Why don't you go on without me."

"Willow." He tilted his head. "When was the last time you ate?"

Her brow furrowed, and her puckered lips twisted from side to side. "If I'm honest, I don't remember."

"That's what I thought." He tugged for her to follow him, feeling rather like he was trying to encourage a skittish mare to trust him. "I don't either. And you will need your strength for this journey. Come on. Just a few bites, hmm?"

With a sigh of seeming resignation, she gave in and took a few steps, and he was satisfied to see that she wasn't trying to pull away from him either.

It felt good to walk with her hand in his, her small fingers laced with his, her shoulder gently bumping his. She was smaller, more delicate than Verona had been. Her hand was practically engulfed in his.

He adjusted his hat and glanced at the first couple of stars that poked holes in the gray-blue of the darkening sky. *Lord, You know I want to care for her and comfort her out of duty to my word. She's going to need a companion. May she feel my friendship as a blanket of comfort in these dark days ahead of her. Give her the strength to endure. And if You could,* he swallowed, *please somehow help me to resist falling for her.*

He led her up the stairs to the diner and held open the door.

Ahead of him, she stumbled to a stop. He peered past her shoulder to see the table where they had sat together so many times with Wayne. Knowing so well the dark grief of her loss, he also knew it would be best for her to face the reality of it sooner than later. It would be good to experience this one last familiar place and to feel her father's absence, for it would hammer home the reality of it even more. Certainly, their next few months would be anything but familiar and routine. She needed this.

He nudged her forward. "You're strong. You can do this."

That seemed to unfreeze her. She gave a jerky little nod and took a step.

He released a breath. Their road wouldn't be easy, but with God's help, they would make it through.

Corbin stared at the cover of his blasted wagon, ignoring the aching muscle in the arm he had tucked beneath his head. It was done then. She had gone and chosen Riley.

His chest heaved as he tried to calm the anger coursing through him. He forced himself to slow. Drew one long sustained inhale through his nostrils and then pushed it through pursed lips.

On top of that, he had spent the afternoon learning how to yoke his oxen to the wagon and wrassling the stubborn beasts to do his bidding. And now he felt achy, sore, and angry to boot. But he'd gone into town and bought a whip, and tomorrow, he would show those beasts who they ought to listen to.

Cranston planned to pull the train out at first light. And Corbin would be ready.

And Gideon Riley and that uppity minister's wife would be sorry they ever interfered.

He fingered the tin of arsenic that he had also purchased in town this afternoon.

Not yet.

But soon.

Chapter 15

Willow ate with mechanical gestures, more to keep Gideon from hounding her than anything else. She tried not to picture Papa sitting in that chair just there with his head tipped back in laughter. Tried not to see him standing there in the aisle smiling at Miss Felicity. Tried to hear the sound of his voice whispering wisdom in her ear, but it was drowned out by the chatter of all the excited patrons who were soon ready to pull out for the Oregon Territory.

Gideon nudged her soup closer to her. "Just another few bites."

She pushed the bowl back from the edge of the table. "Honestly, Gid. I can't. I'm fine."

He didn't look any too happy about it, but he did give her a nod. "All right. Best we turn in then. First light will come mighty fast."

And just like that, Willow's concerns turned in a different direction.

Turning in . . . Just exactly where were they going to turn in? And what was she going to sleep in? She owned absolutely nothing but the dark-blue dress she'd donned this morning.

Miss Felicity stopped beside their table with a basket in her hands and tears streaming down her cheeks.

Willow rose and enfolded the shorter woman into her embrace. "I will miss you so much."

Felicity nodded. "Yes, child. I'll miss you too." She pushed herself back and looked up. "You be sure to write, you hear?"

Willow smiled at her motherly tone. "Yes, ma'am. I will."

Felicity gave a firm nod. "Good. Now…" She thrust out the basket in her hands. "Just a few things that I put together for you from the kitchen. Some spices, a crock of butter, that sort of thing."

"You didn't have to do that." Willow started to accept the basket, but Gid snagged the handle from her.

"I'll carry it," he offered, touching his brow in Miss Felicity's direction.

Miss Felicity drew Willow in for another hug. "He's a good man," she whispered in Willow's ear. "God bless you, dear girl. God bless you."

With that, the woman bustled back to the kitchen, swiping at her cheeks with one corner of her apron.

The warmth of Gid's hand settled at her back, but he seemed content to give her a moment. She took in the familiar room, every last table, the entryway where Papa would pause to snatch off his cap and give Miss Felicity a nod of greeting and a smile when they entered.

With just a few steps, they were on the porch where Papa had spoken his last words to her. *You're strong. Remember, you can do all things through Christ who strengthens. Love you.*

She felt a tremor work through her. She couldn't. Wasn't strong enough.

How did one go about doing that with a shattered heart? What she wanted to do was collapse right here and refuse to do one more thing. She wanted to die and go to heaven with Papa.

And yet, the realistic part of her knew that wasn't a solution. She had no other option but to trudge onward, no matter the ache in her heart.

Gid's hand slipped around hers, engulfing it with a gentle but sturdy grip. "It's time."

She nodded. And took a step.

The moon shone gloriously bright, hanging large and low on the horizon. Overhead, stars spangled the inky sky.

Gid led her out of town and across the field to a wagon that looked exactly the same as all the others they'd passed. How would she ever remember which one was theirs?

She didn't have time to ponder long because Gideon handed her up into the back of the wagon. She found a narrow aisle between strapped-down boxes and crates and a perpendicular pallet at the front, at the height of the wagon's sides.

Relief washed through her. The bed wasn't nearly long enough for a man to stretch out on, so Gid must have somehow added it for her? She turned back to ask where he would sleep and gave a little squeak of surprise to find him looming in the aisle behind her.

Oh. Did he expect . . . ?

A tremor shot through her. "Gid, I'm not sure I'm ready for—"

His hands settled against her arms. "Easy. I don't want anything from you. But I do intend to sleep in my own bed."

She blinked. Glanced back at the narrow pallet. Tried to process the words. Where was she to sleep then?

He squeezed past her and moved to the pallet. He lifted the tick and, to her surprise, folded back a hinged section of wood that extended over the side of the wagon. He leaned over the edge of the box and moved something to prop the hinged section up. He repeated the whole process at the other end of the bed. Both hinged sections of wood pushed the oilcloth sides of the wagon's covering out slightly, but the ingenuity of it struck her. Gideon had built the bed at just the right height to give himself a little more room to stretch out at night. What she had thought were pillows on one end were actually an extra length of the ticking that he now unfolded so that the tick stretched the complete length of the pallet's base. From a small cubby that extended into the space beneath the driver's bench, he withdrew a pillow.

He gave it a few pummels and dropped it on one end of the pallet. "Only the one pillow, but you can have that."

She could have—

Willow felt her eyes go wide. He intended for them to sleep in the same bed? She cast a glance at the narrow opening at the back of the wagon. Maybe she could sleep underneath?

But Gideon side-stepped past her again and, with a few deft movements, cinched the opening tight. He turned and faced her.

She could barely see the reflection of his eyes in the oilcloth-filtered moonlight.

He remained where he stood. "Do you trust me?"

"Enough to marry you." The words popped free before she thought better of them.

With her eyes adjusting to the darkness, she caught his nod.

"Good." He stepped toward her. Motioned for her to turn around. "If you're anything like Verona, you'll need help with the buttons."

Willow's chin shot into the air. She held her ground. "I don't need any help, thank you just the same. I've nothing to change into at any rate."

He reached into a crate beside him and withdrew a shirt. Held it out to her. "You can't sleep in that dress. You'll never rest properly." He brushed past her in the aisle again and paused facing the pallet with his hands propped at his hips. "Go on. I won't look."

Willow remained frozen.

He cocked his head as though listening for her movement, and when she made no move, he said, "Best you turn your back, Willow Girl, lest you see more than you bargained for." With his thumbs, he unhooked his suspenders from over his shoulders.

Eyes shooting wide, Willow spun to put her back to him, refusing to think on what Gideon was doing behind her.

Had there ever in all the world been a marriage night like this one?

Mechanically, she slipped out of her dress, undid the pins in her hair, and tugged the cotton work shirt over her head. It fell only to mid-thigh—not nearly long enough. And the laced neckline plunged much too low. She yanked it tight and tied a bow, still feeling exposed.

Tugging on the hem of the shirt as though she could make it longer, she turned slowly to find that Gideon had already crawled beneath the blankets on the bed. He lay pressed up against the boards near the wagon bench, with one arm tucked beneath his head as he stared up at the oilcloth above him. The blankets were folded back enough for her but covered him from his chest down.

Thank the Lord for small favors. She set the stack of her folded clothes and pile of hairpins on top of a crate and eased onto the tick beside him. For a long moment she simply sat on the edge of the bed, willing herself to find the strength to lie down.

Gideon didn't move. In fact, only a moment later, she heard his deep inhales as though he may have already fallen asleep.

Relieved, she eased her head onto the pillow and pulled her side of the blankets over herself.

Then she willed herself to sleep through her first night as a married woman—and failed completely.

Gideon woke with the first chittering of the birds and stretched his neck to work out a painful kink. He bit back a groan and reached for the sore muscle, but his arm grazed something firm and warm, and memories of the evening before flooded in.

He propped himself on one elbow, pressing his eyes with fingers and thumb.

Willow must have grown cold in the night, for she had encroached on his half of the bed. It *was* cold out here with nothing but an oilcloth separating them from the spring night. Her back was to him, and she lay curled in on herself as though she might be cold even now. A curtain of red curls splayed around her, and one dainty foot protruded from the end of the covers. With his toes, he moved the blankets so her foot would be covered again. Her shoulders rose and fell in a rhythmic sleep, and the half of her face that he could see had lost the lines of tension that had etched it the day before.

He reached for one of the curls and twirled it around his finger. Silken soft, just as he'd suspected it would be. He let go of the curl and scrubbed his thumb over his fingers. If he were to keep himself distant from her, he'd best not go appreciating her attractive features at every turn.

This desire for resistance was new and something he'd have to set his mind to. He'd never even tried to resist Verona. He'd given himself to her heart, mind, and almost soul without thought of the pain that could—would—bring. But he knew better now. He just had to keep reminding himself to be strong in the moments when her beauty called to his baser nature like a Siren.

She needed time to heal from her loss. Time to adjust to him. Time to reconcile herself to their future together. For that matter, he did too, he supposed. This would all feel natural after a few days.

She made a soft sleepy sound and turned into him, settling her forehead right against his chest and slinging one leg over his, exposing a long expanse of pale skin to the dawn light.

He swallowed and pinned his gaze on the sunrise breaking through the eyehole in the cinched oilcloth. He tried to dredge up another prayer to strengthen his resolve not to lose his heart, but all he could think about was how much he wanted to wake her with a kiss. There had been that peck at the wedding, but he didn't count that as any sort of kiss at all. It was contractual. Kisses were not meant to be contractual. Especially not when . . . He lowered his attention once more to the woman nestled against him. Especially not when a woman had lips as sumptuous as Willow's.

Right. That was his cue to summon the willpower to exit the wagon and hopefully find a nice cold creek to plunge into before he faced this long day.

He chastised himself for letting his guard down. What had he been thinking when he'd insisted the night before that they share a bed? If he wasn't careful, he would lose his heart. Not that desiring a beautiful woman meant that he loved her. Her beauty was bound to tug at him from time to time, but he could resist it.

Right?

He swallowed.

Yes, he could, but it would be best if he made his escape immediately.

He tried to ease his legs out from under hers, but she came to with a start. For half a second, she pressed one hand to her forehead as though trying to come to grips with where she was, and then her gaze shot up to him.

In the dim light of morning, her eyes were more gray than blue.

He worked some moisture into his mouth. "Morning." He said the word softly so as not to jar her awake too quickly. But he needn't have bothered.

She gasped and lurched back from him so quickly that she scooted herself right off the pallet and landed in a heap in the aisle, arms and legs all a tangle. Before he could even move to help her, she popped to her feet and scooped a handful of that tempting red hair out of her face.

He remained propped on his elbow. No sense rushing to escape the wagon now, especially not with her blocking his exit. "You all right?"

"Yes. What were you doing?" Her tongue darted over those lips he'd been studying a moment ago.

Heaven help him. This battle was shaping into an outright conflict, and she was painted for war and didn't even know it.

He flattened one hand against the helter-skelter beat of his heart. "I wasn't doing anything." He couldn't stop the corners of his mouth from lifting. "Nothing, that is, except for enjoying the fact that my wife pressed herself against me and draped her leg over mine." Somewhere in the back of his mind a warning sounded that those were not the words of a man winning the fight to keep his heart safe, but he was having too much fun at this moment to pay it any heed.

"I did not—that wasn't—oh. This will never do." She stomped one small foot, drawing his gaze downward.

Now that she was awake, he had no qualms about studying her, and heaven help him, she looked much too good in that shirt with those shapely legs showing beneath. Too bad his shirt hung so long on her.

It really was time to find that creek before he gave up on the battle altogether and tried to coax her into something that would take much too long on a morning when they were expected to be ready to pull out in just a few minutes.

He rose and reached past her for a shirt to don. Since he couldn't seem to tear his attention from her sleep-flushed face, it took him a moment of fumbling to find the right stack.

Her gaze flitted down to his bare chest, and her lashes fluttered a little.

He grinned. Had she not noticed the evening before that he'd stripped to his breeches? After tugging his shirt over his head, he tapped the end of her nose with one finger. He needed to get out of here, now.

"Sorry, Willow Girl. No time this morning for the shenanigans I can see you are thinking of. We don't want to be the last ones in line. That would surely set tongues to wagging."

"I'm not—" Her chin shot into the air. "I have no idea what you're talking about!"

Those plump lips again, and this time within reach and not off limits. Hang willpower. Right now, all he wanted was to see if those lips were as soft as he figured they were, so he dipped his head and captured them with his. She gave a little gasp but didn't try to push him away, so he propped one hand against the stack of crates behind her, let his weight rest there, and explored the softness—yes, exquisite softness—of those tempting lips. Definitely a better kiss than the one at the wedding, but still much too short. Still much too contractual—and one-sided.

However, it gave him great satisfaction when he eased back to see that he'd left her quite speechless. She remained still, face tilted up, small white teeth working over her lips as though trying to memorize the feel of him. Good. Let her linger on that thought today. Maybe it would help her through the grief.

He scooted past her but paused at the oilcloth and glanced back for one more sweeping glance. He allowed a sly grin and pumped his brows. "I'm sad to say that you best dress quickly, Willow Girl. I'll be back inside five minutes to hitch the team." With that, he left her there.

And headed for the creek.

Maybe somewhere in the cold water he would find his sanity and remember why it was loco to flirt with a woman he didn't want to grow attached to.

Chapter 16

Adam felt more than ready for a break from the wagon bench as one of the scouts pulled his horse alongside his wagon.

The man wore a bandana over his face, and gave his hat brim a tug.

Adam did a double take. It was the scout who had pulled him from the fire.

Letting the cattle have their heads, he angled toward the man. "Was hoping I'd see you sooner than later."

The man's blue eyes crinkled at the corners. "How's that hand?"

Adam held up the bandage. "I feel it, but I'd rather that than the alternative, and I have you to thank for that. I'm Adam Houston. You are?"

"Name's Jeremiah Jackson, and I was right glad to mosey on in and fetch you." He reined his horse around a bush as he cut a look in Adam's direction. "Seems the good Lord ain't done using you yet, Parson."

The lead pair of oxen started to drift, and Adam turned his attention back to the reins. "I hope that's true."

"I'm certain it is. Came over to say that Cranston gonna be calling a stop for nooning soon." He gave the brim of his hat another tug, and then put his heels to his mount so he could catch up to the next wagon.

"Thanks again!" Adam called.

The scout waved over his shoulder.

Willow sat on the wagon bench beside Gideon, feeling like a crock of cream in danger of turning into butter. She would jostle right out of herself if she had to sit here much longer. And maybe that wouldn't be such a bad thing. Escaping this ache that threatened to destroy her from the inside out would be heavenly.

She wrinkled her nose at herself. What she was actually in danger of was going off her rocker. Gideon would pack her up and consign her to the asylum for certain if he could discern her thoughts.

The front right wheel of the wagon banged into a hole and jounced out the other side, shooting her up and then slamming her back onto the bench before she could even grab hold of the arm.

"Sorry about that," Gideon offered.

She flicked her wrist to indicate she was fine.

She had to ride like this the whole way to Oregon?

Thankfully the day had dawned warm and sunny, despite the chilly late-March breeze. It was a perfect balance of warmth and wind. She only wished she could find some enjoyment in the beauty stretching in every direction.

Gideon glanced up at the angle of the sun. "Shouldn't be long now till we break for the nooning."

She nodded, but couldn't seem to dredge words from the dryness of her soul.

Gideon glanced over, then did a double take. "You're burning. We'll need to see if we can borrow a bonnet for you from one of the other ladies."

She would burn even with a bonnet. It was simply the nature of her fair skin. But all she did was dip her chin in agreement and study the line of green scrub brush on the horizon.

Gideon's fists tightened on the reins until the oxen bellowed and bobbed their heads in protest. He shifted and eased his grip.

Was her silence making him tense?

She wished she could find words to reassure him that she would be fine, but she wasn't certain she believed it.

Except . . . She remembered that gentle kiss he'd given her this morning. It seemed she'd been longing for such a gesture ever since she'd laid eyes on the man all those months ago when he'd first walked into the mercantile to sell his sister's china.

His kiss ought to have thrilled her, filled her with hope for the future, and giddy excitement to finally have the man of her dreams paying her mind. And yet, all she'd felt was the heartache of it—the realization that he never would have chosen her if Pa hadn't passed.

What kind of a woman would she be if she relished a relationship that she'd only been granted because of the death of dear Papa?

A callous, heartless one.

So she determined not to relish it. Not to let Gideon tempt her to feel.

It wasn't right, this living on without Papa. It was unfair. Incomprehensible.

Ahead, a bugle played several notes, and the first wagon pulled to a stop.

Gideon reined their wagon in behind the one ahead and set the brake, but instead of jumping down to assist her descent, he leaned his elbows on his knees and simply stared across the prairie.

Declan Boyle rode up, so dusty from driving the cattle that even his red bandana seemed to be of the same color as his cotton shirt. She could read concern in his eyes, this boy who had become like a brother to her. Was he missing Papa as much as she?

After he searched her over and was seemingly satisfied that she was all right, he offered. "Guid day."

She returned the greeting with one of her own, but it felt stiff and hollow. "How's the herd?"

He glanced back the way he'd come and swept his hat in that direction. "Happy to be on the shift, I reckon. Thay were getting right antsy bein' kept in one field for so long. That Hereford bull o' Micah's, he has a mind o' his own, he does." Concern filled his face when he turned back to her. "Are ye doin' okay?"

Her cheeks ached from the lie of the smile she sent him. "I'll be fine, Declan. Thank you for asking. Of course, I miss him. And it will take me some time to adjust."

The gleam of moisture in the lad's eyes was almost her undoing, but she clenched her teeth and refused the tears, still concerned that she'd never stop if she started. Then Gideon would be doubly burdened. First, with a wife he didn't want, and then with one he didn't know what to do with.

Without another word, Declan tugged on the brim of his hat and then reined his mount toward Mercy and Micah's wagon just ahead, likely to give a report on the cattle.

Beside her, Gideon angled toward her. "I'm sorry if I overstepped this morning and made you feel . . . uncomfortable."

She darted him a look. "Why would you say that? You've the right to do as you wish. I am your wife, after all."

He shook his head. "That's not true. I've no desire to distress you." He frowned and searched her face. "You haven't spoken to me all morning. I just thought it might be something I did."

"I've spoken." Hadn't she?

He sighed and seemed resigned to letting the matter go. "Give me a moment, and I'll help you down."

Her brows slumped into her vision as he leapt from his side of the wagon, and she heard his footsteps retreat toward the back.

She'd hurt him somehow. And yet she couldn't seem to find it in herself to know how to make reparations. She was the one suffering, couldn't he see that? She was the one who'd just been torn from her home and forced to marry just so she could travel to a far-off land that she didn't even want to go to!

Her blood boiled hotter and hotter as she heard him approaching. By the time he paused by the bench on her side of the wagon, she felt like she might be able to happily strangle him. Her breaths came fast and steady. Her heart hammered so hard that she could feel each pulse in her wrists. She knew the feelings were irrational, yet somehow couldn't bring herself to care.

"Willow?"

She snapped to her feet, pivoted to face him, and allowed him to help her down from the bench.

His hands lingered at her waist, and his blue eyes filled with empathy as he searched her face. She pressed her lips into a tight line lest she cave to the welcome of his lingering touch and the softness in his eyes. "I'm not mad at you, Gid."

She wasn't? Until that very moment, she would have sworn that she was indeed angry with him. So if not him, who?

God.

The thought struck her with such force that she took a bracing step of retreat.

Gid tilted his head, his concern still evident. "I know this is hard, Willow, I—"

"No! You don't!"

He blinked and withdrew a step. Gripped the back of his neck as he looked down at her.

She could see the disbelief in his expression but was too filled with rage to care.

"Well? Do you? Do you know what it's like to lose your entire home, community, and family all in one day? Do you know what it's like to be so relieved and think your father will live, only to have him suffer for hours and then pass? Do you know what it's like to have nothing? So much of nothing that you're forced to marry a person who doesn't want you?"

"That's not true, Willow." He swept a palm over the lower half of his face and propped his hands on his hips. But he made no other comment, and a hardness seemed to have settled in his jawline. Instead of looking at her, he studied the grass before his boots.

"You know it's true. Now if you'll excuse me, I'm going to walk for the rest of the afternoon. I can't take any more jostling on that hard bench."

She pivoted and marched toward the back of the train, intent on finding some solitude.

"Willow?" he called, despair touching the edges of his tone.

She kept walking.

"Please don't wander too far from the wagons."

Wandering from the wagons . . . There was a thought. Maybe she should just walk back to Independence.

Men at each wagon were swapping out their oxen for fresh ones. Women bustled about, starting small cookfires and dipping water from the barrels strapped to the sides of each wagon.

Willow pushed down her guilt for leaving Gideon to do for himself. This was so unlike her. She didn't ever remember shirking her duties a day in her life. But today . . . She grabbed up two fistfuls of her skirts and started to run.

Chapter 17

Eden stood at the back of the wagon, layering together some quick sandwiches with the leftover biscuits from breakfast and the hare that Tamsyn had helped her roast the evening before. The meat was quite tasty, and she knew Adam would be thankful for the easy meal because one of their oxen had already gone lame for some reason, and he needed to tend to the poor critter's foot before they moved out after lunch. He'd led it away as soon as they stopped to see if he could discover what was causing it to limp, and he might not have time to down a proper meal before they needed to head out again.

She'd just offered up her thanks and picked up one of the biscuits to take a bite when a blur of red and blue darted past. What happened? Had someone been injured?

With concern rising in her chest, she set her biscuit down, laid a towel over the preparations, and stepped out to where she could see. It was Willow, the girl whose father had died in the fire—running away from the wagon train like she had a mountain lion on her tail.

At the next wagon, Tamsyn stood with one hand to her eyes, watching the poor girl's retreat, as well. Tamsyn glanced over her shoulder, eyes wide. "I'd go, but I can't leave Edi."

"Not a problem. I'm happy to go after her." Eden dried her hands on her apron. "If Adam returns, will you tell him there are some sandwiches on the tailgate?"

"Of course."

Eden slipped off the apron and left it in a heap by the sandwiches. "Tell him I'll try not to be long."

Tamsyn touched her arm as she passed. "I'll say a prayer."

"Thank you." Eden swallowed as she hurried in Willow's wake. She'd already disappeared into a thicket of brush, but a clear trail showed the way through broken branches.

Lord, You know that I'm not the best at helping people. Give me the right words to ease her distress. Don't let any harm come to her or let her harm herself.

That thought propelled her into a jog to catch up.

But no matter how fast she ran, she never caught a glimpse. Goodness, the girl could run!

She continued the chase for thirty minutes, following her trail out of the thicket and across another rolling plain similar to the one they'd been driving on all morning. She was gasping for breath and just about to give up and return to the wagons when she rounded a bend in the path and saw Willow.

She had collapsed on a rock on a little knoll overlooking the prairie. She held a wild daisy and methodically shredded the petals from the head, one by one.

Willing down the rapid beating of her heart and gulping for air, Eden approached slowly. She stepped on a rock that turned over beneath her boot and grated against another.

Willow leapt to her feet, spinning toward her with a gasp.

Eden lifted her hands. "It's just me. My name is Eden. I'm Parson Houston's wife."

A firm frown settled on Willow's brow before she plunked down on her rock again. "I came out here to be alone."

Eden hesitated, a little taken aback. She hadn't expected such animosity. Should she go and leave her alone? No, definitely not. She likely would have responded the same way after she'd lost her son.

She took a bold step forward. "Sometimes, when we're grieving, the last thing we need is to be left alone. Trust me, I do know." The grassy patch she sank onto not too far from Willow's rock felt warm and had a loamy scent that made her want to inhale of it, long and slow. She plucked a blade of prairie grass instead. Marveled at the intricacy of the head with the fluffy little seeds. Had no idea what else to say. So she simply remained silent.

Willow had torn off all the daisy's petals and now methodically shredded the yellow center, her agitation plain in her movements.

Eden despaired. Why did she never seem to have the right words to say?

"I lost my son." The statement blurted out of her before she thought better of it. Her eyes fell closed. She didn't want to talk about this. But when she opened them again, Willow was looking at her, so she continued. "I was full term. We were so excited, Adam and I. We had everything prepared. Adam had made a little cradle. I'd sewn a tiny quilt. The diapers were folded and stacked on a blue shelf in the corner. My mother had made the most beautiful christening gown. And then . . ." Her throat closed off. She shrugged. "For some reason, God chose to take our son home."

Eden snatched another piece of grass and plucked off the seeds.

"I closed in on myself. Left Adam and went back to my parents' home. Refused to talk to him for months. Was furious with God."

Willow shifted, leaned to the side, and snatched another of the wild daisies from its stem.

Eden pressed ahead. "I'm telling you all this so that you'll know I do understand the grief of tragic loss. It's a pain so severe that it almost killed me. But I made it worse with my choices. Almost lost my husband—*did* lose him for a good while, actually."

"And what brought you around?"

Eden looked up in surprise. She hadn't expected Willow to respond.

"Did the pain fade?"

So much hope filled Willow's eyes that Eden wished she could say yes.

"No. Sorry. I don't know if the pain of that will ever fade. Be a more distant memory? Maybe. One that won't come to mind every single day? Maybe that too. But I will always grieve that loss, I think. Will always wonder the why of it, you know?"

Willow rubbed a petal between her thumb and fingers. "So, what brought you around?"

Eden pondered. Willow probably wasn't going to like what she had to say. But she'd asked, and Eden had prayed for God's guidance, so . . . "There's a passage in Philippians chapter four where Paul talks about how he had learned to be content in whatever state he found himself. Whether he was full or hungry, living in bounty or living in need." Eden tossed aside the blade of grass and dusted her hands. "I realized that I was wallowing in sorrow and that it was a choice I could let go of. Paul goes on to say that he learned that he could do all things through Christ who gave him strength."

Willow jolted and pegged Eden with a glower.

Cautiously she pressed ahead. "Some people might take that to mean that I ought to have prayed in faith and God would have given me back my child, or that I should never have grieved at all, but I see the passage as speaking more to our options when it comes to mindset. Another passage says that in this world, we will have tribulations, but we can take heart because Jesus has overcome the world. One day I'll get to see my sweet, innocent baby once again. In the here and now, though, I had to decide if I would trust God with the pain. I realized I could choose to wallow in self-pity—and trust me, I was very good at it—or I could choose to accept the bad, grieve the loss, but not let it define me in the sense that it stole all other joy. If I'm honest, I'm still working through that every day. But I'm trying."

"I don't know if I'll ever get there." Willow let a few of the petals blow on the breeze.

Eden reached to settle her hand against Willow's arm. "I know the pain is so strong right now. I understand. Really, I do."

"I feel all hollowed out. Like a hole ripped through me and stole all my feelings."

Finally, they were getting somewhere. Eden breathed a sigh of relief to have the focus off her own pain.

"You've been through the unimaginable over the last couple of days. I think what you are feeling is very normal."

"What you said . . . Those were some of the last words my father said to me."

"What was?"

"That I could do all things through Christ who strengthens me."

Eden smiled wistfully. "Your father knew the Lord then?"

"Oh, yes. I reckon Papa is eating popped corn with the Lord right now, and chatting over the latest wagon improvements."

It was good to see Willow joking a little even if she wasn't smiling. "I'm glad you have that hope. The knowing that he's in a better place, despite your loss. It does help." She angled the redhead a glance. "It also helps to let all those feelings that are bottled up inside of you out."

Willow's brow furrowed. "I don't think I rightly know how to do that."

Eden pondered for a moment, then asked, "Do you love your husband?"

Willow spun to look at her so fast that she nearly fell off her rock. She sputtered for a moment, seeming unable to find the right response. Finally, she offered, "I don't think I've had enough time to process that I'm a married woman, much less figure out if I love him."

Eden plucked another blade of grass. "So your marriage last night was . . . unexpected?"

"You can say that again." Willow's mirthless bark of laughter rasped through the air. "He only married me on account of my father asking him to take care of me."

"I see. Well—"

"Willow! Thank God!" The very man they'd just been speaking about stormed from the brush toward their little knoll. He paused before his wife and plunked his hands on his hips as he assessed her. "You had me worried."

Behind him, Adam strode toward them as well. His gaze sought her out, and he swept her with an assessing look and cocked one brow.

Eden gave a little nod to let him know she was fine.

He motioned with his head that she ought to join him and give the couple some privacy.

With a sigh, Eden rose and dusted off her dress. She cast a glance between Willow, who hadn't answered her husband but remained seated on her rock shredding another daisy, and Gideon who hunched toward his wife in concern.

He raised a questioning look as though asking what he ought to do.

Eden offered him a shrug. This was one situation they would have to work out together as a couple.

But as she joined Adam and they retreated a little way off, she knew one thing . . . If a man had only married a woman out of duty to her father's request, he wouldn't have such a look of misery on his face at the thought of his wife's distress.

Gideon trembled with fear and anger over Willow's actions. Did she realize how far she'd come? Did she understand the dangers of this untamed frontier?

Best that she'd done it now, he supposed, while they were still so close to Independence. But he needed to make it clear to her that she could never do this again.

"I thought you heard me ask you to stay close to the wagons!?" He closed his eyes. He hadn't meant for such bite to ring in his tone. "I'm sorry. I don't mean to sound angry. I was concerned for your safety." And it made him tremble with the fear of it.

Willow remained silent, seeming wholly concentrated on destroying the remains of a daisy in her hands.

He let the silence linger for a beat. "Adam also feared for Eden."

She did squirm a little on her rock at that.

Good. If she couldn't find it in herself to care for her own safety, maybe she would care for someone else's.

He squatted to his haunches to get a better angle on her downturned face. "I'm so sorry, Willow Girl, for all the pain you're feeling. I'm sorry that you don't want to be married to me. Lord knows I wish I could take your pain. And I think that talking about it would ease some of your burden. Care to tell me what you're feeling?"

She held her silence, only twisting her lips to one side as though to prevent herself from speaking.

He sighed. Hung his head. *Lord, give me patience and the wisdom to know how to help her through this.*

When he lifted his head again, he found her watching him.

His heart picked up a beat. Maybe he was getting through to her? He kept his voice soft. "I do know some of what you're feeling. I lost my wife and child and sister, as you know." And Lord help him, he was terrified of losing her too. He gritted his teeth against the emotions that he never wanted to feel again.

She turned her attention back to the mangled flower. Continued holding her silence.

He sighed and glanced toward where Adam and Eden waited for them. "The wagons went on without us. Cranston said we should catch them not too far ahead because he only plans to go seven miles today, and we've already come five. Once we catch up, you can rest in the wagon. But we do need to go. It's not safe for us to be out here on our own."

She tossed the daisy to one side, stood, and brushed off her skirt, then started toward Adam and Eden.

He scrambled to regain his feet and followed in her wake. He may not have succeeded in getting her to speak to him, but at least they were together once again and returning to the wagon train.

Adam led the way, with Eden close on his heels. Gideon wished Willow would stick closer to them, but she seemed content to hang back by several feet, and he didn't want to keep harping at her, so he held his silence. Though Adam led them at a good pace, by the time he could see the canvas tops of the wagons, they'd been gone for over an hour.

Ahead, Eden gasped and gripped her husband's shoulder. "Adam!"

Adam's hand shot into the air in a sign for them to halt and keep silent.

Gideon strained to see what had caught their attention, not for the first time in his life wishing that he were just a few inches taller. He rose on his toes and felt everything inside him go cold.

Gideon stepped forward and scooped Willow behind himself.

Their two wagons had been left in the prairie tracks by the wagon train that had moved on ahead.

And standing at the back of his wagon were several Indians. Most of them mounted on ponies, but one of them had handed his horse off to a friend. He stood on the rear step with his head shoved inside the flap.

From behind, he heard Willow gasp. "Gid!"

He spun to find a warrior standing behind them in the path they'd just created through the brush. How had the man moved so silently through the thick tangle? However he had accomplished it, he was upon them and in his hand, he held a long spear, pointed in their direction.

Chapter 18

Willow called herself every manner of fool. How many times had Papa cautioned her about wandering away from town on her own because of the Osage?

The one standing in the trail just behind her certainly didn't look any too friendly. He had a broad, blunt nose and a face that almost seemed rectangular for the wide square jaw and the shaven fore part of his head. A lock of hair dyed a bright red spiked from the back of his head. At his throat hung a long, beaded necklace that ended in a large white medallion that seemed to have been carved from stone. His bare chest glistened with sweat, and the long spear gripped in a brawny hand was decorated with black and white feathers. An animal-hide breech cloth hung about his hips, but other than that, he wore nothing. Even his feet were bare.

He nudged the spear and indicated they should move with a grunt and a jut of his chin.

Gideon once again tried to sweep her to the other side of himself. "Get in front of me again."

Willow shook her head. She had put them in this situation, so it really ought to be her putting herself in danger. "Just move, Gid."

"Now is not the time," he snapped. "Get in front of me and walk."

She tipped her head back and pegged him with a look. "This is my fault, and I'll be the one to—"

The man behind them grunted a sharp phrase and Willow glanced back and realized he'd come quite close. So close that she could smell the acrid scent of sweat and animal hide. So close that he reached out to touch her hair.

She gasped and recoiled from his touch, scampering in front of Gideon to make her escape.

"We're moving. We're moving." She heard Gideon say. And when she glanced back, it was to see her husband with his hands in the air as he strode in her wake, the Indian fast on his heels.

Their captor prodded them into the open space between their two wagons. The man's companions spread out to surround them, and he grunted something at them that made them all laugh. Suddenly, all pairs of eyes fell on her!

Willow squirmed under the collective scrutiny. Despite her earlier resolve, she sidled closer to Gideon.

The captor uttered another phrase that again had all the Indians laughing.

Beside them, Adam wrapped his arms around Eden and held her fast to his side, but Gideon hadn't moved. He remained beside her with his hands in the air, his jaw hard, and his attention never wavering from the square-jawed man with the spear.

Square-Jaw jutted his chin in Willow's direction and said something to Gideon.

Gideon shook his head. "No." He pointed at Willow and then back to himself. "She's mine."

The man grunted and took a step closer to her.

Willow's heart hammered. What was happening here?

With one short, sharp movement, the point of the man's spear hovered at Gideon's throat.

Gideon stiffened but held his ground. He leveled narrowed eyes on the man.

Keeping half an eye on Gideon, the Indian approached Willow.

She tried to scramble to the other side of Gideon, but the man grabbed her hair and gave a tug.

"Ow." She felt her hairpins give way, and her long curls fell about her shoulders.

A murmur of awe rose from the Indians gathered around.

Enough!

Willow's anger flared. She spun to face the man and took a step toward him. Just like Papa had taught her, she punched the heel of her hand from her hip upward at the man's nose. He lurched back, and she missed, but his spear bobbled in the process.

Gideon moved so fast that Willow hardly had time to register it. He snatched the man's spear and leveled the pistol that had somehow appeared in his hand at the Indian's head. The man thrust his hands high. Gideon tossed the spear to one side. "I ought to—"

"Gideon! Think before you get us all killed!" Adam snapped, still hugging Eden with one arm as he held his bandaged palm toward the rest of the men surrounding them in a universal gesture that said he wanted no trouble. Several of them had cocked their arms back, ready to throw their spears!

"Begging your pardon, Parson," Gideon's voice was low and calm as he motioned for all the Indians to cluster to one side. "But the only way to deal with bullies is to show no fear." He continued talking as though they might all be having tea in a grand hotel. "Now you and I, sir, are going to walk to my wagon, so I can help my wife inside. Willow, for crying in your cups, please do as I say this time."

Yes. That was probably a good idea. She swallowed and nodded.

They all moved to the back of the wagon, the Indian seeming to understand what was required of him.

Gideon held his free hand out to help her mount the short ladder at the back of the wagon. He thrust his chin, never taking his eyes off his captive. "Inside, toward the back, you'll find a few five-pound sacks of sugar. Bring one out."

Willow shook so badly that she could barely climb into the back of the wagon, but the warmth of Gideon's hand lent her strength. Once she stood behind the canvas, such relief flooded her that she felt tears burn the backs of her eyes. She clenched her teeth. She would not start crying now. Not when Gideon had risked his life to save her and in the face of her own foolishness!

With trembling hands, she tucked her flowing hair behind her ears. She wished she could pin it up, but there was no time.

Sugar. Where had he said it was? Every thought seemed scattered.

"Toward the back. By the pallet on the right." Gideon's calm voice soothed her nerves a little and she found the bags of sugar just where he said.

When she emerged, Gideon still held his pistol toward the man's head. His companions didn't appear to be any too relaxed, but neither did they want to get their friend killed, it seemed.

"Go on and open the top of that bag," Gideon said.

It was woven shut with a thick thread, but she'd dealt with these at the store all the time. All she needed to do was pull the right strand, and the top of the bag would come open. Her hands trembled, and at first, she grabbed the wrong thread.

"Easy, Willow Girl."

How could he be so calm in this situation?

She finally found the right thread and tugged the top of the sugar sack open, then held it toward him with both hands.

Gideon licked his finger and thrust it into the sugar. He withdrew it and held it up for the square-faced Osage to see. "Sugar. Good." He slurped the sugar off his finger and then pointed for the man to try some. "Go on and try it."

Cautiously, the man touched his finger to the end of his tongue and then touched the white crystals. Slowly he tasted it.

"Sugar," Gideon said.

"Sugar," the man repeated with surprisingly no accent. He uttered a few words to his tribesmen, and it was clear that they all knew what the bag contained. A few of them motioned for their friend to join them.

Gideon smiled, but Willow knew him well enough to see the forced nature of it. He pointed at the man. "You take the sugar." He pointed from Willow to himself. "I take my wife." With his free hand, he grabbed the top of the bag and thrust it against the Indian's chest, being sure to keep his gun leveled.

"Trade." The man thrust the sugar back at Gideon and motioned that he wanted to take Willow for himself.

"No." Gideon's voice held firm. He shook his head. "No trade."

The Indian's expression slid into irritation, but he lowered his gaze to the bag of sugar in his hands. "Sugar good. Two sugars better."

Gideon's eyes narrowed. He never took his gaze off the man. "Tell you what. One sugar as a gesture of friendship. One sugar for that pony there." He pointed to the only pony in the group without a rider.

It was a beautiful, dainty horse that looked like a palomino, only smaller in stature—maybe twelve hands high. It had a creamy golden coat with lighter spots all over and a light cream main and tail. A white blaze painted the pony's face from mane to nostrils. The mare's large brown eyes seemed intelligent, and from the way she stood quietly waiting for her master through the conversation, she was also well-trained.

Several of the Indians laughed at the predicament the square-jawed man found himself in. He looked from the bag of sugar in his hands to his pony and back to Gideon.

One of the older Osage said something in a tone that gave Willow the sense that the man encouraged an end to this so they could move on.

She swallowed. But would it end with them all skewered? Or would the Indians ride off peaceably?

Square-Jaw gripped the top of his sack of sugar and twisted it to seal it shut. Then he nodded. "Two." He held up his first finger and his thumb.

"Willow Girl, fetch one more bag of sugar, would you? I think you just got yourself a pony." Once again, Gid held out a hand to help her into the back of the wagon. When she returned to the opening, she didn't bother descending again. She merely leaned down and held the bag of sugar out to the Indian.

He accepted it, but only after he captured a strand of her hair that had fallen forward. He splayed it on his fingers and muttered something with a bit of awe in his voice. Several of the men laughed again. One of them motioned more emphatically for him to rejoin them.

He took the second bag of sugar and backed away, his gaze never leaving Willow. "Walks with Fire," he said, leveling her with a cheeky grin. "Go with No Fear and be good to my pony." And then he hugged both bags of sugar to his chest with one arm, snatched up his spear with the other, and vaulted up behind one of his companions with such athleticism that it took Willow a moment to believe what she'd just seen.

The Indians galloped away, several of them laughing at the top of their lungs and obviously giving their friend a hard time about his loss.

Had the man been able to speak perfect English that whole time?

Adam and Eden slumped against each other in relief, and Gideon thrust his pistol back into his holster and strode to the horse. He took up the lead—the only piece of tack on the animal—and led her over to the back of the wagon. After tying her off to the tailgate, he dipped some water from the water barrel for her and allowed her to drink from a bucket.

Without a word, he strode to the front of the wagon and did the same for the oxen that Willow only now realized had been hitched to the wagon in the sun as they waited for the wagon's brake to be released and the "get up" command to start them moving.

That done, Gideon returned and paused to look at Adam and Eden.

Adam had just finished watering his own stock, and as he returned the bucket to the hook on the side of the wagon, a spark of anger lit his eyes. "How did you know they wouldn't attack us?"

Gid swept a hand around the back of his neck. "Guess I figured that if they'd have wanted us dead, we'd have been dead before we knew what hit us. And cowering to a bully generally only makes him bolder. We were better off taking our chances with some strength."

Adam closed his eyes and settled one hand on Eden's shoulder. After a long moment he drew his wife close and pressed a kiss to her temple, then urged her toward their wagon. "Well, we survived. More likely because the Lord watched out for us than because of your show of strength. But let's be thankful while we move, shall we? I've no desire to remain separated from the rest of the train for any longer than we absolutely have to."

Gideon nodded. "Agreed."

And then he turned a hard gaze on Willow.

She swallowed. "I know. I'm sorry."

A puff of breath escaped him, and he motioned toward the front of their wagon. "We can talk more later. For now, let's get going."

Willow strode to his side of the bench and allowed him to help her up. She scooted across to her side and tucked her trembling hands beneath her legs, letting her eyes fall closed as Gideon swung up beside her, released the brake, and said "get up" to the team.

Oh Lord, how merciful You are to me in my foolishness. Forgive me for putting so many in danger, and thank You for keeping us safe. Please, Lord, please help me find my way through this sea of grief that has me all a muddle. And continue to keep us safe from those who intend to harm us. You are good and gracious, abounding in love. Your mercies are new every morning. Great is Thy faithfulness, oh Lord. Great is Thy faithfulness.

Once the ox team was headed at a good clip down the road, Gideon reached over and took her hand. She felt a tremor work through his fingers as he raised hers to his lips and pressed a kiss to them, then he tugged her close and pressed a kiss to her temple, followed quickly by another.

After holding her close for much too brief a time, he released her. "Pin your hair up, please," was all he said.

But his actions and his words were enough to make her ponder for the first time about whether he really might have feelings for her.

Chapter 19

Mercy paced with one thumb tucked between her teeth as she studied the trail to the east. The wagons had circled up on a flat plain, leaving space in the circle for the last two wagons to close the corral that would hold all their animals in for the night.

Water was scarce here in this place, but Cranston had assured everyone that tomorrow they would camp on the other side of the Blue River at a camping place known as Elm Grove.

They'd only been on the trail for less than a day and already she looked forward to a bath in fresh running water.

But what she wanted right now was to see Gideon and Willow's wagon, followed closely by the parson's. The horizon remained empty.

Footsteps approached. She didn't have to turn to recognize them as Micah's. What made his tread distinguishable? She couldn't have said.

The same as she couldn't have explained what comfort settled deep inside her when he slipped an arm around her from behind and tucked her against him.

"Gid's fast with a gun and a good shot. They'll be fine." His low words rumbled in her ear, and then he pressed a kiss into her hair.

She leaned her weary head on his shoulder. "I hope you are right."

The warmth of his soft laugh wafted against her temple. "Married for less than a day and already you are doubting my word?"

She smiled and angled her head to dawdle a gentle kiss against the stubble of his jaw. "Is this a rule?" She lifted a brow. "That I'm not allowed to doubt you?"

He pretended to ponder long and hard. "Yes. I think this is a good rule."

She laughed and spun to get a better angle on smacking his chest. "Listen to you go on."

He splayed one hand against her lower back and drew her closer as he grinned down at her unrepentantly. Then his head dipped, and he kissed her, long, slow, and sure. He eased back but didn't set her from him. "I think this should be a rule too. I like being able to kiss you any time I want."

She felt her smile slip. Pushed away the flash of a memory and focused on the top button on Micah's shirt. It had a loose thread. What an odd time to notice that.

"Hey now." Micah touched her chin. "All in good fun. Don't let your thoughts wander to that cretin you were married to. I'm sorry to bring him to mind for even a second."

She tucked her lower lip between her teeth. "I'm sorry, Micah. I know you are nothing like him. I don't know why he comes to mind at the most inopportune moments."

He grunted and gritted, "I do." His hand curved around the back of her head, and he nudged her close. "Tell you what. We'll change that rule to you can kiss me any time you want."

She laughed. "Even when you are chewing the fat with all your friends around the fire nights?"

He snorted a laugh. "Even then. They'll all be jealous, and I'll love it. Besides that," he whispered in her ear. "I know you'll never do it."

She giggled. "Just you wait. You never know. I might surprise you."

"Ah." He turned her to face the trail once more. "I guess you will have to admit I was right at least this once."

"Oh! Thank the Lord!" She threw her hands to her mouth as she watched the two missing wagons trail each other toward them in the late afternoon sun.

Gideon, Willow, the parson, and his wife had finally returned!

But as the wagon passed, Mercy frowned at the pretty little pony trailing the O'Riley wagon.

"They have a horse. Why do they have a horse, Micah? Where did they get it?"

He drew her toward the circle of wagons as Gideon and Adam filled in the last two spots. "I'm sure they'll tell us. Come on and we'll invite them to our fire for tonight's meal, if that's all right with you? I think the last thing Willow needs to think on is dinner preparations."

"Yes. Of course. I'll put those grouse you bagged this morning in a stew. There will be plenty."

"All right, then. Let's go see how they got that horse and extend the invite." He stretched out his hand for her to take.

Which, of course, she gladly did. And as her fingers slipped between his, she was struck with how much hope filled her at the prospect of the future. It was an emotion she hadn't felt for many dry years.

It felt good. Like coming home.

So they were back. Good. Corbin smiled.

He wouldn't miss out on the anticipation of killing the man.

He lifted the bucket of water from his tailgate and strode toward the group that gathered around the arriving wagons.

People dashed from all directions of the encampment to hear what had happened.

Riley and the parson were busy unhitching their oxen and filling the crowd in on some story about a group of Indians that they'd run into, and Willow stood to one side, hands folded and head downcast as though embarrassed to have caused the ruckus.

As she should be.

He approached her with a smile and held out the bucket. "Afternoon. Figured you might be thirsty." He lifted the dipper and offered it to her with a raised brow.

She stepped forward and accepted it. "Thank you. Very kind."

"I'm just glad you made it back, is all."

Her hands were small and pale around the dipper. He watched her sip daintily from the bowl of it. The column of her throat, long and slender, worked in and out as she swallowed each mouthful. Her delicate pink tongue swept over her lips as she handed the dipper back to him with a smile of thanks.

His heart pounded in his chest. She would have come around to him if he'd had more time to convince her. If Riley hadn't butted in where he didn't belong. Well, no matter. He would soon have the opportunity again. Then she would be his. But now was not the time to press his suit.

He gave her a sketch of a bow and forced himself to turn and offer water to her walking dead man of a husband.

Riley hesitated, surprise lifting his brows as he glanced from the water bucket to Corbin and back. Then he gave a perfunctory nod of thanks and gulped down several dipperfuls. His grip was like an iron trap when he clapped Corbin on one shoulder. "Thanks," he offered as he strode to the front of his wagon and continued unhitching his team.

This was good. Setting the tone for them to trust him.

Corbin continued on with the bucket to the parson's wife. But his thoughts were never far from Gideon Riley and, more to the point, his wife.

How long did he have to wait?

Soon.

Not too long, now.

Just a few more days.

When the man approached with the water bucket and a dipper, Eden couldn't have been happier. She hardly glanced at his face, so focused was she on her anticipation of a cool drink of water. She'd grown quite parched through their little ordeal. Her legs were still trembling at the thought of what might have happened with those Indians.

It made her a little queasy to think that she and Adam were purposefully heading west to be missionaries to such men. Were the Snohomish as savage and uncouth as those men back there? Of course, why would she expect them to be anything else when they hadn't been offered a chance to know the Lord? And yet, in this moment everything in her longed to run back to the safety of her parents' home. Back to civilization. Back to stores, doctors, diners, and theaters.

As she drank thirstily from the dipper, she cast her thoughts heavenward.

Lord, You know how scary that was, right? You knew what You were calling us to. I don't want to be of those who put their hand to the plow and then look back. I've already done enough of that in my life. So please, help me. Give me strength, stamina, perseverance, and fortitude.

The man with the bucket cleared his throat, snapping her back to the present. She'd let her mind wander and was standing with the empty dipper in her hand.

She handed it back to him. "I'm so sorry. I was lost in prayer there for a moment."

He frowned and reached for the dipper. "Not to worry, ma'am."

As he took it from her, the late afternoon sun glinted off something at his cuff. It reflected painfully into Eden's eyes, and she shot up one hand to block it.

"Sorry about that." The man adjusted his coat sleeve, tugging it down. "These cufflinks could put an eye out."

Eden felt her lips form a smile, but she was suddenly back in the hotel room, looking down on the alley, watching the man in the black hat turn the corner at the end of the alley.

There had been a similar reflection! At first, she'd chalked it up to the flare of the match or maybe the glowing end of a cigarette. But no. It had been much brighter—just like the reflection of the sun off that cufflink just now. And she distinctly remembered that the flare of the match had come after the brighter flare.

She lifted her gaze to the man, taking in his features as he moved over to offer Adam the dipper of water.

Oh! It was the man who'd saved Willow's father from the fire.

Eden frowned. So it couldn't have been him then, right? She gave her head a little shake. Of course, right. It made no sense that someone would start a fire and then go into the building and risk his life to save a practical stranger. Besides, would that kind of man be thoughtful enough to bring water to people he barely knew?

No. She was seeing ghosts in places because of their recent scare with the Indians.

That was all. She needed rest. But first, she needed to make dinner.

Chapter 20

After her short night and the ordeal with the Osage, Willow felt weary to her very core and simply wanted to crawl into the wagon and sleep, but she didn't feel right about going into Gideon's wagon without him knowing.

She had tried to rest earlier this afternoon when they'd first returned to the camp, but the wagon had been stuffy and hot, and she hadn't succeeded in more than closing her eyes.

Now, with dinner concluded, Caesar Cranston had sent his scouts around to ask that everyone attend a short meeting before turning in.

The cattle and horses had been corralled in the middle of the large circle of wagons, so the gathering had been moved to a flat spot near a bend in the trickle of water they had camped by. And that was really all it was, too—just enough to dampen a hanky, if she'd had one. She'd walked along it for a ways with several of the women, hoping to find a spot deep enough for bathing; however, their hopes had been deflated.

Nearer to camp, several of the men dug a hole and lined it with rocks that they'd removed from the dust. After they'd let the mud settle, the shallow pool ran clear enough to dip buckets of water for the oxen, but it filled back up slowly, taking much longer than if it had been a larger stream.

Gideon had left with the scout named Jeremiah a few minutes earlier to attend to a sore on one of their oxen's shoulders where the yoke had rubbed a spot raw. Apparently, Jeremiah was quite a hand with animals and had brought along an ointment that he felt would help.

She was trying to decide whether to walk out to the meeting place alone or wait for Gideon to get back when Eden and Tamsyn stopped by.

"We wondered if you'd like to walk over with us?" Eden asked.

Relieved, Willow dredged up a smile. "Yes. Thank you. Do you mind if we stop to see if Mercy wants to join us?"

"Of course." Tamsyn smiled. "By the way, my name is Tamsyn. I don't know if you remember, but we chatted for a bit in your store the other day . . ." Her words trailed away as though she was second-guessing her decision to remind Willow of that.

But Willow took comfort from the memory. What she wouldn't give to go back to the bustle and craziness of normal, everyday life in the mercantile.

Tamsyn hurried to add, "And this here—" she gestured to the man trailing them "—is my brother, Edison. But everyone calls him Edi."

Edison didn't seem to want to meet her gaze, so Willow gave Tamsyn a smile. "Yes, I remember meeting you, but it's lovely to see you again. Have you met Mercy?"

Both women shook their heads.

"Not yet," Eden offered.

Willow nodded for them to follow. "Let me introduce you."

Mercy placed a lid on a dutch oven filled with biscuits as they approached. She greeted them with a smile. "Good evening." She motioned to the fire that was not much more than coals. "I thought I'd get the morning's biscuits baking while we are at this meeting."

"What a good idea." Willow wished she'd thought of something similar. But all she'd been thinking of was how much she wished Papa were here. How she wanted to hear his hearty laugh just once more. How she longed to feel his sturdy hand on her shoulder and hear him murmur how much he loved her.

She gave herself a shake. "May I introduce you to Eden, and Tamsyn, and Edison."

"Edi!" Tamsyn's brother frowned at her as though she'd committed a grave sin.

"I'm sorry. Edi." His stubborn frown almost made her want to giggle. "This is Mrs. Morran. And these two—" Willow slung an arm around each of the boys "—are her sons, Avram and Joel." She ruffled Joel's hair and dropped a kiss on Avram's curls.

Edison perked up immediately. "Want to play ball?" He directed the question at Joel.

Tamsyn laid a hand on her brother's arm. "Maybe for a little bit after the meeting, Edi. But first, we must go and listen to what Mr. Cranston has to say."

Edi's shoulders slumped. "Okay."

Joel glanced up at Mercy and then returned his attention to Tamsyn's brother. "I'd be happy to play catch with you for a little while after the meeting. And my little brother has a good arm too!"

The pride in those words drew an unexpected grin that did Willow's heart good.

Mercy rolled her lips in and pressed them together, blinking hard as she settled one hand atop Joel's mop of curls. The little jostle she gave him said more than words could ever express about how he had touched her heart.

The three other women fell into step with each other then, and Willow was happy to trail behind the two boys and Edi as they all moved toward the meeting place.

If Mercy and Micah had been able to form a family out of their shared pain, could she and Gideon do the same? Of course, their circumstances were different, but certainly less traumatic than Micah and Mercy's beginnings.

Hope raised its head, but Willow stomped it down. It was too soon to be thinking about a happy future.

When Gideon returned to the wagon and found Willow missing, his heart nearly stopped beating.

Surely, she hadn't gone off alone again?

With a frown tightening his brow, he hurried toward the crowd gathered on the creek bank, hoping upon hope to find her there.

Mercy was there, seated on a log near Micah, who stood talking with the parson. The parson's wife and the tall brunette woman and her brother stood behind them. He scanned the rest of those gathered and didn't see her.

His heart thudded dread. His palms turned clammy.

He wasn't sure until this moment that he'd registered just how many of them there were in this wagon train. Sixty-two souls, Cranston had said. He'd realized that was a large group. But seeing them all gathered together now hammered home the task that lay before them. When feed and water were low, it would be a problem for all of them. When storms swept in, many would get sick. So many little children darted through the meadow grasses, playing tag in the growing dusk. Men clustered in groups, some laughing, some deep in discussions of one sort or another.

Cranston stepped up on a log round and called the meeting to order.

Gideon's pulse spun in his ears. Where was she? He didn't want to miss the meeting, but finding her was more import—

There!

A group of men sat down in the grass, and Willow stood behind them, with one hand to her eyes as she studied the sunset on the distant western horizon.

Such relief swept through him that it sent a tremor from the top of his head all the way to his toes. He snatched a blade of grass and tucked it into his mouth.

Apparently realizing the meeting was coming to order, she turned and glanced his way, as though his scrutiny were a magnet that had attracted her gaze. She started to lift a wave, but her hand died in mid-air, and she searched his face as though wondering if something was wrong.

Yes, something was wrong. Hang it. He'd gone and fallen for her despite his best intentions. He shouldn't have stubbornly shared the bed with her, and then he wouldn't have kissed her, and then he wouldn't have this constant worry filling him! So much for keeping his emotions out of it!

He swiped a hand over his face and did his best to council his features. Tried not to think about the dangers of the trail or what might have happened if those Osage had chosen a more aggressive tact. Tried not to think about how beautiful she was or how her blazing red hair would be like a flag, attracting attention from all sorts of undesirables.

His hand trembled, and he leaned into his heels and crossed his arms.

Willow's hand fell back to her side, and she lowered her head as she walked over to stand beside the parson's wife.

His eyes fell closed. That wasn't what he wanted. Her hurting and wondering why he was upset.

He sighed.

"Thank you!" Cranston spoke from the front of the gathering. "Now that I have everyone's attention, I would like to talk to you about what to expect over the next few months as we travel together. I will try to keep this meeting short, so please grant me your attention for just a few minutes."

Yes.

Yes, please.

At least listening to what the wagon master had to say would give his mind a few minutes' break from his frustration with himself and his worry for Willow Chancell—Riley. She was Willow Riley now.

He shifted his feet and released a breath.

And there she was, right back in his mind again.

He was done for.

Chapter 21

Willow tried not to think about that glower on Gideon's face. How had she irritated him? She tried to focus on the wagon master as he droned on about how Cody Hawkeye would blow his bugle at four in the morning to wake up the camp. By five, he wanted the cattle to be rounded up and sorted out.

She angled a glance at her husband, only to find him looking at her in return, but as soon as their gazes met, his darted back to Cranston.

She pressed her lips together. She had upset him. Maybe it still had to do with her earlier jaunt into the wilds. Or maybe he wasn't happy that she hadn't waited for him at the wagon?

"By seven," Cranston continued, "Each family should have their oxen hitched and everything stowed. This provides approximately two hours for breakfast and cleanup. We will blow another bugle at that time to indicate *wagons ho*. Every family must be ready. We need to get that early start in order to make good progress. We hope for at least fifteen miles each day—after tomorrow, which will be another short day. Twenty will need to be traversed on some days to keep us on schedule. It is imperative that we make it over the Rocky Mountains before snow begins to fly."

Willow pondered that. Back when Mama was alive, their family had taken a train to the east and spent a day in the Appalachians.

Though it had been October—a slow month for the store, which was what had allowed them to make the trip—there had been only a skiff of snow in the mountain pass they had crossed.

How bad could the Rocky Mountains be?

Willow folded her hands. She wanted only to sleep. She didn't want to think about how Mama and Papa had laughed with one another and held hands as they stood at the top of that mountain and looked out over the rolling foothills of that range. She didn't want to think about how lonely Papa must have been for Mama all these years. And she certainly didn't want to think about how lonely she would be for both of them for the rest of her life.

She forced her attention back to what Mr. Cranston was saying and realized she must have missed most of it.

"The guard will change again at midnight," he said.

Thankfully, she wouldn't be among the guards, so she didn't need to know when the first posting of the guard would happen, she supposed. What else had she missed?

"For now, that concludes our meeting. Everyone get some rest, and we'll take it easy in the morning since we will have another short day." He lifted a hand. "Good night, everyone. Thank you for coming."

The crowd began to disburse, but not Gideon. He remained fast where he stood, with his gaze fastened to her.

Since the other women were already wandering back toward the wagons, Willow fell into step behind them. She paused when she reached Gideon and lifted her gaze to his. Might as well get it over with. "I'm sorry if I upset you again."

He shifted. Resettled his hat. Swept a hand around the back of his neck. "I was just worried when I didn't see you at the wagon is all."

So that was it. Had he feared that she'd run off again? She curled her fingers together. "I promise I won't run off again, Gid."

He stared at her for a long time and then finally offered a succinct dip of his chin. "Thank you for that."

In the distance, cattle lowed, drawing her attention. She cleared her throat. "I'm rather weary tonight. Would you mind if I simply turned in a little early?"

"Not at all." He swept an arm for her to lead the way. "I think I'll do the same."

She swallowed. Didn't he need to find out about the rotation of the guards? "Will you have to stand guard at some point?" Maybe that would send him off to talk to Cranston. Then maybe she'd be able to fall asleep before he returned.

"You must have missed what he said. This first week, the guard duty will be divided between Cranston, Cody, Striker, and Jeremiah. That lets all of us settle into the routine. Next week, we'll draw for spots in the schedule."

"I see." She hoped her disappointment didn't ring too loudly in her voice. But, the thought of trying to sleep with him beside her once more weighted her with weariness. At some point, he was going to expect her to fulfill her wifely duties, wasn't he?

And would that be so bad? She felt heat blaze through her cheeks and touched them to cool them. Would he, though? If he'd only married her at Papa's request? And yet . . . Earlier, when they had climbed onto the wagon after the Indians had departed, she'd thought . . . well, she'd thought that Gid might be feeling something for her. But based on his frustration with her tonight, she'd obviously been wrong.

A thought flashed into her mind, and she lifted her head.

Maybe it would be best for her to simply return to Independence. That would unburden her of a husband who didn't want her and unburden Gideon of a wife he didn't want. And yet, she'd just promised Gideon that she wouldn't run off again, and she highly doubted he would give her permission to return.

Dread worked through her as she strode toward their wagon, hearing Gideon's footsteps fast on her heels. What kind of life had she consigned herself to? All her life, she'd hoped for a loving marriage like her parents had shared. And now . . .

She pushed the thought away lest it overwhelm her.

When they reached the wagon, Mercy stood there waiting for them.

Willow felt overly relieved to see her. "Don't tell me the boys have chased you off in search of female company?" She smiled.

With a laugh, Mercy held out a blue bonnet. "The boys are playing catch with Tamsyn's brother, but I wanted to bring this by. Georgia had several. More than I need. Please take this to wear tomorrow. It will keep some of the sun off at least."

Slowly, Willow accepted the offering. "Thank you. I appreciate it."

Mercy tugged her into a quick embrace. "Of course. I'd best be off to see if I can encourage the boys back to camp so I can get them into bed." She chuckled. "Edi was so thrilled at the prospect of Joel and Av playing catch with him that they practically raced to that flat spot near the creek."

With a smile, Willow turned her attention to where the three still tossed the brown belt ball to each other as Mattox lapped from the watering hole the men had created in the creek. Edi's boyish laugh cut through the chorus of cicadas, crickets, and bullfrogs.

Willow smiled at the sound. "I imagine it's a lot of work for his sister to keep him happy—a man his size and yet still with the mind of a boy."

Mercy nodded. "Yes. We all have our challenges, I suppose. She seems determined to face hers with grit."

Willow nodded absentmindedly, however the comment struck a nerve deep inside.

"Good night, now." Mercy waved and walked toward the boys. One of them tossed her the ball, and with a laugh, she tossed it back but also motioned for them to head to their wagon.

Tamsyn appeared from behind her wagon and called to her brother. His shoulders slumped, but he did shuffle toward her as Joel and Avram called goodnight.

Tamsyn glanced Willow's way, and she lifted a hand. The woman smiled in return, then settled one hand on her brother's shoulder and said something to him in a voice too soft for Willow to hear. The pair disappeared behind the covered wagon.

Facing her challenges with grit.

Willow certainly didn't feel like she had even an ounce of grit left inside her, though she wished she did. If she had grit, maybe this feeling of terror and fear of facing a future with a man who didn't want her wouldn't be dogging her all the time. This feeling of hopelessness over what was to come would be transformed into hope. This feeling of . . . thirst would be quenched.

If anyone thirsts, let him come to Me and drink.

The words from the book of John struck her with such convicting force that she withdrew a step. She turned her face to the sky. The first stars poked through the gloam of dusk, and a bat darted through the air above her on a hunt for bugs.

"I've not been drinking of You, You're right." She whispered the words. "I don't know if I have the strength right now. Please help me."

A picture formed in her mind. Eden sitting by her earlier out on the plain. She had said something about contentment and Philippians chapter four.

With a sigh, she turned to the wagon and found Gideon watching her from where he had leaned one shoulder against the tailgate.

"You all right?" he asked.

She concentrated on her fingers, skirting his question. "Do you have a Bible?"

"I do."

"Would you mind, that is, would it be all right if I read in it for a few minutes?"

He straightened and motioned toward the inside of the wagon. "Of course. We'll light the lantern."

She glanced up and found him waiting to help her inside. She lifted the bonnet. "Thank you."

He shook his head. "I hadn't gotten around to asking anyone yet. She offered the bonnet on her own. But I'm glad she did. Shall we?"

Willow settled her hand in his, hoping beyond hope that he couldn't feel her trembling as she stepped into the narrow aisle between the crates once again.

But when Gideon climbed in after her, he settled his hands on her shoulders. "You're so tired you're trembling. I'm sorry you had such a distressing day." His thumbs worked into the hard knots that had formed in her shoulders and she almost groaned at the pleasant feel of his strong hands working to relieve the tension.

He stopped suddenly and all too soon. She felt cool air rush between them as he withdrew.

Willow took a breath. He meant only to comfort and had no idea how his nearness undid her. She longed to turn into the comfort of his arms, and yet knew he wouldn't welcome the gesture.

And she wanted to face the future with grit.

Maybe that did mean she needed to stand on her own and return to Independence. She had no place to stay, but she could let a room— maybe from Miss Felicity. And maybe that dear woman would even have a job to offer her.

Behind Willow, Gideon lit the lantern and then nudged her forward so he could hang the lamp from its hook in the stay nearer to the bed. "If you don't mind . . ." He reached past her and lifted a Bible from one of the crates. "Would you read it out loud?"

Her gaze flew to his as she accepted the book.

He lifted a hand. "You don't have to."

She smoothed her fingers over the leather cover. "No. It's fine. I'm happy to. I wanted to refresh my memory about a passage in Philippians."

"Sounds good to me."

Behind her, she heard his boots *thunk* onto the floorboards. After that, he scooted past her, went through the steps to lengthen the bed, and then crawled to the far side of the mattress, patting the place next to him as he lay down and tucked one arm behind his head.

Thankfully, tonight he kept his shirt on! And if possible, he was pressed even closer to the wagon bench end than he had been the night before.

The Bible. Right. She was supposed to be reading the Bible.

Willow swallowed and sat on the pallet, angling the book to catch the best of the light. She opened to Philippians and found chapter four. "'Therefore, my beloved and longed-for brethren, my joy and crown . . .'"

The passage was the closing portion of a letter.

The first conviction that struck Willow to the core came from verse four. "'Rejoice in the Lord always. Again I will say, rejoice!'"

Willow paused and stared at the words, rereading them silently to herself.

"I imagine that strikes hard in the face of your loss." Gideon's voice rumbled softly.

"Yes. I don't know how to rejoice right now." She glanced over her shoulder at him.

With one hand still tucked behind his head and his other resting on his chest, Gideon continued to stare at the oilcloth overhead. "When my Verona, our unborn child, and my niece Jess passed, and then later when I lost my sister, I felt the same. Still find it hard to rejoice in all that loss. But I think that's because we have our eyes fixed too much on this world. When I pause to think, to really think, about where they are and what they are doing, well, I can't be anything but happy about all that they must be experiencing. Little Jess didn't have to grow up in a world where she was bound to be hurt by sin—whether her own or someone else's. Verona escaped a world where sickness, toil, and loss wear us down. She and Georgia are living in the very presence of God now because as the Word says, to be absent from the body is to be present with the Lord for those who know Him. And they did. They'll suffer no more dying, tears, or sorrow. And my baby . . ." His voice broke, and he cleared his throat. It took him a moment to resume speaking. "So yeah, when I think about the eternal blessings, I can find it in myself to rejoice. It's only when I concentrate on myself and all I lost that I find the rejoicing hard."

Willow spread her palm over the precious pages. "That's very true, I suppose. Papa won't have to stand guard for long night hours or change any broken wagon wheels. He won't have to fret about whether he calculated supplies correctly. He simply gets to exist in the Father's love. Worship. Rejoice."

Behind her, she heard Gideon move, and when she glanced back this time, it was to find that he'd turned on his side, propped himself on one elbow, and was watching her intently. "There's another passage in the Bible where it talks about how we don't grieve as those without hope. But we still grieve, Willow. What you're feeling . . . it's natural. And to be expected. So try to rejoice, but in the moments when you fail, don't despair. Give yourself the grace to get back to the foundation of truth and the joy of trusting it."

Willow nodded, closed the Bible, and set it back into its crate.

Gideon pointed. "Your nightshirt is there."

As soon as she had it in hand, he rose to his knees and blew out the lantern.

By the time she changed and lay down beside Gid, he was once again breathing the deep breaths of sleep.

If she had to be married to a man who didn't want her, she supposed she could rejoice that he at least loved the Lord enough to talk about the scriptures with her.

Willow turned on her side and tucked her hands beneath her cheek.

Lord, tonight, that's what I choose to rejoice in. Thank You for this man and for his kindness to me. He took me in when he didn't have to. He could have driven off and left me in Independence, so thank You for that, at least.

Only as she was drifting off to sleep did she realize that the very thing she'd just said she was thankful for was the thing she was thinking about throwing away.

Weariness overwhelmed her. She would ponder her problem again tomorrow.

Chapter 22

Tamsyn nearly groaned with relief when the bugle sounded on the second day, and Edi called a loud "Whoa!" to the horses. It seemed to take forever for the wagons to circle up. If her muscles ached from today's jarring ride of only eight miles, how was she going to handle days when they traveled fifteen or more? She might have to leave Edi to drive on his own and join the other women who she'd enviously watched walk along behind the caravan, visiting—and collecting firewood towards evening time.

But how would he handle sitting alone without periodic instructions during the long days ahead? Sometimes his mind wandered, and she feared he might get a notion to pull out of line and start across the prairie to see what some land formation or another looked like up close.

She stood and arched her back to ease some of the tightness. Sakes alive, it felt good to stand!

"Miss, allow me to help you down from there."

She gasped and nearly lost her balance.

Striker Moss stood just below her, holding up his hand to assist her descent.

She quickly surveyed their surroundings, feeling her face heat. There were any other number of women in the wagon train who could have also used some help, but she supposed she was the only one Striker Moss felt the need to keep an eye on—or more to the point, whose brother he was checking up on.

"Edi did a fabulous job today I'll have you know."

From his side of the wagon bench, her brother grinned as he meticulously wrapped the reins around the brake handle just as he'd been taught.

Striker gave a nod, continuing to hold his hand aloft. "Noticed that. Nice job, Edi."

Tamysn hadn't thought it possible for her brother's grin to grow, but it did.

Striker cleared his throat. "If I may be so bold, Miss, Jeremiah and I would love to join you and your brother for supper this evening? I hope that won't be an inconvenience to you?"

Taken aback, she sputtered a stream of nonsensical sounds before finally blurting, "Of course. That would be lovely." Inwardly, she groaned. She'd thought it bad enough to have to satiate Edi's ravenous appetite for six months on the way to Oregon, but would she now be required to feed the two scouts as well? She schooled her features to withhold a wince. She had very carefully calculated the required supplies to keep her and Edi fed. But adding two more mouths would tax those supplies before even half the journey was complete.

"I also hope you won't leave me standing here with my hand in the air for the rest of the evening?" His lazy smile, full of charm, stretched from ear to ear.

Giving him a pinched-lip squint, she leaned over the edge of the wagon and took his hand, intending to jump down as she always did. "I thank you for your consideration, Mr. Moss."

But his grin grew as he transferred her hand to his shoulder and then reached up to settle his large hands about her waist.

Why the nerve of the man! If she didn't need him to be fully on her side for the entirety of this trip, she would give him a piece of her mind about propriety! She bit her tongue to keep quiet. If only she didn't like the feeling of safety and security that his strength lent her—or the feel of his nearness quite so much.

He swung her to the ground and immediately stepped back, tipping his hat.

She retreated and dusted her hands, willing away the awareness of the sheer strength of the handsome scout. "Much obliged."

There. That had been a very polite and acceptable response, despite the irritation swelling through her.

"We're the ones who are obliged, ma'am. I'm sure your cooking will be a sight better than either mine or Jeremiah's."

She kept her face placid, tamping down her irritation once more.

"Now, if you'll show me where you'd like your cookfire built, I'll get it started for you—and fetch the brace of hares that Jeremiah bagged a few miles back."

Her gaze shot to his as surprise widened her eyes.

He grinned, leaned toward her, and offered conspiratorially, "The first law of trail etiquette is never invite yourself to someone's fire without bringing something to contribute." His brown eyes sparkled with mischief.

He'd purposely withheld that information just to see what she would do!

"Jeremiah is taking a moment to fill Cranston in on what we found when we rode ahead today. He'll be along any minute now with the meat." He raised his hand as though in pledge. "Sure as I'm a rascal of the lowest sort."

Biting back a grin lest she encourage his teasing, she smoothed her skirts, scanning the area. She had no idea where the best place to put a cookfire might be. "Uh . . ."

"If I might suggest . . . That dip there." He gestured to a hollowed-out spot in the dirt to the inside of the wagon.

"Y-yes, that will be fine. Thank you."

"Firewood?"

She pressed her hands together to hide her agitation. "I'm afraid I wasn't able to gather any as I needed to stay close to Edi. I will try to do better tomorrow." She glanced around the area of the encampment. She'd heard someone call this place Lone Elm, but she didn't see even one tree standing nearby. Nothing but grass and prairie vetch. "Perhaps we could just do a cold supper from some of my supplies? I'll keep an eye out for wood tomorrow as we travel."

"Nothing doing. A man needs meat after such a long day, doesn't he Edi?"

Edi nodded from the spot where he'd started to unhitch the team. "I like meat!"

Striker grinned at Tamsyn. "There, you see. We must cook the hares. Give me a minute to fetch some wood from my wagon. I'd heard it was mighty scarce at this camp. Future camps should offer better fuel."

He jogged off and, true to his word, returned a few moments later with an armful of logs and one very large branch trailing behind him.

Tamsyn couldn't help a chuckle. "Where did you find all that?"

He dropped the armful of wood near the place he'd said would make a good firepit. "I have a compartment under my wagon that can open on one end. It's made for tossing in wood as I find it."

She hadn't realized he had a wagon. "Aren't you out scouting most of the day? Who drives your wagon?"

He spoke as he formed a teepee of bark in the dip. "Edi, best you get those cattle on to the creek there. They'll be thirsty after such a long day."

"Edi thirsty too!" her brother groused.

Tamsyn hurried to fetch the canteen from beneath the wagon seat where she'd hoped it would stay as cool as possible. "Here, Edi. Take a drink first. But then water the oxen, okay? After that, drive them back here because we need to turn them loose in the grass here in the middle of the wagons."

Her brother guzzled thirstily, and only after he'd driven the six cattle off toward the creek did Striker speak again. He looked up at her with one of his forearms resting on one knee. "Best you take a drink yourself. Sitting in the hot sun all day can tax a body."

Biting back a retort about how she was more than capable of taking care of herself, Tamsyn lifted the canteen her brother had just drained dry. "I'll have to fetch more water from the creek." She would need to fill the canteen in a few minutes after she moved upstream away from where the thirsty cattle were stirring the creek into a muddy cascade.

Without a word, Striker rose and stalked off.

Tamsyn frowned at the half-built fire that he hadn't even lit yet, wondering what she'd said. But before she could decide what to do, he was back and thrusting a canteen into her hands.

"Go on and quench your thirst."

She wanted to protest that she was fine, but she figured silence was the better part of valor. She opened his canteen and took several hearty swallows, then wiped the mouth of it with her sleeve and handed it back. "Thank you." She did have to admit that it was lovely to have someone think about her needs for a change.

He accepted it with a nod and drank several swallows himself before recapping the canteen and setting it on the wagon's bench. He then returned to his task with the fire. "I hired a man to drive my wagon. I've scouted for several wagon trains now, but this one will be my last. I already got a section of land in Oregon, and I plan to settle down, build a cabin, and start a ranch."

"Once you are given a tract of land, don't you have to live on it to prove up?"

He nodded and struck a match. Blew on the small flame as it licked hungrily at the dry grass he had wadded into the hollow beneath the teepee of dry wood. "You do. My little brother and two of my cousins are all out there now. We needed a little more money to get a herd going so . . ." He shrugged. "I'm doing what I can."

Tamsyn hung her canteen from the arm of the wagon's bench. "So your ranch will be a joint effort with these other men?"

He nodded and adjusted the position of the logs.

Gracious! The way he moved those logs with his bare hand, he was going to come away burnt for certain!

But he didn't seem concerned about his hands as he said, "Sure will. The way we see it, pooling our land and resources will help us all get to ranching four times faster and with four times the help."

Once the fire was going, he motioned for her to follow and strode to the back of the wagon, where he lowered the tailgate. He patted it with one palm. "Makes a right good countertop for food preparations."

Tamsyn offered her thanks, but she couldn't help wondering why he was being so kind to her. She dared not explore the question further. Even though he wasn't close enough to breach propriety this time, she took a step away, feeling the need for more distance between them.

Knowing Edi would want coffee and expect dessert with his dinner, she rolled up her sleeves and dug out the apron from the foodstuffs box.

As she hung the apron around her neck and started dinner preparations, she studied her surroundings.

Tonight, the dusty blue sky brought to mind a sea of sun-bleached cornflowers. The sun, a golden orb of calendula, hung low on the horizon. And the small tufts of clouds, turned pink by the setting sun, could be pink astilbe like she'd planted in the garden back home.

She fetched Striker's canteen and worked some water into the flour, salt, and lard, trying not to think about how much she missed that garden. When they got to Oregon and Edi got his land, she would plant herself another. She'd brought plenty of seeds.

Once the dough was thoroughly kneaded and resting, she dusted her hands and lifted the lid on the box on the side of the wagon. She had invested in a cooking station, but now she wished the box on the wagon wasn't so high. That cast iron was heavy, and it was hard to get a good grip and lift it out at such an angle! She grunted and stood on her tiptoes to get a better grip. If the unit helped her cook half as well as it was heavy, it should do a fine job.

Made of two double tripods connected by a bar, the unit stood like a tent over the open flames. From the center of each tripod a chain hung to support a level grate. Included with the cooking station were a cast iron frying pan, a set of three dutch ovens that could be stacked on each other—each with lids formed to hold hot coals so a cooking tower of sorts could be formed, and a cast iron coffee pot. Any of the pots could rest on the grates or be hung from the central bar by chains and hooks.

As she tried to tug them out, two of the metal bars smashed together, catching her finger in between, and she hissed out a gasp and shoved the throbbing knuckle into her mouth. If she were going to cook with the blasted thing, she first had to get it set up over the fire.

She stood as tall as she could and reached for it again.

"I'll get that for you." Striker appeared at her side.

She jumped back and smoothed her hands down her skirt. She massaged her still throbbing knuckle with her thumb. "Thank you. I'll just finish preparing the food while you set it up. If you could just put the two biggest dutch ovens on the tailgate, I'd appreciate it."

"My pleasure."

She felt, more than saw, him touch the brim of his hat before she scurried back to mix her dumplings and chop the potatoes and carrots.

She was out of water now and there was nothing for it but to go fetch some. Since they were near a creek, she ought to use that water instead of what was in the barrel on the side of the wagon. It was her understanding from all the journals she'd read that sometimes they would camp in a place that had no water. The water barrel would best be saved for those nights.

She took up both canteens and headed toward the creek, passing by Edi as he returned with the watered cattle. "Good job, Edi. Drive them through that gap"—she pointed—"into the center of the wagon circle and then see if Mr. Moss needs any help. I'll be right back with water."

"Okay." He touched one of the cows with his big broad hand. "Come on, Bessy."

Tamsyn almost choked on the laugh she tried to swallow. The steer would likely be highly offended to be given such a feminine name if the poor dumb beast could understand.

The water of the creek flowed smooth and clear and how she wished for a moment to soak her feet, but there was no time for that with dinner needing to be cooked. By the time she got back, the pans were set out for her on the tailgate. Edi didn't like to be kept waiting, so she hurriedly dropped some bacon grease into the largest of the ovens and scooped the onions, potatoes, garlic, and carrots in on top. She covered it all with water and sprinkled in some salt and thyme for good measure. She lined the other dutch oven with half the pie dough, filled it with chopped apples, and topped it with the remainder of the dough. The fresh apples wouldn't last out the week. Then what was she going to bake to make Edi happy? She pressed that worry aside for another day.

Bent slightly to carry the heavy cast iron, she hurried to the fire. Jeremiah must have come by because a pair of rabbits had been spitted over the flames. She gave them a quarter turn and hung the vegetables beside them over the hottest part of the flames, then set the apple tart off to one side. She would need to remember to turn that every few minutes to keep it from burning. She rushed back to the tailgate to do a little cleanup and to gather plates and forks.

When she turned, Striker was standing in her path. "Heavens!" She almost dropped the enamelware, and the forks clattered loudly against the metal. How did he appear without a sound?

He raised his palm. "Sorry about that. Just wanted to see if you needed any more help?"

"No. I think it's just a matter of waiting for things to cook now."

"All right. Jeremiah and I will be back in time to eat. We have to ride out for one more quick scout around the area. Have Edi help you do any heavy lifting, huh?"

She frowned. She'd been taking care of herself long before he came around. "We'll be fine. Thank you. See you soon."

She hurried toward the fire but was well aware of him walking to his paint and mounting up. She heard the sound of his horse's hoofbeats fading into the sunset and prayed that he and Jeremiah would be safe.

She wrinkled her nose at herself. This was no good—no good at all. Becoming attached to a man would only set her up for disappointment. They would have to part ways at some point, and the last thing she needed while taking care of Edi was to tend to a broken heart.

Okay then.

No more thinking of Mr. Moss. No more hoping that he would be safe. No more praying for him—at least not with such concern filling her heart.

As she set the plates and utensils on a rock near the fire, she angled a glance at the sky that had transformed from sun-bleached cornflowers to deep blue delphinium.

Lord, I would appreciate a little help on that score. Don't I have burdens enough? Please help me avoid a broken heart on top of it all.

The heavens rang with silence.

Tamsyn pressed her lips together and gave the brace of hares another turn. She smiled at Edi when he tromped up to the fire and collapsed into a heap on a barrel one of the men must have rolled near.

"Edi hungry!" he snapped.

Tamsyn sighed. "I know, Edi. Just a little while longer. We can't eat it raw. Why don't you walk around and see if you can find us some firewood?"

His brow slumped lower as Tamsyn scrambled to turn the pie a quarter turn. But he did get up and stalk off into the golden gloam that had settled over the prairie.

It was good they'd had a shorter day, but she feared that Edi had just enough energy left to be irritable, and she was probably going to catch the brunt of it.

She only hoped the scouts wouldn't be around to see it.

Chapter 23

Adam felt every one of his twenty-eight years as he swung down from the wagon bench with his hand throbbing as though it had been set afire rather than just touching something that was.

Eden had chosen to walk along behind the wagons for the past several hours and now he found himself looking intently for the women on the trail behind them.

Indians wouldn't try to attack them, would they?

Most reports that he'd read spoke of the Indians being peaceable, but there had been that Cayuse attack on the Whitman Mission a few years back—the results of which were still causing conflict in the Oregon Territory, from what he understood. And the Battle of Coon Creek far to the south just the year after that, where a troop of soldiers had been attacked by Comanche and Apache Indians.

Despite his love for the Native Americans he was called to reach, he wasn't naïve. Settlers coming in and demanding land that the Indians had claimed as their own for hundreds of years created a situation fraught with tension that was bound to explode from time to time. Also, since their exposure to diseases was different than the settlers, they didn't have the ability to fight off some of the sicknesses travelers were bound to bring with them.

The first group of women straggled into the circle of wagons on the far side, and Eden was . . .

There! *Thank You, Lord.*

She held something in the swoop of her apron with one hand and struggled with the other to tuck some stray strands of hair into the blond braid wrapped around her head as she paused to speak to a woman. After a few moments of conversation, Eden smiled and gave the woman a one-armed hug, then they parted and she sauntered his way.

Since she still seemed unaware of his scrutiny, he let his gaze linger on his wife. His *wife.* He was still trying to comprehend the miracle that had brought her to him in the nick of time. If she'd come even a day later, they would have been gone. Would she have followed all the way to the Territory on her own?

With all the busyness of the last few days, they really hadn't had a chance to talk much yet. The evening before, she'd asked him to stay in the wagon with her, and the pleading in her eyes had almost been his undoing, but he'd held to his decision and fought the cold and the bugs on the grass beneath instead. Because the moment he'd seen her standing in the street back there in Independence, he'd promised himself that she would not fall with child again until they reached the Territory and had a qualified doctor nearby. And that meant he needed to keep himself occupied and as far from her as possible.

As though sensing his study, she turned and lifted a wave of greeting. He returned the gesture and then pivoted to unhitch the team.

His hand throbbed and the thick bandage that was now brown with dust made his fingers nearly useless. One of the oxen shifted and almost stepped on his foot as he fumbled to pull the pin on the yoke.

"Here, Adam, let me help." Eden spoke from beside him.

He opened his mouth to decline, but she'd already bumped him aside, and the press of her hip against his own had him clamping his teeth tightly enough to prevent speech.

She must have left whatever had been in her apron at the back of the wagon because her hands were now free.

Standing on her tiptoes to reach the pin, she said, "I had a lovely afternoon walking and talking with the ladies. I even found some wild mushrooms growing when we walked through that shady glen a few miles back. And don't worry, Cook was very careful to teach me the things to look for in a poisonous mushroom. These are not colored, nor did they turn blue or yellow when broken open. They don't have white gills, nor do they have a—" She took one glance at his face and fell silent.

Maybe he hadn't done such a good job of disguising his aversion to mushrooms. "Sorry. I'm not much for mushrooms, poisonous or otherwise."

Eden nodded and moved to the other side of the yoke. "Yes, I remember that now."

The ox bellowed at the unfamiliar feel of her skirts, but Eden patted his cheek. "There, big fellow. Best we get used to each other, you and I, hmmm?" She hefted the yoke.

"Eden, it's too heavy for you," he protested.

But she only gave him a deprecating look. "Nonsense. But I will let you lead them to water while I get dinner started," she ended with a wink.

A wink!

He scrubbed two fingers at the rapid tattoo of his pounding heart. Willing himself not to put too much hope in her transformed attitude. When they were first married, she'd . . . struggled to fit into the life of a working man. He'd often cooked his own breakfasts, which he honestly hadn't minded. But when she'd begun to let the garden go and then the housework, his concern had prompted him to speak to her about it. And to her credit, she'd stepped up and done her best to learn what she needed to do.

And then they'd lost the baby, which had sent her running straight back to her parents.

His jaw ached, and he realized that he was in danger of cracking a tooth if he didn't loosen it. Hauling in a huge breath, he worked to relax the tension in his chest with a long slow exhale.

By the time he returned and staked the watered stock where they could graze in the corral of wagons, Eden had a pot of soup bubbling over the fire and what smelled like cornbread baking in the coals. His stomach rumbled loudly at the delectable scent.

"Smells wonderful." Using his good hand, he scooped some water from the bucket Eden had placed on the tailgate and sluiced it over his face, flinging it free as best he could.

Beside him, his wife giggled.

It was a sound that he used to take for granted. A sound that filled him with contentment and nostalgia. He cut his eyes in her direction only to find that she was giggling at him. "What?"

She stepped nearer and he steeled himself not to flinch at her touch as she took up the corner of her apron and rose on her tiptoes to wipe his face. "You just have a few . . . smears . . . is all. We'll pretend it's not mud running down your face." She wrinkled her nose and held up the corner of her apron for him to see the dirt she'd wiped free.

Problem was, he was having trouble looking anywhere but into those captivating blue eyes of hers.

She rolled her lips in and pressed them into a tight line, batting her eyelashes at him coyly.

An invitation if ever he'd seen one.

She dropped the corner of her apron and settled her hand against his side.

Adam lurched back and used his sleeve to swipe at another rivulet he could feel streaking down his temple. "Sorry about that. I'd give anything to find a good watering hole for a bath, but—" he lifted his bandaged hand "—the doc said not to get this wet for a few days."

"Speaking of which . . ." Eden motioned to a spot in the shade of the wagon. "Best you sit and let me have a look and bandage that with clean cloths."

Adam swallowed, wishing that redoing the bandage was a task he could competently do on his own but knowing it was not. He would just have to find enough resolve to resist the temptation of her touch, the lure of her invitations, and her consarned batting eyelashes.

Willow pressed her hands into the ache of her lower back as she studied the golden wash of the sunset. She had come out to look for firewood, but enjoying this beauty for a few minutes wouldn't hurt.

Maybe it would help her mind to settle.

All day, she'd been warring with herself over the choice she needed to make. Continue west toward the setting sun with Gid? Or go back to Independence and try to make a life for herself there?

She'd settled on one option or the other more times than she could count, and each time, she came up with a reason to reverse her decision.

She held one hand to shade her eyes as the bright globe of the sun touched the horizon and shot brilliant light across the skyline. Golds began to meld into pinks and peaches. Her heart ached at the beauty of it.

With a sigh, she turned her attention to her task. Firewood had been scarce nearer to the wagons. She bent to pluck a twig from the ground, twirling it between her fingers before she tossed it to one side.

She skirted around a lilac bush, flush with the tight buds of spring, and finally found a larger branch that would do nicely for burning. She tucked it into the crook of one arm.

Not far away, she saw Edi, hunched and searching the ground like she was. He glanced her way, and she waved at him. He lifted a hand, gave her a shy smile, and quickly returned to his task.

He stooped and reached for something but froze, arm extended. Something about his immediate stillness raised the hair on the back of Willow's neck.

"What is it?" she called.

Edi remained frozen, his gaze fixed steadily on the ground before him, and his arm still outstretched.

Willow lifted her skirts with one hand and gripped the piece of wood like a club in the other as she slowly approached him.

She heard the chilling sound before she saw the danger that had frozen Edi in place. A rattler! The warning rattle sent a chill up Willow's spine. She pushed down panic and willed herself to breathe calmly.

Edi remained bent with his unmoving hand only a foot from the snake's beady eyes and flicking tongue.

"Don't move, Edi. Don't move."

Thankfully, he already seemed to know not to move.

What was she going to do? She glanced toward the wagons. Too far. By the time she ran back to the wagons and fetched someone, Edi could already be bitten! She was the only one who could do anything about this!

Willow swallowed. She must be strong. Please, Lord, don't let me get Edi killed.

She angled herself so that she would approach from behind the snake, which seemed to have its full attention on Edi.

Her palms were slick with moisture, and the branch, her only weapon, trembled in her hand. Pausing a ways behind the snake, she stretched the piece of wood out, but it was too short. She had to get closer.

Her knees felt about as sturdy as the swaying grasses all around her. Did snakes travel in packs? She tucked her lower lip between her teeth, wishing she hadn't thought of that!

It was impossible to walk silently with her skirts sweeping against the prairie grasses.

The snake heard her coming, and now its head wavered and twisted to eye both her and Edi. When Willow froze, the snake returned its slitted gaze to Edi.

One more step . . .

Willow's foot came down on a bit of dry brush, and the rattler hissed.

Mouth dry, she paused behind the snake and adjusted her grip on the club. She must be fast. Her aim must be true!

She kept her voice soft as she inched closer. "Edi, I'm almost set. You jump back as soon as I swing, okay? Just in case I miss." Her nose wrinkled. She hadn't meant to say that last part out loud.

"Don't miss," he whispered, continuing to hold himself steady.

Right. So much easier said than done.

Willow leaned forward, keeping her attention fixed on the snake's head. Its tail vibrated another warning. Its head writhed through the air, tongue flicking.

The grating sound of the rattle set her teeth together. She assessed the length of her club again.

Just another inch. She scooted forward.

The snake coiled tighter. Raised its head higher. Reared back to strike!

Willow swung!

Edi lurched away. He tripped and landed on his back!

Willow's stick connected with the snake just below its head. The impact lifted the creature out of its trajectory and sent it careening through the air headfirst, followed by the branch.

The snake landed with a whump, and the firewood crunched end over end through the grass in the distance. The sound of the snake slithering away sent a shiver up Willow's spine.

She hurried forward to offer Edi her hand. "Are you okay?"

He let her haul him up and then enveloped her in a crushing hug that lifted her off her feet.

She giggled and fought for a breath. "I'll take that as a yes. Okay, Edi, okay. You can put me down now, please."

"You saved me!" He set her down and thumped her shoulder so hard that Willow wondered if she would have a bruise.

She rubbed the spot and took a retreating step from his exuberant gratefulness. "I didn't do anything that anyone else wouldn't have done." She smiled at him. "I'm glad you're okay, Edi."

"Willow?"

"Edi!"

Gideon and Tamsyn charged toward them from the direction of the wagons.

Gid searched her from head to toe, and from his expression, it was clear that he must have seen at least the last moments of her ordeal. He narrowed a suspicious glance at Edi even as he spoke to her. "What happened?"

Willow wrapped her arms around herself. "We were gathering wood. And there was a rattler." She jutted her chin to where the snake had slithered off.

"She saved me!" Edi proclaimed to his sister.

Tamsyn tucked her arm into her brother's and gave Willow a heartfelt look. "Thank you so much!"

Willow shook her head. "It was nothing."

She felt the tremor of the lie course through her as Tamsyn nudged her brother back toward the wagons.

"Come on, Edi. Dinner is ready."

"She didn't miss." Edi glanced back at her, a bit wide-eyed.

A nervous chuckle escaped her. She gave Gid a smile. "I was strong. I didn't miss."

He blew out a breath and settled one hand to squeeze her shoulder. "I've no doubt that you were strong. I'm glad you're not hurt. Come on. Let's get some dinner."

Willow scrunched her nose. "We still need wood."

Gid laughed. "Since it seems that I can't leave you alone even for a moment, I'll help."

Chapter 24

Gideon glared at the canvas overhead long into the night, the words he'd spoken to Willow about focusing on the eternal eating at him. How he wished that his own beliefs weren't coming back to haunt him. Sure, it was one thing to believe that his niece and sister, along with his wife and baby, were in a better place—and he truly did. But it was another to realize that despite the heartache he'd experienced, the Lord had seen him through those times of loss and that there was no sense in hardening his heart to the joys of love again.

Why hadn't he kept his mouth shut? It was one thing to know the truth and quite another to be willing to risk such pain again in the future. He may have made it through that dark valley, but that didn't mean he wanted to experience such heartbreak again.

Beside him, Willow stirred and loosed a soft whimper in her sleep. He turned on his side and settled one hand on her shoulder. His touch seemed to soothe her, for she released a long sigh and turned her face toward him, her breaths coming easier now.

He withdrew his hand, but only far enough to capture one of her soft tresses. He stroked his thumb over the silken smoothness of it in the dark.

Today, if that snake . . . He frowned and tore his thoughts from what might have happened.

Lord, haven't I lost enough?

Of course, freeing himself to love Willow didn't guarantee him pain and heartache in the future. The Lord might see fit to protect her and keep her safe, but He might also see fit to test Gideon's faithfulness.

Again.

Unbidden, Wayne's voice drifted into his mind. *You can do all things through Christ, who gives you strength.* The last words he'd spoken to his daughter now echoed in Gideon's mind.

What did those verses mean? Surely not that he could snap his fingers and never experience heartache again. Nor that he could demand that God never let anything bad happen to Willow.

Paul, after all, had penned the words from a jail cell. And they were spoken in the context of being content whether he had much or little.

Can do all things . . .

All things like finding the capacity to make right choices even when wrong choices were easier. He hadn't wanted to marry Willow—not because he wasn't attracted to her, but because he feared the future. Yet, he'd somehow found the strength to do the right thing despite himself.

And now . . .

His heart hammered with dread and yet a parallel excitement.

He could choose to love his wife. He knew that would be the right thing to do, and God would give him the strength if he asked for it.

He swallowed in the darkness. *Lord, You know this fear that fills me each time I think of how it would feel to lose her . . .*

His mind froze on a thought, and his hands fisted into the quilt.

He'd already come to the realization that he'd fallen in love with her. And here he was dreading the prospect of being in love rather than enjoying the pleasures of it for whatever time God granted him with his wife.

Rejoice always.

He bit back a groan and flopped down to stare into the expanse of darkness overhead once again.

Lord, aren't You asking too much of me? I never want to lose my faith in You, and I fear what might happen if I experience such heartache ever again.

Verses that he knew well from the next section in the chapter Willow had read flooded his mind.

Be anxious for nothing, but in everything by prayer and supplication, with thanksgiving, let your requests be made known to God; and the peace of God, which surpasses all understanding, will guard your hearts and minds through Christ Jesus.

A sob caught him unaware in the darkness. He pressed a hand to his eyes and blew out all his anxiety on a long, slow breath.

Okay, Lord. Please help me. Help me to love her with everything in me and help me to trust You with the future. Protect her. Keep her safe. But help me to have faith no matter what comes.

And just like that, a warm love flooded his heart and filled him with peace. He would be okay. God would see him through no matter what came his way.

He turned his head and glanced at the shadow he knew to be Willow. He could hear her slow and steady breaths and see the outline of one shoulder rising and falling with the cadence.

Relief rushed through him. This place of resting in the Lord, this perfect peace, this was what he'd been missing for so many months.

Lord, help Willow find her way through this sea of grief that I know threatens to overwhelm her right now. It would be wonderful if You could help her learn to love me as much as I suddenly realize that I love her.

Love . . . He smiled in the darkness.

He ought to tell her, yet she was in no place to hear the words. Maybe in a few weeks, once she'd passed through the deepest of the grief over her father. Until then, he needed to keep this revelation to himself. He didn't want to overwhelm her with emotions to sort through while she was still trying to grieve for her father.

Willow woke the next morning to find Gideon in a lighter mood. He smiled and laughed and even teased her by stealing her cup of coffee when she wasn't looking and then, when she set about to look for it, producing it from behind his back.

She gave him a mock glower and plucked the cup from his fingers, to which he only laughed unrepentantly, started off to fetch the oxen, and lifted a hand of farewell over his shoulder.

As she watched him walk away, Willow sighed. Moments like these made her wonder if they could make a go of it. Maybe Gideon could learn to love her?

But did she want a man who forced himself to love her because he had no other choice? And did she want to be such a burden to Gideon? The woman he didn't want but was stuck with because of his good nature?

The sun lit the eastern horizon with a golden wash sure to fill the day with suffocating heat. Yet eastward was where home lay. It could be home once again if she chose it.

With a sigh she watched Gideon returning with six of his oxen. He spoke softly to the creatures, and they seemed content to do his bidding.

She really ought to free him. What was holding her back?

She glanced toward the east once more, but this time it was the expanse of empty land that drew her attention. Thoughts of the Indians that had accosted them on the prairie filled her mind. If she was going to return, she would need an escort. That was all that held her back.

An urge to do so quickly filled her. She was growing to feel too much for Gideon. If she didn't make the decision soon, she wouldn't be able to make it at all because her heart would tether her to the man tighter than the water barrel was tied to the wagon.

At the next settlement, then.

She would find someone to help her get back to Independence. Until then, it was best she not say anything to Gideon. He would likely be relieved to be shut of her, but there was no sense in telling him too early because then he might ask questions that she didn't have answers to.

Like how she would support herself.

She swallowed and turned her gaze to the brazen sky. *Lord, that's the right thing to do, right? Let Gideon go? I'm trying to do as Your Word says and rejoice and I'm finding it hard. If I go on with Gideon, I'll struggle to rejoice because he doesn't love me. And if I go back to Independence, I'll struggle to rejoice because Papa is gone, and life won't be the same. I don't know what to do. Please show me what to do.*

Somewhere in the back of her mind rang the reminder that she'd spoken vows. But surely their situation was unusual enough that she shouldn't be held to them. She'd been reeling from Papa's death. Not thinking things through clearly. And yet . . . Was that reason enough to break her vow?

As though the brass dome of the heavens had bounced her prayer right back to her, no answer seemed to be the right one.

She sighed and set about packing up the breakfast things. If neither answer seemed like the right one, she would choose to go back home. At least things there would be familiar, and she wouldn't feel like she was consigning Gideon to live with a woman he didn't want.

She tried not to think about how leaving him would add another layer of grief to her upturned life. Better do it now while she was already in turmoil. Then she could do all her healing at once.

She gave a short nod. Good. The decision was made. Now she simply had to figure out a way to let Gideon know that he would be a free man.

Corbin Donahue stood in the brush to one side of Gideon Riley's wagon and watched Willow. She hadn't seen him yet because he'd approached with the water bucket through the tall brush from the creek. She seemed to be deep in thought about something. Kept looking toward the sunrise and then back toward where Riley was probably fetching his oxen for his wagon.

Corbin ground his teeth. He should have fought harder. Made himself more indispensable. Of course, if her old man hadn't died, things would have gone better for him, he felt sure. Too bad the man had been so weak.

He was trying not to live in the regret of the past. However, even he would have to admit to himself that he was struggling to accomplish that.

Which was what had brought him here this morning. The next step on the way to the completion of his plan. It was too soon. But things could be explained away. And he didn't want to wait another day.

Clearing his throat, he stepped forward. "Good morning."

Willow spun toward him, causing the hem of her skirt to flair for the briefest of moments. "Oh. Good morning. How can I help you?"

She tossed a glance toward where he presumed Gideon stood, though he'd purposely kept the wagon between himself and the man so that his scrutiny of Willow would go unnoticed. She was a comely woman, and he hadn't wanted his perusal to be interrupted.

Corbin pushed away thoughts of her beauty. He had to keep his mind on his task and not make her feel uncomfortable.

He lifted the bucket. "Watered my stock and refilled my water barrel. Wondered if you could use some more water for yours?"

She tilted her head and seemed perplexed by his offer. Her gaze lowered to the bucket.

He held his breath. Was she going to send him packing? If so, he would have to devise a different plan.

"I suppose we could. Thank you." Her lips lifted in the barest of smiles.

But that minuscule smile, along with her acceptance of his offer, sent his heart soaring. Carefully he kept all his exuberance from his features and only gave her a genteel nod. "Good. Carry on, and I'll just make sure your barrel is full to the brim."

"That's very kind of you. Thank you for your thoughtfulness."

Had that been a touch of hesitation in her tone?

Corbin pushed that worry away. The important thing was that she'd said yes. Of course, he couldn't poison the whole water barrel. He needed the dosage to be concentrated, and he also didn't want to injure Willow, nor the animals for that matter. But this would give him the opening he needed to get close enough to Gideon to finish him off without drawing suspicion on himself.

He was simply being neighborly, after all. If he himself complained about a bit of a stomach bug at the same time as Gideon started having stomach trouble, no one would suspect that Corbin had anything to do with it. Finishing off the minister's wife would also lend credence to his story. No one would suspect the real connection between the three of them getting sick all at once. He'd already visited their wagon this morning and snuck the arsenic into the coffee cup he'd seen her set on the tailgate of their wagon as she had her back to him while she packed up their breakfast things. All it would take would be one more swallow of the coffee, and she would join Gideon in feeling sick for a few days before passing from this life.

His conscience panged him, for she seemed like a nice enough woman. But she'd seen too much. Not only that, but she'd spoken of what she'd seen and there had been something in the way she'd looked at him when the sunlight had reflected off his cufflink. Had it triggered a memory for her?

He shook his head. It didn't matter. She was already taken care of, and now he needed to see to Gideon.

He lifted the lid from the Rileys' water barrel and carefully poured his bucket inside, then headed off to the creek for more, whistling as he went.

It was good for people to see that he was willing to work on behalf of others. He waved grandly to the black scout who stood talking with the half-breed, careful to keep his disgust from his features. Such men should not be allowed in positions of power.

Once he gained control, he would do everything he could to amend that.

Gideon placed the last pin into the third yolk that tethered the oxen to his wagon. The injured ox's shoulder had looked much improved this morning, which filled him with relief. He would give the beast a few days to rest and heal, and then it could resume its duties. Thankfully, Wayne had encouraged both him and Micah to buy two full teams. They'd thought it unnecessary, but now, only a day out, he was thankful for the advice.

He rested one hand on the nigh ox and tipped his face to the rising sun. His heart felt light, happy, carefree.

A honeybee droned near his head, and he brushed it away. Overhead, a vee of geese squabbled as they flapped their way north. One dilatory gander trailed at the end of one side of the vee as though he might be having trouble keeping up. Small patches of clouds shone gold against the lighter bronze of the sky.

Gid smiled. It was going to be a glorious day.

With satisfaction coursing through him, he gave the ox a pat and turned.

He stilled.

Hoyt Harrington approached with a tin cup of water in one hand and a bucket of water in the other. He smiled and stretched out the mug. "Listen, I just wanted to say no hard feelings about Willow. I'm not the kind to hold ought against another man for winning the hand of a fair maiden." He winked. "I finished watering my own stock and spoke to your wife, and she said you all would be happy for the help. I've filled your water barrel and thought I could water your stock?"

Gideon shook his head, even as he accepted the cup of water. "Already watered the stock but thank you for this." He lifted the cup in a little salute. "Been meaning to talk to you about Wayne's wagon. I know Cranston gave you his spot and that her uncle sold you her pa's wagon. But I wondered if you'd found anything inside that might belong to Willow? Wasn't sure if her pa may have packed some of her things without her knowing? She lost everything in the fire, as you know." He twisted the cup in his fingers as he waited for a response.

Harrington seemed to ponder thoughtfully, his gaze fixed on the cup in Gideon's hands. "Can't rightly say that I've poked through the crates in there too much. I'll try to take a look tonight." He offered a smile.

"All right. Thank you."

"Of course. Not a problem." He stretched out his hand. "If you want to down that water, I'll return the cup to your wife for washing."

Chapter 25

Corbin held his breath as Gideon gave him a nod and started to lift the cup.

The clatter of hoofbeats drew their attention to a group of riders galloping into the center of the wagon circle.

Gideon Riley lifted his gaze and lowered the cup.

Corbin cursed his luck, and then he felt the bottom drop out of his stomach as the rays of the early morning sun glinted off the badge pinned to the lead rider's chest.

Willow appeared by Gideon's side. "That's the sheriff from Independence and his deputy."

Gideon nodded to where the two men were just dismounting. "I'll go see why they're here." He tossed the water and thrust the cup into her hands.

Corbin almost cursed aloud. He bit his tongue just in time. Sunlight reflected off a droplet that clung to the rim of the cup as though to taunt him.

"Wait for me." Willow set the empty cup on the wagon bench and hurried in her husband's wake.

Corbin closed his eyes in defeat, and then his chin shot up! The minister's wife!

If it were to be believed that it was the local water making people sick and that Gideon and the minister's wife had been the ones to succumb, it all needed to happen at once! He dashed back toward the minister's wagon, hoping upon hope that the woman hadn't already drunk the dregs from her mug.

Eden was halfway to the trickle of water the wagon folk had been generously calling a creek when a yawn reminded her that she'd left her coffee cup on the tailgate of the wagon. With a sigh, she tucked the tub of dishes against her hip and returned to the rear of their wagon to fetch it. She frowned at the mug that lay turned on its side and the brown stain that puddled across the boards of the tailgate.

Misery and depression!

She'd spilled it? She felt certain that the cup had been upright the last time she'd seen it. Too bad she'd already tossed the dregs of what was in the pot. And even more upsetting was the fact that she'd put a whole teaspoon of sugar in that coffee. What a waste!

She stifled another yawn.

It was cold and lonely in the wagon all by herself at night. She hadn't slept well the night before for wishing that Adam wasn't being so stubborn about her return. She could tell that he was still in love with her by the look she caught in his eyes sometimes when he didn't realize he watched her.

She sighed, picked up the mug, and dropped it in with the other dishes. So far, she hadn't been able to break through his wary distrust. Just recompense, she supposed, for her own stupidity.

A commotion drew her attention to the middle of the wagon circle, and she saw Mr. Harrington striding toward two riders who must have just dismounted from the two horses she could see above the heads of those gathering.

With a frown, Eden set the tub on the wagon's tailgate and followed in his footsteps to see what might be happening. As soon as she learned who the new men were, she could wash the dishes.

Willow's heart hammered as she hurried to catch up with Gideon and find out why the Sheriff was here. Surely he wouldn't have ridden all the way out here if he didn't have news.

And yet, that wasn't the only thing that had her heart pounding. This was her opportunity. This had to be an answer to her earlier prayer, right?

The perfect escort back to Independence. Gideon wouldn't be able to protest that the sheriff and his deputy wouldn't be able to protect her.

Somehow, she had to make this work!

Standing at the center of the still-gathering crowd, the sheriff was already speaking when she stopped by Gideon's side. ". . . soon as everyone gathers 'round."

Willow nudged Gideon with the back of her hand. "What did he say?"

He leaned closer. "Said he has something to show all of us as soon as everyone has gathered around." He studied her thoughtfully. "You look pale beneath that sunburn. You doing okay?"

Her hands trembled as she clasped them before her. There was no time like the present to tell him her wishes. She opened her mouth but then closed it again. There were simply too many people nearby for this conversation. She tried to look him in the eye but couldn't manage to hold his gaze. "I'm fine."

She felt his searching look drilling into her as she concentrated on massaging the fleshy part of her left hand with the fingers and thumb of her right.

"Willow—"

"Now that most of you are gathered," the sheriff spoke over top of Gideon, much to Willow's relief.

Going back was what she really wanted, wasn't it? Shouldn't she feel more at ease if that was the right thing? She shook away the concern and focused on the sheriff.

"As all of you know, I've been investigating the big fire that happened back in town just before you all pulled out." His gaze landed on Willow with brief sympathy as he shoved his hand into the pocket of his vest, withdrew an object, and thrust it high into the air. "A day ago, we found this. And our investigation leads us to believe that it belongs to someone in this wagon train. Does anyone know who it might belong to?"

Willow squinted to see the tiny object he held aloft as Eden stopped beside her.

"What's happening?" the parson's wife asked.

Willow gestured. "He wants to know if any of us know who that belongs to." She leaned forward, trying to see the small piece that the sheriff held between his thumb and forefinger as he twirled in the center of those gathered so all could see it. He held it close to each person in turn, and each person shook their head.

Until Eden.

When the sheriff came to Eden, she gasped as soon as her eyes settled on the item that Willow could now see was a bit of metal. She bounced a glance from it to Eden's horror-struck face and back before she leaned to examine it more closely.

It looked like a large silver button inlaid with mother-of-pearl, only it had a stud protruding from the back of it. A man's cufflink, except it was missing the crossbar that would hold it in the buttonhole.

"Ma'am?" The sheriff hadn't taken his eyes off Eden. "Do you know anything about this?"

Eden clutched at the lace of her blouse's high collar, her gaze traversing the circle until it paused somewhere in the section that the sheriff hadn't yet had a chance to show the piece to.

Willow followed her gaze to Hoyt Harrington and felt her heartbeat begin to pound in her chest. What did this mean?

She glanced back at Eden, waiting for her to speak.

Eden swallowed and opened her mouth.

But before she could speak, Mr. Harrington stepped forward. "May I see that, Sheriff?"

Surprised, the sheriff turned toward him, holding the piece of jewelry in his palm.

"You found it!" Hoyt exclaimed. He thrust out one of his arms for the sheriff to see what Willow presumed must be a matching link on one of his sleeves. "I noticed just the other day that one of mine went missing, and I was so disappointed. My grandfather gave them to me, you see."

Both the sheriff and his deputy stiffened.

The deputy settled one hand on the butt of his pistol.

The sheriff said, "So you don't deny that this is your cufflink?"

Willow shifted forward, not wanting to miss a word of the exchange.

Hoyt shook his head. "No, sir. As you can see . . ." He thrust his arm out again. "It's a match to the one I'm wearing."

The sheriff and his deputy exchanged a look, and Willow tried to follow what was happening.

"Where did you find that?" she blurted before she could stop herself.

Hoyt relaxed into his heels and curved his hands around his elbows. "They found it in the ashes, of course, and were hoping that it would lead them to someone who may have started the fire."

Willow darted her scrutiny to the sheriff's face. Was that true?

"Actually," the sheriff said as he yanked a pair of clanking metal bracelets from his belt, and his deputy drew his gun and leveled it on Hoyt, "we found it behind the store, not even anywhere near the ashes. Now what were you doing back there, Mr. . . . Harrington is it? I believe that's what Grant Moore said your name was."

Mr. Harrington, who only a moment ago had been the picture of calm, raised his hands and cast a glance from the deputy's gun to the sheriff's handcuffs and back again. "Now listen, you all know that I was at the store the other day. I'm the one who brought Willow's pa out of the building, remember?"

The sheriff stepped toward him. "We do remember. And yet, we found this behind the store. Why would we have found it out back? Near where we figure the fire started, I might point out."

Hoyt showed the man his palms in a "just wait" gesture. "I went out to use the privy. I must have dropped it then."

That made the sheriff hesitate. He turned, and Willow was surprised when his gaze fell on her. "Is that true?"

Willow fought to think even as she noted that the deputy kept his gun leveled on Mr. Harrington. She frowned. She didn't remember Mr. Harrington going out back, no. "After the wagon train meeting, he was at the store for a few minutes while Papa showed him around. Then he signed the contract and went out the front door. Not out back." She shifted her gaze to the man, heart pounding. Was she looking at Papa's killer?

Hoyt waved his hands. "I went out the front door, yes, but then down the alley to the outhouse!"

The sheriff looked at her again. "Well?"

Willow felt despair shift through her as she shook her head. The man may have made her uncomfortable with his looks, but she wouldn't condemn a man without evidence. "I can't say if he did that or not. I didn't watch him leave."

Gideon stepped forward. "I was out back, helping Micah finish packing his wagon, and I never saw him." He looked to Micah. "You?"

Micah shook his head but then frowned. "We were inside the barn for most of the time, though."

Gideon nodded. "But that privy door squeals like a scared rabbit. I think we would have heard it."

Micah tilted his head with a shrug of acknowledgment. His gaze shifted to Hoyt. "Probably."

Hoyt sputtered. "I used the privy! I swear it! You have to admit that you might not have heard the door, what with the work you were doing."

Micah and Gideon both lowered their heads.

After a moment, the sheriff prodded again, "Well?"

Both men nodded reluctantly. "Could be."

The sheriff still looked uncertain.

Hoyt thrust a hand toward Willow. "I saved her father! Why would I start a fire and then risk my life by going in to save him? Also, I'd just bought the store from him! Why would I burn down something I'd just worked so hard to attain?"

Gideon's head snapped up. "To attain for Willow's uncle, you mean!"

Hoyt shrugged and spread his hands. "Yes. I was working for Grant Moore. You already know that. My point stands! Why would I work to close a deal for him and then burn the place down?" He pinned the sheriff with a look. "I did not start that fire!"

The sheriff tilted his head. "That's not what Grant Moore says. In fact, he's the one who told us we should come out here. He said he was almost certain you started the blaze."

Hoyt's jaw dropped and he huffed a sound of exasperation. "Of course he said that! Would you be happy if you acquired a building and only hours later, it burned down? He's upset over his loss and looking for someone to blame. Look, I'm the one who stepped forward and claimed the cufflink as my own. Would I have done that if I was guilty?"

The sheriff and the deputy exchanged glances. The deputy waggled his head, his eyes squinting in uncertainty, even though his pistol remained leveled on Hoyt.

Shoulders slumping in defeat, the sheriff batted a hand for the deputy to lower his pistol. He twirled his hand through the air. "You're all free to disburse." After a moment, he turned to Willow and stepped toward her. His head tilted to one side, sorrow weighing his shoulders. "I'm very sorry to say, Miss Chan—ah, Mrs. Riley—that I don't think we will ever find enough evidence to learn what started that fire. It's clear from interviews we conducted and from examination of the scene that it started on the back side of the store and then spread to the hotel, but that's all we can ascertain."

Eden thrust out one hand. "But what about me saying that I saw a man with a bright reflection at his cuffs going around the corner? Surely that has to be the same cufflink as this one?" She swept a hand to the cufflink the sheriff still held in his hands just as Hoyt Harrington drew near to get the piece of jewelry.

He gasped a protest. "Why is everyone determined to pin this on me?"

Willow narrowed her eyes. "Maybe because you did deal underhandedly with my father, Mr. Harrington, by buying the store and then handing it over to my uncle. What did you get paid for that, by the way?"

Mr. Harrington snatched the cufflink that the sheriff held out to him and thrust it into his pocket. "What I got paid is irrelevant. I already told you I wouldn't have worked with the man if I'd known what an underhanded crook he was."

Willow thinned her lips, not sure that she believed him.

The sheriff touched her shoulder. "We may never learn what happened, but I want you to know that I greatly admired your father. He never once ran up against the law, not even in very lean years. He was a man to ride the river with." He motioned for his deputy to mount up. "Let's head back to town. I'd like to get this case wrapped up so that Moore and Darnell can get on with rebuilding the store and the hotel."

Willow clasped his arm. "Sheriff, will you give me a few minutes before you ride away?" At his frown, she hurried to add, "I'll be fast, I promise. I just need a few moments to speak to Gid—Mr. Riley."

The sheriff didn't look too pleased at the delay, but he did give her a nod. Then he shouted to his deputy, "Take a few, William, and water my horse while you're at it, would you?" To Willow, he said, "I'll be over there in the shade of that wagon. I'm getting too blasted old for this heat." He departed with a wink.

Willow turned to look for Gideon only to find him standing just behind her and to one side, with his hands propped on his hips and a hard glitter in his eyes.

Eden glanced between them and then bustled off after wishing them a good day.

Willow's palms started to sweat.

Chapter 26

Corbin strode casually until he reached his wagon and hoisted himself inside. He barely made it to the pallet stretched the length of one side of the wagon before collapsing onto it.

His hands shook, his knees shook, his whole body shook. That had been much too close for comfort. Thankfully, his intelligence had saved the day, and he'd come up with an answer for every accusation. But had it been enough?

Maybe he should simply cut and run. Oregon was a vast territory. He didn't need any of these people to make it out west. He could find another town far from wherever they settled and rise to leadership on his own.

However . . .

Grant Moore would be a problem. The man might talk. So far, it seemed like he'd only said a little. But . . . He could share his real name with the authorities. He could cause Corbin a lot of trouble, and the last thing he wanted was for the law to dog him for the rest of his life.

He needed leverage. Leverage the man would understand. Leverage that would make him comply.

He needed Willow.

Dread clawed at Willow's chest the moment she saw the look on Gideon's face as the sheriff walked away.

He started to shake his head. "Willow, don't—"

Her hand shot out, and she gripped his arm. She must speak before he changed her mind! "Gid, I appreciate everything you did for me, truly I do. But this—" She swung a finger between them. "You and I, it will never work. I want a man who loves me, and you want a wife you can love."

"Willow." He stepped close and settled his hands at her waist, stealing all her words with the surprising firmness of his grip—as though he wanted to hold onto her forever. The softness in his eyes as they searched her face almost stole the strength from her knees.

She memorized the firmness of his chest beneath her palm, the glint of sunlight in the stubble on his jaw, the way her heart seemed to be having trouble beating with him this close. All things she would never experience again. She swallowed the lump in her throat.

Gid raised one hand to touch her chin. "I do love you. I realized it, oh I don't know when I realized it really, but definitely last night when you weren't at the wagon. Maybe when you ran off or when the Indian wanted to trade for you. It doesn't matter. The point is, I do love you. Don't leave me." His knuckle caressed her jawline. "I know things are hard, and you're feeling overwhelmed by all the unexpected changes. But please, let's stick it out together."

Willow tucked her lower lip between her teeth. Oh, how she wanted to believe his words. How she wished he wasn't simply being gallant.

But she would know if something had changed, wouldn't she?

She pondered his demeanor this morning. He had seemed happier and more carefree, yet he'd not said one word to her about his feelings—until now.

She summoned all her courage and took a step back, putting enough space between them that his hands mercifully fell to his sides. "You fulfilled your duty, Gid. Be free."

"Listen, I know I haven't been the easiest on you the last few days. I fully admit that I was afraid to love you like I should because of my wife and—" he waved a hand "—all that I lost. But after our talk the other night about rejoicing, I realized that I was a fool and that I was already in love with you."

Willow's heart stuttered and then galloped to catch the missing beat. She rubbed her palms together to remove the clamminess. She heard his words, and yet, he'd often seemed so unhappy to have her in his life. "Papa never would have wanted us to suffer each other's company."

His blue eyes narrowed as his hands plunked onto his hips. "Are you saying that you are suffering in my company? Because I'm certainly not suffering in yours. And if you are suffering in mine, I'm willing to do whatever necessary to fix that."

She pondered that. Had she been suffering? Only because of Papa's death, not because of anything Gid had done. In fact, despite his sometimes gruffness, he'd always treated her with gentle kindness.

She reluctantly shook her head, unwilling to malign him in such a way. "No. I haven't suffered. You've been more than good to me." She couldn't bring herself to meet his gaze. He was making this harder than it should be. She hadn't expected her heart to feel like it was breaking in two.

Once more, he stepped close, but this time, he didn't touch her. He simply spoke soft and low: "I meant my vows, Willow Girl. What about you?"

She felt her shoulders slope and turned her face to the side. "Gid, I was beside myself with grief."

He reached one hand to caress her arm with the backs of his fingers. "You're *still* beside yourself with grief."

That did make her hesitate. Maybe she was. But that didn't mean that she didn't know what she was doing.

Slowly, he reached to take her hand. He tucked it against his chest, curving his hand around hers and pressing her palm against the beat of his heart. "I'm sorry that I haven't made you feel welcome in my home, our home, our marriage. I'll do better."

He said that, but could she trust it? Or was he simply forcing himself to say what he knew she wanted to hear? If only there was a way to know for certain.

A thought increased the beat of her pulse.

If she insisted on going back to Independence and he chose her, that would be enough, right? Him choosing her over his family?

Her eyes fell closed.

She was the lowest of women. How could she ask him to choose between her and his only remaining blood relative?

And yet . . . she must know if his heart was truly hers.

Slowly, she withdrew her hand and focused on the whites of her fingernails. "I *am* still grieving, but I'm in a better frame of mind. And I really feel this is best. I'll go back to Independence and find a job. I'll be fine. We didn't even—" She felt her face flame. "There's been no consummation. No judge will contest our separation, but . . . you'll have to grant it to me."

"I won't."

She shot her gaze up to meet his, seeing the glitter of ire reflected in the blue of his eyes.

He thrust a finger toward the east. "If you are going back to Independence, I'm coming with you."

"You would actually leave your family?"

"No, Willow, I won't leave my family." Defeat rang in his tone when he said the words and her heart plummeted.

So, she'd been right. Yet, there was an undertone that made her search his face.

The creases at the edge of his mouth deepened as he continued, "Like it or not, Willow Girl, you're my family now."

Willow felt her mouth drop open. "You mean it? You would really choose me over Joel and Micah? Over Av and Mercy?"

"Of course I—" His eyes narrowed. "Wait a minute. Has this been a test?"

Willow lowered her gaze to her fingernails once more.

"You *were* testing me!" He took a step back, hands fisting even as his arms folded and his eyes glittered blue flame. "Let's get one thing straight right from the start. And please remember it well. I'm not a liar. Nor will I ever be. If I say something, I've thought it through, and I mean it. Got it?" His jaw bunched as his nostrils flared. "Now, are we going back to Independence or staying with the wagon train? Whatever we're doing, we're doing it together!"

She notched her chin into the air, determined that if she hadn't yet cried for Papa, she certainly would not cry for Gideon Riley! But there was no use in pursuing all this now. The stubborn man seemed determined not to let her go. *Thank You, God.*

"We can stay." She pressed her fingertips against the emotion in her throat.

"Good." He pivoted on one heel and stalked away but paused only a few paces from her and turned back, searching out the sheriff. "Sheriff, she's staying."

The lawman gave Gideon a nod.

With one more glower in her direction, Gideon stomped off.

Willow felt her shoulders deflate. That had not gone as she'd expected.

And yet, her heart pounded with hope.

Even though he'd just stormed off and left her standing in the center of the wagons, Gideon Riley loved her!

Gideon stalked to the wagon, propped his hands on the wagon bench, and hung his head between his arms.

Breathe, just breathe.

The woman was infuriating.

And yet, he must remember that she wasn't in her right mind at the moment. He, of all people, knew that grief could make people do things they normally wouldn't. They would get past this. *Please, Lord.*

Something nudged his back, and he turned to find Willow's pony, which had still been grazing in the grass between the wagons this morning. Gideon settled his hand against the horse's nose and pressed his forehead to hers, breathing in the soothing scent of the mare that must have sensed his distress.

"It's all right. I'm all right. She's all right. We're all right." He lifted his head and rubbed the mare's cheek.

She whuffled his hair with a soft whicker.

He smiled. Okay, maybe she was here more for her morning scoop of grain than to comfort him.

"After one day, you already like this routine, eh?" He chuckled. "All right, come along."

He took up her halter rope and led her to the other side of the wagon, where the grain bin was. He scooped a generous portion into the bucket stored there.

At the wagon just behind his, Parson Adam was just finishing hitching his oxen. "Morning," he called. "Some doings, aye?"

Gid nodded. "I wish we could have figured out who it was." He strode closer to the tailgate and set the bucket within easy reach of the horse.

The parson nodded. "The good Lord knows and will one day bring justice."

Gid wished he could be as content with that as the parson seemed to be.

With a happy bob of her head, the pony set to munching while Gid tied her rope off to the eyebolt inset into the wagon's back post. Willow might choose to ride her for some time today, but he wasn't sure how she would accomplish it without a side saddle. He made a mental note that they needed to get one at Fort Kearny.

He pulled in a long breath and pushed it out slowly. Now that he'd had a chance to cool off, he realized he shouldn't have stalked away from her immediately after proclaiming his love for her. But when he glanced to where he'd left her, he saw that she'd started this way. He returned to the front of the wagon and waited for her. She would probably want to ride at least until they all got underway and formed into a straight line. Then he could pause to let her down as soon as she wanted to.

When he reached the front bench, an intermittent buzzing drew his attention down, but the only thing he saw was the tin mug that Hoyt had brought him this morning. He lifted it to return it to the bin at the back of the wagon but stilled when he saw a half-dead bee in the bottom of the cup.

The critter staggered and buzzed and then collapsed before rising to repeat the process. Then it flipped onto its back and began spinning so fast that it disappeared into naught but a blur in the bottom of the cup.

Gideon's heart began to beat in earnest.

He glanced from the cup to the place where he'd tossed out the water Hoyt had given him and then on to Willow's pa's wagon, where Hoyt had disappeared only moments earlier. Then he looked back to the struggling bee.

No!

He surely conjured threats because of the meeting they'd all just had with the sheriff.

The bee could have already been old and ready to die. It could have gotten too hot in the tin cup.

And yet . . .

From the wagon behind, Gideon heard Eden call, "Adam? Can you come here for a moment?" The tension in her voice drew him in that direction.

Adam glanced his way, then hurried to the back of the wagon to see what his wife needed.

Gideon ought to stay out of it, but his curiosity kept him walking, nonetheless. When he peered around the rear of their wagon, Adam and Eden both stared at something on the tailgate. Adam's back blocked his view.

Gideon stepped to the side, and the sight of the boards before him stilled his breath.

A damp brown circle on the wood was surrounded by bees, all of them dead. He worked some moisture into his mouth. "What is that?"

Eden shrugged her shoulder. "Spilled coffee. I put a teaspoon of sugar in it, which is what attracted the bees, I suppose. But I didn't know coffee would kill them."

Gid's heart was suddenly beating from the region of his throat. "It wouldn't. At least not in such a small amount as they must have ingested." He thrust the tin mug into Adam's hands and clapped him on one shoulder. "Don't let your wife out of your sight!" He started across the field toward the sheriff as he continued to call quietly over his shoulder, "Don't lose that cup, and don't clean up that mess. I'll be right back."

Halfway across the field, he met Willow, who gave him a searching look. Not wanting to let her out of his sight, he scooped her hand into his and tugged her with him. "Come with me. We need to get the sheriff to see something."

"What is it?" Her voice sounded a little breathless as she trotted to keep up.

"I think Hoyt Harrington just tried to kill me—and maybe Eden too." He spoke the words low as he glanced around to make sure the man didn't linger nearby. His wagon remained in its place, and the man was nowhere to be seen.

"What!?" Willow squeaked.

"Shhh. We're both okay. But I need to get the sheriff."

When they reached the man, it only took Gideon a moment to quietly explain what had happened and then he led the lawman back across the circle of wagons toward the Houstons.

Chapter 27

Willow wrung her hands as Gideon explained to the sheriff about the cup that Hoyt had brought him this morning and how he'd found the dead bee in it when he returned. And then he swept a hand at the spilled coffee on the Houstons' tailgate.

"And this is what Mrs. Houston here found after we returned from your meeting."

The sheriff rubbed his jaw thoughtfully, then reached for the tin cup and angled it. "There's still a drop or two of liquid in here." He fished in a nearby tub of dishes until he withdrew a spoon, which he used to remove the dead bee from Gideon's cup. Then he leaned close to the cup and sniffed it. "Either of you ladies have anything copper?"

Eden stepped forward. "We have a copper kettle."

"Perfect." The sheriff reached into his pocket and withdrew a pocketknife. "Somebody light me a candle. And someone find William."

While Adam dashed off in search of the deputy, and Gideon lit a candle, the sheriff took the copper kettle from Eden and shaved a tiny flat sliver of copper from the bottom rim. Then as Gideon set the candle near, he dropped the shaving of copper into the drops of liquid in the bottom of the tin cup and then held it over the fire. It only took a few moments for Willow to hear the liquid popping and bubbling in the bottom of the mug.

The sheriff stared into the bottom of the mug intently.

Adam and William returned, both breathing hard.

The sheriff spoke to William. "Saw that Harrington fellow climb into the back of his wagon. Stand guard and make sure he don't go nowhere."

The deputy nodded. "Yes, boss." He dashed off.

Willow clenched her hands so tightly that each knuckle ached. Why would Mr. Harrington try to kill Gideon and the minister's wife? It had to be because of Eden telling the sheriff about the man she'd seen in the alley by the store! And why would Mr. Harrington care about that unless he had indeed started the fire?

Of course, the only things linking Eden's tailgate with Gideon's cup were the dead bees, and the only thing linking Mr. Harrington to Eden's situation was that Mr. Harrington had handed Gideon a cup of water. Were they all jumping to ill conclusions?

The sheriff pulled the cup away from the flame, looked intently into the bottom of it, and then uttered a mild oath. "Well, I'll be." He used Eden's spoon to withdraw the sliver of copper and held it out for Gideon to see.

Gideon's jaw bunched. "Arsenic."

The sheriff nodded. "Sure enough is!"

Heart pounding, Willow stepped forward to see the piece of copper. It had turned a chalky gray-black color. She lifted her gaze to Gideon. Did this all mean what she thought it meant?

Gid settled a hand on her shoulder. "Arsenic turns copper that color when it's heated."

The sheriff thumped Gideon and Adam on their backs. "Let's go catch ourselves a murderer."

Willow reached for Eden without thinking and felt a measure of her trembling ease when the woman wrapped both arms around her as they stared after the men.

Confusion swirled through Willow as one question pounded at her. Why? They hadn't even known Mr. Harrington. He'd contacted them based on Papa's newspaper advertisement for the sale of the store. Why would he want to burn down the store he'd just purchased? Did he have a dispute with Uncle Grant?

"None of this makes any sense," she lamented aloud.

"It's going to be all right," Eden said as they pressed their heads together. "They're going to catch him, and we're going to figure out why he did all this."

Gideon breathed slow and steady as the deputy indicated quietly that he'd seen no one leave the wagon. Harrington had to be inside.

He, Adam, and the two lawmen surrounded Harrington's wagon. Despite Adam's earlier protest about peaceably handling resolutions, he seemed comfortable with the gun the deputy thrust into his palm.

The deputy and the sheriff took the front and back of the wagon; he and Adam, the sides.

When they were all in place, the sheriff barked, "Gig's up, Harrington. We've got you surrounded. Come on out with your hands up."

Hand steady on his Colt, Gideon watched his side of the wagon for movement. None came.

"I mean it now, Harrington. Don't make me come in there or I'll come shooting!" The sheriff's words were sharp and loud and began to draw attention from others in the wagon train now.

As the silence stretched, Gideon's heart pounded. Something wasn't right.

The sheriff signaled to his deputy, who climbed aboard the front of the wagon and poked his head inside. He jerked his head right back out. "Wagon's empty!"

What? Gideon lurched toward where he'd left Willow at a sprint.

Willow remained with Eden, watching the men as they approached Harrington's wagon. She was still scrambling to discern the how and why of all this when a rustling sound came from the bushes behind them.

Willow released Eden and whirled toward the sound, feeling her new friend do the same beside her.

Hoyt Harrington eased from the brush with a pistol in his hand. Anger glittered in his eyes. "You two have caused a lot of trouble for me," he gritted quietly.

Anger hot and sure burst to life in Willow's chest. She stepped forward and to the side to block Eden from the line of his gun. "*We've caused problems for you?* What are you talking about? We've both simply been minding our business. Did you kill my father?"

Hoyt lurched toward her and had a handful of her hair gripped in his fist before she'd hardly registered that he'd moved.

Willow ground her teeth, stumbling a few steps to maintain her balance, which put her closer to the man. She willed herself to breathe and not pass out.

He yanked her head back and pressed the pistol beneath her chin. "Shut up, woman! If I didn't need you alive to convince your uncle not to blather my name, I'd be done with you, here and now."

A shiver of terror slipped through her. His name? They all knew his name already, including the sheriff. Unless . . . Did he mean that none of them knew his real name?

Suddenly Hoyt jerked the gun away from Willow's chin and thrust it behind her. "No! No, you don't," he snapped sharply, though keeping his voice low.

Willow angled her head.

Eden, who had apparently been trying to dart around the corner of the wagon, froze and spun to face them, shoving her hands into the air. "Sorry. I'm not moving!"

"Get over here." The pistol never wavered.

Eden took two faltering steps closer.

Keeping hold of Willow's hair, Hoyt held his pistol trained on Eden. "I need you to deliver a message for me. You tell the lawman that I have Grant Moore's niece. And you tell him that he needs to pass that message along to Moore. Moore will know what it means. You tell him that no harm will come to her ... unless it's necessary. Oh, and while we're here, let me add that if you say one more thing about it maybe being me behind the mercantile that afternoon, you'll never see your friend here again, understand?"

Eden looked as pale as flour sacking. Her hands still in the air, she nodded and lowered her despondent gaze to Willow.

Willow shook her head. If they tried something, one of them was bound to get killed. She didn't want anyone else to be hurt by this madman.

Eden swallowed and nodded. "O-okay. I'll keep silent. I swear I will. And I'll tell the sheriff," she whispered. Her eyes shifted and then settled on Hoyt again. "Unless you want to tell him yourself?" Her volume rose by several notches. "You could, you know! Turn yourself in. The law would most likely go easier on you in that case. Kidnapping a woman is a hanging offense. Probably something you want to avoid, right? I mean—"

"Shut up, woman!" Hoyt moved as fast as lightning. He surged forward, and the barrel of his gun *thunk*ed Eden's temple.

Eden toppled like a felled tree.

"Dear, Lord!" Willow gasped and then shuttered the sight away. She hid in the darkness behind her eyelids. Had she just witnessed Eden's death? She trembled so badly that she could hardly remain upright.

"Great," Hoyt muttered. "Now look what she made me do."

Suddenly, a footstep grated against a stone, and a loud hollow *crack* came from behind her. Hoyt fell to the ground. His fingers, still tangled in Willow's hair, took her with him.

She flopped onto her back, kicking against her skirts and fighting to loose herself.

But Hoyt wasn't fighting back.

She stilled. Breathed. Tried to figure out what had just happened.

And then Edi leaned into her line of sight, concern etching his features. "You okay, Willow?"

Relief coursed through her. Had Edi knocked Hoyt out?

She tried to sit up, but the dead weight of Hoyt's fingers tangled in her hair kept her tethered each time she rose partway up. "Edi, help me, please. Was that you? What happened?"

"I didn't miss!" Edi reached none-too-gently to extract her hair.

Willow winced, holding her breath as he yanked on her hair.

"He a" *yank* "bad" *yank* "man," Edi proclaimed.

"Yes. Thank you for saving me. But can we just—" She reached to still his attempts to free her.

Gideon was suddenly there, leaning over her also. "Dear Lord, have mercy! What happened?"

"Gid!" Willow had never felt so relieved to see someone in her entire life. "Help me, please!" She fought down the panic that suddenly clawed for preeminence. She wanted to get as far away from Hoyt Harrington, or whoever he was, as possible.

Gid reached to untangle her hair. "Hold on. I've got you. There!"

Willow felt the tension on her scalp give way.

Relieved, she scrambled to her feet and spun to stare down at the man who had only a moment earlier held her and Eden captive. "Eden!" She fell to her knees by Eden's head. "Where's the parson? Someone, get the parson! Eden? Oh, Eden!"

Blood trickled from the woman's temple into her hair.

Footsteps crashed toward her from all directions now.

"Eden!" Adam dropped beside his wife. "Dear God, please. Please, not Eden!" He reached as though to gather Eden into his arms.

"Stop!" The command was sharp, short, and authoritative. "Don't move her!"

Willow glanced up to see Tamsyn pushing through the gathering crowd.

The woman sank to her knees on the other side of Eden and leveled the parson with a look. "She may have hurt herself when she fell. We have to be careful with her neck and spine."

Adam rocked, scooping both hands into his hair.

"What happened here?" Caesar Cranston bellowed the question as he and the sheriff arrived together.

Silence fell over the gathering and Willow glanced up to see every eye upon her. It was Gideon whose face she paused on, willing herself to find the strength to figure out where to begin.

He gave her a nod, and reached for her hand, drawing her up and away from Eden as another woman she hadn't met yet took her place.

"We left you and Eden here by the wagons and went to get Harrington. Then what happened?"

Willow looked at the prostrate Harrington. His mouth hung open, and one of his legs lay twisted behind him at an odd angle.

"Eden and I were talking when suddenly—" she swept a gesture to Harrington "—he just appeared from nowhere. He had a gun, and he . . . He told Eden to tell you, Sheriff, to tell my uncle that he had me and that no harm would come to me unless it was necessary. He said he didn't want Uncle Grant telling you his name."

Hoyt stirred and moaned. Tried to roll to his side.

Terror surging, Willow leapt closer to Gideon. "He's moving!"

Edi, who hadn't moved more than a step from the spot where she'd first seen him a moment ago, shot out his foot. The toe of his boot connected sharply with Hoyt's temple.

Hoyt grunted and his head lolled to the side. He slumped onto his back as his jaw went slack again. His arm flopped to one side.

"Got him!" Edi proclaimed with a proud grin.

A glint of gold on his hand drew Willow's gaze. "What's that?" She pointed to the ring on the man's hand. But it appeared to have a crack in it beneath the red stone. Had it broken somehow when he fell?

Gideon bent down to examine the man's palm more closely. "Well, I'll be!" He took up a twig and prodded at the ring that had been twisted to the inside of Hoyt's palm. A small lid lifted to reveal a compartment beneath.

Gideon looked up at the sheriff. "I bet that's where you'll find traces of that arsenic." He pressed his hands against his knees and rose to his feet, coming to stand beside her once more.

The man readjusted his hat, then gave a dip of his chin. "We'll make sure to test it."

Gideon's hand settled warmly at the back of Willow's neck as the sheriff and his deputy worked to turn Hoyt and secure his hands behind his back. "It seems clear that Harrington there, or whoever he might be, was working with Willow's uncle in some capacity or another."

The sheriff tugged the thick metal manacles from his belt. "Sounds like."

As Gideon massaged his hand over the tight muscles in her shoulders, Willow felt tension easing out of her. "He also told Eden that if she said anything about seeing him in the alley, he would hurt me."

The sheriff clamped the knobbed ends of his handcuffs around Hoyt's wrists. "My guess is we're going to find this man's dandy mug on a wanted poster buried somewhere back in my office."

Beside her, Gideon released a sigh of relief. "Yes. I think so too."

"Don't worry." The sheriff and the deputy hauled Hoyt to his feet and heaved him onto the back of a horse someone had brought close. "We'll speak to Willow's uncle and see what we can learn." The man leveled his gaze on her. "If there was foul play in the death of your father, I'll be sure to see justice served and send you word."

"Thank you." Willow leaned against Gideon's strength, wanting nothing more than to disappear into their wagon and try to gather her thoughts.

On the ground, Eden groaned, and Adam leapt to lean over her. "Don't move, Eden. I'm right here, honey. Don't move."

Willow stepped to one side so she could see Eden's face through the small gap between Adam and Tamsyn.

Tamsyn pressed the backs of her fingers to Eden's forehead. "Just be still for a moment. We want to make sure you aren't injured worse than it seems." She held up three fingers. "How many fingers am I holding up?"

Eden blinked. Worked her lips. Then mumbled, "Three."

"Good. That's real good." Tamsyn nodded. "Now, do you have pain anywhere?"

Eden touched her temple. "My head."

"Anywhere else?"

A complete silence fell as the whole crowd seemed to be holding their breath in anticipation of her answer. Willow leaned forward, fists bunched around handfuls of her skirt. She felt Gideon's hand still.

Eden frowned and seemed to be thinking. Finally, she shook her head. "Something—a pebble maybe—is poking me in the back of my head, but otherwise I feel fine."

A collective breath whooshed from those gathered around.

But Tamsyn remained unsatisfied. She instructed Eden to remain still as she gently prodded her neck, arms, torso, and legs, all while asking if she felt any pain. To each question, Eden responded that she was okay.

With a smile, Tamsyn finally pronounced that she could rise.

As Adam reached a hand behind Eden's back and helped her sit up, Willow collapsed against Gideon's chest.

His arms came around her, and his chin tucked her close. Just as quickly, she felt one of his arms release her, and he said, "Edi," giving a little nod.

"I saved her!" Edi said proudly as Willow felt the men shake hands.

"You did. Thank you."

Willow reluctantly left the security of Gideon's arms and turned to give Edi a hug. He stood stiffly with his arms by his sides as she squeezed him, but he smiled from ear to ear when she pulled back.

"Thank you, Edi."

He nodded. "You're p-pretty."

Willow chuckled and hung her head in embarrassment, seeking out the solidity of Gideon's chest for her shoulder once more.

Gid's hand rubbed across her back as he rumbled, "That she is, Edi. That she is."

Caesar Cranston swung an arm above his head. "All right, folks. I'm giving everyone an hour so's we can clear up this here craziness, and then we all need to be ready to head out."

Slowly the crowd began to disburse.

Willow walked to a place where she could watch the sheriff and his deputy head back toward Independence, leading the spare horse behind them.

She rubbed her hands over her arms, feeling tremors begin to work all through her.

Gideon paused beside her, then took her hand and led her to their wagon.

As soon as they had both climbed past the pony and stood in the concealing darkness, Gideon pulled her into his arms and rested his chin atop her head. "I'm so sorry. I never should have stalked away from you the way I did. Forgive me."

Willow shook her head as she tilted her face up to see him. "I never should have planned to leave you like that. It's I who should ask for your forgiveness!"

Gideon cupped her face, and in the light slanting through the uncinched canvas at the back, she could see moisture glimmering in his eyes. "I'm so glad you are okay."

A sob caught her unaware, and it was quickly followed by another.

With a frown, Gideon stepped back, but Willow stepped after him and threw her arms around him, suddenly crying uncontrollably. She cried so hard that she lost the strength in her knees and felt a moment of weightlessness as Gideon lifted her onto the bed and snugged her against his chest once more.

As though a dam had burst open inside her, Willow felt no control over the wracking sobs that shook her.

"Shh, Willow Girl. I'm here. I'm right here." Gideon's hand caressed the length of the curls that cascaded down her back and then returned to the base of her neck. His fingers fumbled in her hair and she felt him begin to remove her already loose hairpins, and still, she cried. He pressed a kiss to her temple. "I know it's going to take some time, but I'm going to do my best to fulfill your father's last request."

Willow stilled. Sniffed. "What was it?" She lifted her head, just enough to see his face through the blur of her tears.

Gid stroked her cheek and tucked a strand of hair behind her ear. "He told me to make you happy." He tilted his head. "I'm not so sure I've done such a good job of that."

Willow nestled against his chest again with another sniff. "You do make me happy. I just need time. Time to adjust to all the changes."

Gideon settled his lips against her ear. "Take all the time you need. I'm here. I know it's been overwhelming."

Content with that, Willow continued to let her tears fall. She cried for what had almost happened. She cried for the joy of Gideon's proclamation of love. She cried for the relief of no longer feeling so alone. She cried for missing dear Papa with such an ache that she felt she might crack right open.

And all the while, Gideon murmured words of comfort and soothed his hand over her back.

Willow pressed a palm to the ache in her chest. "I don't . . . think . . . I'm strong enough for this."

She felt Gideon shake his head. "When we are weak, Christ is strong. Rest in the Lord's strength and let Him carry you."

Papa's words washed over her again. *You can do all things through Christ, who strengthens.* That was the component she'd been missing. *Through Christ.* She didn't have to be the strong one! Relief rolled through her even as another sob wracked her. "I'm sorry." She hiccupped.

Gideon's hand soothed over her shoulders. "You've nothing to be sorry for."

Willow lifted her face and pressed her fingers to Gideon's cheek, relishing the freedom to do so. She curled the fingers of her other hand into the curls at the base of his neck. Lifted her mouth to his.

He caressed her lips with the gentlest of kisses. "I love you, Willow Girl."

She breathed out a contented sigh. "I love you, too."

His lips found hers again, more firmly this time.

Outside, thunder rolled, and great fat drops of rain began to hammer the wagon, but Willow couldn't find it in herself to worry because despite being here in the middle of nowhere with nothing but a taut oilcloth separating her from the elements, she suddenly felt as if she'd come home.

Please Review!

If you enjoyed this story, would you take a few minutes to leave your thoughts in a review on your favorite retailer's website? It would mean so much to me, and helps spread the word about the series.

You can quickly link through from my website here: https://www.pacificlightsbookstore.com/collections/the-oregon-promise-series/

Coming soon…

ACROSS

Barren Plains

 OREGON PROMISE - BOOK 3

You may read an excerpt on the next page…

Excerpt

Eden Houston pressed one hand to the base of her throat as she stumbled to a stop. All around, the rest of the women who had been walking behind the wagon train with her did the same.

The day was perfect. Warm and breezy. But now they studied the large column of smoke blotting the blue of the western sky just over the next rise.

"What do you think it means?" Tamsyn Acheson asked, voice filled with trepidation.

In her arms, she carried a large chunk of wood that she'd found on the trail a few hours earlier. Eden figured she had brought it with her due to firewood being so scarce on this stretch of the trail.

Eden shook her head gingerly. "I'm not sure." She felt the familiar pulse of the pain that had tormented her head ever since she'd been pistol-whipped and knocked unconscious by the man they'd all known as Hoyt Harrington. She was careful to keep any evidence of the pain from her features. The last thing she needed was word of it getting back to Adam. "I don't think it can be anything good."

"Do you think it's from Fort Kearny?" The blond girl was one of the seven Hawthorne children that Eden had a hard time telling apart since there were three sets of twins among them. This one was either

Wren or Whitley. They were the oldest Hawthorne children—about fifteen, she would guess. Their mother was once again round with child.

Eden wanted children, but she hoped the Lord wouldn't bless her with quite so many as eight!

She might have smiled at the thought if their current situation wasn't so dire.

"Do you?" the twin prodded, a bit of wishfulness in her tone.

Eden came back to the present with a start, realizing she'd left the girl waiting for her reply. "Sorry. No. I don't think it's from the fort. We aren't supposed to reach it for a few days." If only the explanation could be something as simple as the fort's cookfires.

Ahead, the wagons of their train stretched in a long line, trundling one after the other up the gentle slope they'd been climbing for the past hour.

Since the first men of their party were about to reach the top of this rise and would likely be able to see what was happening ahead, they should soon have a better understanding of whether the smoke was something of concern or simply a natural event.

Did any folks live this far out from the fort? Could they be burning their fields for planting? Eden hoped that would be the case.

As she and the women continued forward, she kept an eye on the road ahead—paying even closer attention as the first wagon reined to a stop on the crest of the slope with Caesar Cranston riding his big Appaloosa beside.

Outlined against the horizon, Caesar's long white hair billowed around him. He seemed to stiffen as he took in the scenery ahead.

Eden's heart stilled. She held her breath. He didn't move for so long that she'd begun to think she was imagining things.

But then Caesar reined his mount sharply to one side, snatched his bugle from where he kept it hanging down the side of his saddle, and blew the few notes that indicated the wagons should circle!

Eden's heart thrashed painfully in her chest. *Dear Lord. Dear Lord. Dear Lord.*

Where was Adam? Whatever was happening, he'd likely be called right into the thick of it. And injured as his hand was from the burn he'd taken back in town a couple weeks back, she knew he'd be a bit clumsy with a gun, even if he wouldn't thank her for saying so.

She took a breath to tamp down her fear. She might have awoken on this day with frustration pulsing in her chest toward the man she loved, but that didn't mean she wanted to see him put in harm's way. She wished that she could confide in him. However, their lack of trust and confidence in each other could be laid almost squarely at her feet, so she supposed she couldn't complain too much when she had been the one to break their connection.

As though all of them had just found their feet unfrozen from the ground, several women surged toward their wagons at once.

Tamsyn hoisted a handful of her skirts and hurried forward with her wood tucked under one arm. "I have to get to Edi." She spoke over her shoulder as she dashed into the swirling dust that twirled up in dust devils on this side of the slope.

The wind brought with it the sharply disturbing scent of smoke.

Eden gave her friend a distracted wave, unable to remove her gaze from the black mar billowing against the dome of blue sky overhead. Her pulse thundered in her ears, causing the pain in her head to throb with each beat. And her breaths came shallow and rapid even as she hurried to conquer the ascent.

Dread coiled in her belly. Drat this rise that blocked her view of whatever lay ahead. For weeks, they'd crossed open plains where the land stretched endlessly in every direction. But this morning, the terrain had changed. Subtle slopes and dips now rolled beneath their wagon wheels, just steep enough to hide what waited beyond. What could possibly be so urgent that Caesar had ordered them to circle the wagons? In the six weeks they'd been on the trail, he'd never once called for a halt so early in the day.

Willow Riley and Mercy Morran, with her two boys, fell into step on either side of her.

"Lord, have mercy," Willow whispered. "This can't be good."

"My thoughts exactly." Eden pressed her hands to the backs of both women. She ought to pray. It was something expected of the minister's wife, even if she felt dry and deserted by the Almighty. She forced the words out as they continued to walk. "Lord, we ask for Your safety and protection for our wagon train. Give us courage to face what comes next and to do Your will. In the name of Jesus, amen." She swallowed down her guilty conscience. Here she was praying, and yet she had all this anger churning inside. That certainly wasn't the accepting faith a truly righteous woman should display. The person she ought to be angry with was herself, yet all her bottled-up displeasure seemed only directed at Adam recently.

"Amen." Mercy and Willow spoke together, driving another nail into the coffin lid of her guilt.

Mercy clasped the hands of her two boys, her face pale and her eyes wide. "Come on, boys, let's find Pa."

Willow gave Eden a little wave and hurried after them.

Eden glanced back at the three women trailing behind. One was the elderly Mrs. Marigold Hawthorne, grandma to the family of mostly twins. Eden moved toward the woman, taking slow breaths to ease her headache, even as she flapped a hand at Mrs. Goode and Mrs. Hession. "Best hurry to your wagons, ladies. Quick like!" She hoped her voice inspired urgency but not panic.

A panic that she felt to her very core! If this were an attack of some kind, would her health stand up to it?

Several women traded places with their husbands on the wagon bench to take over driving the teams as the men hurried at a run toward Caesar.

But Eden had located their wagon now. It was far up the line— third from the front. Adam must have maneuvered closer to the front of the caravan after they'd all stopped for lunch, because this morning he'd been closer to the middle of the train. She had made cheese sandwiches with leftover biscuits at the nooning, but before she'd had a chance to eat her own, she'd been called away by Tamsyn to help tend to a blistered heel on one of the children. The wagons had been moving out again before she'd been able to return. Her stomach grumbled now at just the thought of food. Had Adam even noticed the sandwich she'd wrapped in a towel and left on the tailgate when Tamsyn had asked for her help?

Giving herself a little shake, Eden forced herself to focus on the present as she swept an arm around Mrs. Hawthorne's shoulders. "Here, ma'am, let me help you up to your wagon. I have to tell you that I love the big red rose painted on the side of your canvas." Eden inhaled purposefully. Now she was just blathering for something to say.

The woman planted her cane into the dusty track they'd been following and gave a nod. "Painted thet myself."

Eden smiled even as she tossed a glance over her shoulder to make sure no one else remained behind. "You did a lovely job. That rose has brought a smile to my face on more than one occasion."

"Well then, it has served its purpose." Marigold gave a pleased hum.

"Mind this rock. We don't need to turn an ankle." Eden helped the older woman navigate the obstruction. "You are quite a talent with a paintbrush, I must say. Did you take instruction?"

Mrs. Hawthorne paused, planted her feet wide, and gave a blank look. She seemed ready to stay awhile.

Eden tamped down her impatience. She wanted to be at Adam's side, no matter that she'd relish the opportunity to wring his neck. She would also love nothing more than to crawl into the wagon and take a nice long nap that might ease her headache. But she was needed here.

"Instruction?" Marigold asked.

"In painting?" Eden pressed one hand to the older woman's back to urge her forward. Thankfully, she tottered onward, if much more slowly than Eden would have liked.

Carefully searching for a sturdy spot to plant her cane, Marigold said, "Oh my, no. A body don't need instruction to copy down what they can plainly see before their very eyes!"

Eden bit back a smile. Mrs. Hawthorne had obviously never witnessed the blobs that fell off the end of her brush when she tried to paint. "Well, I must say you have a singular talent. It's quite impressive. I can almost smell that rose for the perfection of it."

She glanced up to take their bearings and felt the hair prickle on the back of her neck. She and Marigold were quite alone. And the wagon train was still a good quarter mile distant.

Marigold tottered another couple of steps up the incline. "I'm an old woman, dear, so do forgive my meddling ways."

"Meddling?" Eden frowned.

The older woman stopped once more and rested both hands atop her cane. Her rheumy blue eyes settled directly on Eden. "You and the mister don't seem to be on the best of terms?"

Ah! That kind of meddling.

Eden tucked her lower lip between her teeth. She worked her fingers into the tight muscles at the base of her skull. How much ought she to say? She started to take a step, but the older woman's hand shot out, surprisingly quick and strong where it clamped on her arm.

"I can see this ain't something you be ready to speak on, and yet, I've experience with a difficult marriage."

Eden felt her brow tuck into a tight pinch. "I don't want you to think badly of Adam. He's a good man." If only he thought she was a good woman. She would keep trying. One day, he'd see that she was trying to be different now.

Marigold's brows lifted. "A good man who sleeps on a hammock 'neath his wagon nights, 'stead of tucked in warmly by his wife."

Tears sprang to Eden's eyes, and familiar anger, hot and sure, surged. She spun away on the pretense of studying the distant horizon, unable to decide whether it was anger with herself for showing such emotion, anger with Adam for continuing to keep her at a distance, or anger with Mrs. Hawthorne for prying. This constant ache in her head wasn't helping her choose. Yet, if she were to be the wife she wanted to be, she must defend him!

She faced the woman once more as she plucked a blade of prairie grass and shredded the stem. "He does do that, yes. But he has his reasons. He— We— We lost a child . . . a son, you see. And . . . I didn't respond to that loss well. I shut him out for a time and now . . . well, things aren't the best between us." Embarrassment heated her cheeks. Why was she spilling so much to this woman?

Mrs. Hawthorne shifted and tipped a nod to indicate they should keep walking up the track. "My Henry, were he here, Lord bless him, he would tell me I ought to keep my meddling mouth shut." She smiled fondly. "But he ain't here, and your husband, Adam, puts me in mind of my Henry back when we first married—overprotective and trying to do the Lord's tasks 'stead of trusting the Lord to do for Himself."

Eden reached a hand to help the older woman over a rut in the path. Was that what Adam was doing?

"You be wanting children, dear?"

Eden felt her face heat at such an intimate question coming from a practical stranger. She released the woman's arm and strode ahead a couple of paces. They were almost to the wagons now, and she could have left the woman to make it to hers alone, but politeness made her stay and answer, "Yes, I do. More than almost anything."

But would this new pain in her head allow her the concentration to care for a child? Would the knifing shards ever recede? Worrying over that was likely exacerbating the affliction.

Marigold gave an assertive nod. "Thet's why the loss of your first child took you under."

The grief washed over Eden as fresh as it had on the day the grim-faced doctor had told her their son hadn't lived through the birthing. She sobbed, quick and short, before she gathered her strength about her and drew herself together. "Y-yes. I suppose it is."

Breathing hard, Mrs. Hawthorne paused again, settling her hands on the knobby handle of her cane.

Eden was surprised to see tears shimmering in the woman's eyes. One slipped free to sweep down the crepey wrinkles of her cheek.

When it reached Mrs. Hawthorne's chin, she reached gnarled fingers, twisted with age, to swipe at the moisture which she then dried against her skirt.

The woman stared toward the smoke overhead for a long moment as though gathering herself. Finally, she lowered her piercing blue gaze to Eden. "I conceived, carried, and lost seven babes. Two more died when they were no more than walking. Grief takes the legs from under us and sits upon us like a great dragon determined not to let us rise. I been under the weight of that dragon more times than I care to remember. But I'll tell you something the good Lord done for me."

Eden searched the woman's face, willing herself not to put too much hope in her words.

"He give me seeds to sow."

Eden frowned. What nonsense was this? To be polite, she asked, "Seeds?"

A sage nod dipped Marigold's wrinkled chin. "They that sow in tears shall reap in joy. He that goeth forth and weepeth, bearing precious seed, shall doubtless come again with rejoicing, bringing his sheaves with him. From the Psalms. One twenty-six, five and six."

"Don't you think those verses mean the spiritual seed we sow into people's lives? And the sheaves are a picture of people that surrender to God because of our testimony."

Marigold nodded and continued up the slope. "Sure. But spiritual seed isn't just telling others they need the Lord. That's part, but it's also scattered when we show others love, joy, peace, patience, kindness, goodness, gentleness, and self-control. It's honesty. It's respect. It's putting others' needs above our own. And I think the sheaves can also represent other things besides saved souls. Sometimes just the honor of helping another might be the cause of our rejoicing. Maybe God uses our pain to encourage others that they ain't alone. Or thet—" She waved a hand. "—at the very least, someone understands and they don't have to suffer alone."

"I'm not sure I have much to offer others right now, Mrs. Hawthorne. I'm like one of those sheaves, unbound, and facing a roaring windstorm. I'm struggling just to hold myself together, and I don't have any answers."

Marigold's hand fell to rest on her arm once again, but this time it was gentle and soft. "Ah, child. I know just what you mean." After a moment, she released her, and the clunk of her cane beat methodically against the dust of the trail.

Eden fell into step beside her, relieved to at least have someone with a listening ear . . . until the woman continued talking.

"But you listen to me, now, and you listen good. You carry a precious pain inside you. The absence of a life cut down before it even begun. Thet has made you a stronger person than you was on the day before your loss. Sure, it took you some time to escape thet dragon of grief, but the good Lord calls to you now to sow thet seed of pain into ground what needs it. Take your pain, child, and cast it to the soil and see what joy the good Lord will bring from it. You don't have to have all the answers because you know the One thet does!" She gave a definitive nod. "Thet were the gift the Lord done give to me. With every pain, I said, 'Lord, show me how to sow this.' And He'll do the same for you, if'n you'll let Him."

They had reached the woman's wagon now, and Eden had never felt more thankful to see an end to a conversation. "I'm sure He will. Thank you." She offered the placating words as she hurried away, working her fingers once more into the tight muscles at the base of her neck. She shook her head. Sowing the seeds of her pain? No one, least of all her, wanted that crop to grow again.

She put the conversation behind her and hurried off to find Adam and discover the cause of the smoke that still belched into the sky.

ABOUT THE AUTHOR

Born and raised in Malawi, Africa. Lynnette Bonner spent the first years of her life reveling in warm equatorial sunshine and the late evening duets of cicadas and hyenas. The year she turned eight she was off to Rift Valley Academy, a boarding school in Kenya where she spent many joy-filled years, and graduated in 1990.

That fall, she traded to a new duet—one of traffic and rain—when she moved to Kirkland, Washington to attend Northwest University. It was there that she met her husband and a few years later they moved to the small town of Pierce, Idaho.

During the time they lived in Idaho, while studying the history of their little town, Lynnette was inspired to begin the Shepherd's Heart Series with Rocky Mountain Oasis.

Marty and Lynnette have four children, and currently live in Washington where Marty pastors a church.

Printed in Great Britain
by Amazon